THE FIRST DRYAD

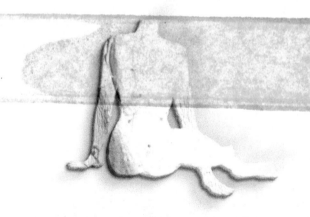

FROM THE MIND OF
TESHELLE COMBS

Of all the circles and all the turns,
I am honored to share this one with you.

The First Collection Reading Paths

The First Collection is a series of standalone novels woven together to create a cohesive fantasy romance experience. Choose your own path to piece together the puzzle, or select one of these 10 paths to curate a journey for your personality!

The Romantic

You are bound to love. Read it all in the most romantic flow, ending with a happily ever after.

1. The First Dryad 1
2. The First Spark
3. The First Muse
4. The First Nymph
5. The First Flame
6. The First Shadow
7. The First Breath
8. The First Dragon
9. The First Stone
10. The First Dryad 2

The Warrior

You are fearless. Attack the most soul-shattering stories first.

1. The First Breath
2. The First Nymph
3. The First Muse
4. The First Shadow
5. The First Dryad 1
6. The First Dryad 2
7. The First Spark
8. The First Flame
9. The First Dragon
10. The First Stone

The Adventurer

You crave a good epic tale. Read it all as one adventurous thrill.

1. The First Muse
2. The First Stone
3. The First Nymph
4. The First Spark
5. The First Flame
6. The First Breath
7. The First Dryad 1
8. The First Dryad 2
9. The First Dragon
10. The First Shadow

The Purist

You don't mess with perfection. Read in the exact order the books were written.

1. The First Dryad 1
2. The First Stone
3. The First Nymph
4. The First Flame
5. The First Dryad 2
6. The First Breath
7. The First Muse
8. The First Dragon
9. The First Spark
10. The First Shadow

The Elementalist

You are one with nature.
Read with each element
grouped together.

1. The First Flame
2. The First Dragon
3. The First Dryad 1
4. The First Dryad 2
5. The First Breath
6. The First Muse
7. The First Shadow
8. The First Spark
9. The First Stone
10. The First Nymph

The Scholar

You crave information.
Read in the order that fills
in the most details first.

1. The First Shadow
2. The First Dragon
3. The First Dryad 1
4. The First Dryad 2
5. The First Nymph
6. The First Breath
7. The First Stone
8. The First Muse
9. The First Flame
10. The First Spark

The Heartcrusher

You aren't afraid to cry.
Read from happiest to
most devastating.

1. The First Stone
2. The First Dragon
3. The First Flame
4. The First Spark
5. The First Dryad 1
6. The First Dryad 2
7. The First Shadow
8. The First Muse
9. The First Nymph
10. The First Breath

The Historian

You are a defender of order.
Read along with the true
timeline of the overall story.

1. The First Breath
2. The First Stone
3. The First Flame
4. The First Dragon
5. The First Dryad 1
6. The First Dryad 2
7. The First Nymph
8. The First Muse
9. The First Shadow
10. The First Spark

The Chaos

You like to tempt fate and tease
your brain. Read in the most
unnatural order possible.

1. The First Dragon
2. The First Spark
3. The First Muse
4. The First Nymph
5. The First Stone
6. The First Shadow
7. The First Dryad 2
8. The First Flame
9. The First Breath
10. The First Dryad 1

The Maverick

You don't color inside the lines.
Choose your own journey in any
order you wish!

I Will Be Punished

I rattled the cellar door, but it was no use. It was bolted from the outside, yet that did not stop me from trying. Hunger does not care if it compels one into dangerous consequences. It only demands. And so I rapped my knuckles on the wood, though I knew doing so would end poorly for me. We had company over, and company meant I'd spend the turns among the shriveled beet roots of last season. Quietly.

"Open the door...please? Won't you open? I will behave. I will stay quiet—"

I paused as I considered to whom I should address my plea. My brother went by many names. None of them were his. Sometimes, when I was very angry with him, I wanted to call him the name I knew belonged to him. The one he was born with. The one he denied as fiercely as he could but could never truly bury. If I called him this name, he would certainly open the cellar door, but it would not be to let me out.

"Aman, open the door!" I could smell the rich, bitter Caram flavors slow cooking upstairs, and it made me salivate, my stomach groaning. I closed my eyes, imagining biting into

coarse bread dipped in the strong, thick sauce. Very different
from our usual plain boiled potatoes, but it would fill my belly
just as much as it would burn it. The pungent smell meant my
brother was pretending to be something he was not yet again.
Caram sauce. It came from far away, he always explained,
warning me not to use it on our potatoes. If my brother was
preparing such an extravagant meal for his guests, they would
know him as Aman.

I sighed, giving the door one last touch, for I knew Aman
would not acknowledge me and let me out until his guests
departed. It would be two more turns still, at least.

The air was stale in the cellar, and there was no light. Not
that the streets above held more color or freshness. The
Neighboring Lands were dusty and soured, with harsh light
and dry soil, cluttered towns and diseased livestock. But I rarely
witnessed these things for myself anymore. I spent so much
of my time in some version of my current arrangement. For
eighteen circles, I followed the rules. In the cellar or under the
storage bins in the pantry. Or, my least favorite, beneath the
bath drain in the washroom.

After a few more hours in the cellar, when I was asleep on the
cold dirt floor, the door creaked open, and firelight flooded
the small space. I sat up quickly, my hands sweating in an instant.
It was far too soon for Aman to let me out. Guests always
stayed longer. Three turns for a visit. Four.

My brother descended the steps like he always did. Same
rhythm. One slow step, two quick ones. *One...two three.*
One...two three.

"There you are," he said, his tired voice dragging from his lips.

Aman knew where I was. Just as he knew I had not been quiet like I was supposed to be when he locked me away. His clean-shaven face and freshly cut hair indicated the effort he went through to impress his guests. *They must be important.* Followed by the realization, *I will be punished for interrupting his meeting.*

"Of course I'm here," I mumbled, a bit groggy, pushing my hair from my eyes. "Where else would I be? You are the one who put me in this place, Aman, and you are the only one with the key."

He made a humming noise in the back of his throat and crouched down in front of me.

"I am sorry about that, Aia."

"You do not need to be sorry."

He smiled, plopping down beside me, his muscular body clearly exhausted from all the hosting. He had no staff to assist him in his work, as we could not afford servants, and once the meetings began, I could no longer offer any help.

"It's not so bad in here," he said, motioning to the dark cellar that stretched out behind us. "And it teaches you to obey. You will need to learn obedience. It's important for your future, remember?"

I nodded, trying to keep the fire out of my eyes. Aman greatly disapproved of my eyes. Too lively. Too awake. Too intelligent. People would ask questions, he always said. And so I was to make myself as dull and blank as possible.

"Well..." he sighed. "You know I would never want you to be unhappy. I am your protector. I am to watch over you until you are ready to be offered for some greater use."

"I am thankful," I said. I was never certain if this was a true sentiment, but it was what I was taught to say. I wondered why Aman was reminding me of his duties and mine. Our father was dead. Our mother was dead. Of course Aman cared for me in their stead. He didn't have a choice. Nor did I. If he said to get into the cellar, I had to go. If he said to be thankful, I had to be.

"I am glad you are thankful. That is precisely what you should be. But...Aia"—he sighed as though there was some heavy burden he carried—"it is time now for me to take a wife of my own."

I had thought about this for many circles. I would have to accept it. That went without question, as Aman was at least seven circles older than me and should already have taken a wife. But it made my stomach hurt. Or perhaps it was the emptiness of hunger. Strange how lack could cause so much pain. "I will support you in this, Aman. Gladly."

"I knew you would. But it means I must change your position in the household. Your usefulness will be...revised. Of course, you will still be useful to me, but in a very different way."

I pulled my knees up to my chest. "My...position? It is only you and me here. What could change?"

"If I take a wife, she would be my priority and, well...you would be a threat to her. Do you understand?"

I shook my head. My chest hurt almost as much as my empty stomach, but neither would be filled any time soon. "Aman, I predict that your wife would hold a superior place in your affections and attention. I understand. I would not question this. I would not attempt to rival her."

"That is not what I mean by a threat, Aia." He leaned his head back on the shelves that I liked to press against as I slept. Those bare shelves made it feel like I was less alone when the nights were very long. My brother continued. "I will arrange for you to come home on festive turns if I can. And you can have cakes with us. When we have children, you will celebrate with us on those blessed turns. In that way, you will remain loved."

I could not help my eyes filling with tears and clutched the hem of my dress, pulling it further over my bruised knees. I was not ready to be taken, to be put to work in some place other than my home. "I will not question your new wife. Ever. I will even stay here in the cellar, if you wish, and only come out when she is asleep. I can be more useful that way and cook and clean while you rest. I would not mind more work or to stay hidden for a very long time. Aman, please. Please let me remain useful here, with you."

Ep 2

The End of Me

"I am very sorry. But I have put this off long enough, Aia. Guests...they do not trust an unmarried man. And if they knew I was protecting you all this time instead of taking a wife, they would not do business with me. If I cannot do business, I will starve. Then who would protect you? This is the best I can do for you. This is how I fulfill my oath to our parents."

My inhale was little more than a shudder. "I would rather you let me make my own way on the streets, then. I do not want to be taken by a stranger. I do not want to trade myself to be useful to someone I do not know. Perhaps I can make my own use. For myself. I could at least try, could I not?"

His eyes still closed, Aman spoke as if talking to himself. "I have an obligation to you."

I could not see, for my eyes blurred with anxious tears. I knew he had already decided, but I had to try. "You could disown me. Then you would have obligations to no one. I would prefer this, Aman, please. Please do this for me." *I would rather be devoured in the streets than be taken to a house where I work namelessly to please lustful or ambitious men.* Besides being married myself, which would be a joyous occasion that would cost Aman a large amount of gold, there were only two options for a young woman in our Realm. To work or be worked.

"Aia...my dearest." He sighed. "I have already informed the Palace."

I spun to face him straight on. "The Palace?" It was as if my mind was arguing with my body, trying to reason it into flight, into an escape. But I stayed seated next to my brother. "I thought you meant a workhouse. I thought you meant labor. Or...or whoring. But you...you *told* them?"

"I could not, in good conscience, let a gift like yours go wandering the streets. You would meet your end facedown in some dusty gutter or face up in some bed, wasting your talent, when greatness could be yours. Aia, this is for your best. A chance to shine. A chance to be who you are."

I hate you. I hate you, I hate you.

"No," I said. The tears mixed with the dirt caked on my cheeks from sleeping on the cellar floor with no blanket beneath me. "No. It is not bearable. I will suffer the same fate you aim to spare me, only some Monarch will be my undoing, Aman. It is a worse end. To be deemed useless in front of the entire Realm."

"This is not being presented as an option, Aia. It is for the good of us both. For my future and for yours."

I stopped listening. I'd never really believed my older brother, but I'd always *listened*. For survival. For food. For hope. But I could not do what he was asking me to. I could not go willingly to such a future. At least in my home, my future was predictable. I would help, I would hide. This went just so for circles and circles. *Why does it have to change?* The pain was familiar. The emptiness a solace of sorts.

"You must go with them now, Aia. They are waiting."

I dug my heels into the dirt. I would not go. My body would not let me. And it did not matter how sweetly Aman worded it. *This will be the end of me.*

Practicing Stillness

"Let's hope she will do nicely for him," the man said. He had a long face and an even longer beard, all white. His eyes squinted out of a countenance crowded with wrinkles. "Heaven knows we need a miracle."

My brother held me still. Well, as still as he could. From behind, he laced his arms though mine, pressing his palms against the back of my head so I could not escape his grasp. The old man squeezed each of my breasts with his spotted, leathery hands.

"Perhaps they will be filled with sap soon enough," he said with a curt nod. "I can sense these sorts of things. That is why he sends me."

The man pressed my cheeks together, wiggling his finger between my back molars so I had no choice but to open my mouth. He examined my teeth, wearing peculiar shimmering spectacles on his eyes. "No signs of disease or decay."

He leaned on the curved, black cane he held in his other hand. "You will want to lay her out on the table for this one. I would suggest the floor, but these bones are getting old. Gone are the

turns when inspections require me to get on my knees."
He snuffed, hobbling over to our kitchen table.

I fought. Only I could not fight. My brother was stronger
than me. Not only was he superior by size, but nutritionally,
I could not compare. So many turns spent in the dark of the
cellar made me weak. If not for the hatred shooting through
my veins, I might have fainted from hunger right there.

My brother dragged me to the table and threw me onto it,
knocking over the dishes my mother had hoped we would save
for my eventual marriage home. They clattered to the ground
as my body was pinned down, my brother crushing my upper
chest with half his torso to keep me still.

The old man lifted the hem of my dress, throwing it up over
my belly with little ceremony.

"I do not want to be here for this part," my brother said,
struggling to hold me still.

"Then you should have gotten a proxy," the old man muttered,
smacking his lips after the last word as he brushed off my
brother's concern.

I also did not want to be there for that part. And worse for
him, Aman could not cover my mouth and crush me into the
table at the same time.

"Aman, no! Please, *please* stop him!"

"You are only making it harder," he shouted over me.
"Practice stillness!"

But I could not because the man lifted a knife to the skin of
my outer thigh and dragged it downwards. To say that there
was pain would not be fair. I wanted to scream, but all that
came from me was a whimper. The muscles in my legs froze,
and my lower back spasmed in resistance.

The man then pressed something tiny into the incision, pushing deeply so that my body convulsed in response.

I knew what it was that he pressed into me. I could feel it the moment it was brought near. A seed. Dead and hardened. I did not mean to make it come to life but I could not help it. I could not say no. I twitched as the seed cracked and I did everything I could to rip myself from my brother's grasp when the baby vines coiled out of me, winding themselves along my thigh.

"Heavens," my brother said, "I have never seen such a thing."

Without consideration, the old man clasped his bony fingers around the vine and yanked it out, the roots tearing my flesh as they were forced to part with me. I cried out and went still, for the feeling in my chest was like no other sadness. As if a child had been taken from me. As if I had lost some great love.

"Well then. She is legitimate," the old man said, removing his hand from my thigh at last. He snorted his disapproval. "Clearly, she is not as obedient as you claimed," he complained. "Nevertheless, she is what we are searching for. And so she will be taken, as we discussed."

"And a bride for me? Also as discussed?"

The man nodded. "She will be sent in due time. If your sister passes muster at the courts. Which is highly unlikely. No one has passed muster for some great time."

Aman removed himself from me, relieving the pressure he'd been putting on my chest. I groaned and then sprang up and slid off the table, racing for the door. But Aman caught me by the ankle, sending me careening into the wooden floor. I scratched my way forward, but he pulled me back until he had a fistful of my pale hair in his hand. He yanked me backwards, eliciting a scream from me, and dragged me back to the man, who had not budged during our altercation.

"It does not look good for you," the man said to my brother, with a click of his tongue. "My estimation is that she survives three turns and not one turn longer."

My brother did not loosen his grip on my hair. "Perhaps a final beating will help?" he asked the man. "It may calm her."

"Perhaps," the man said. "If it is thorough." He adjusted his spectacles. "I, of course, will observe."

I did not care if my brother beat me. I had always given in relatively quickly when he'd done it before. Why fight back if there was nowhere else to go, no one else to run to? But this was different. Everything was different. I would not give in. I would rather Aman beat me to death than for me to go where they were taking me.

Aman dragged me to the bar set just above the ground near our oven. There, he tied my wrists to it. This of course forced me to either crouch or lie down, for I could not stand with my hands bound so low. Aman reached for the whip he kept mounted on the wall, letting it crack once before he took it to my hunched back.

I could not count how many fearsome lashes he laid on me, but he did not restrain himself, and I did not beg him to stop.

Finally, the old man intervened. "She will be no good to us dead," he said, moving toward my brother. "But she will be docile enough now for me to transport her without any further hysteria."

The man was not entirely wrong. I could hardly move, my wrists still bound, my body lying belly down on the floor. Aman clutched me by the hair, holding my head up while he

sliced the ropes he'd kept on that bar for all the circles he'd
taken care of me.

"I will need new ropes anyways," he said, explaining to no one.
"For my wife."

He lifted me over his shoulder, and I was aware how strange
it felt for my arms to dangle as if they were no longer part of
my body.

"Chain her there," the man said once we were out of doors,
just outside his horseless carriage. "You will see the cuffs on the
inside. They should fit her nicely, as they are designed for the
slim wrists of women. We take every precaution. He would
have it no other way."

Aman set me in the carriage. "Do not let me down, Aia,"
he said. "If you do not succeed, I will never afford a wife. Find
a way to make yourself useful to the High Monarchs."

There were no seats, no plush conditions. Only an empty
black cell of sorts on large wheels, with thick doors and no
windows. In the center of the floor was an iron hook with a
series of chains attached to it, and on the end of each chain,
a metal cuff. Aman clicked the cuffs to my wrists, and they
fastened without a key.

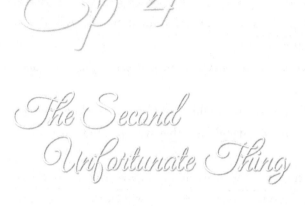

Ep 4

The Second Unfortunate Thing

There are two things no one wants to be in this world. I am one of those things.

The first is the wife of a High Monarch. It is the most stressful role in the entire Realm, and not because it comes without perks. For the High Queen is lavished with luxuries. I do not know what such luxuries could be but I have heard that they sparkle. And she does not even have to take a step if she prefers to be carried from luxury to luxury. But her role in life is to bear the King a son. After which, the High Queen has proven her usefulness and is promptly put to death. As a reward, I've heard. To be so revered, so honored, that no other heir may come from her. The one she made is perfect. And will be perfect forever. So the High King chooses a new wife to be Second Queen. And Third. And Fourth. Each bearing him one son. Each rewarded with death.

The second unfortunate thing one can be is a Tree.

I was spared the destiny of ever being High Queen. But in my heart twisted the thick vines of some ancient arboreal line. I could not bring a crowned heir to the line of Monarchs ruling

over the Realm, but I could do something far more mysterious.
I could give one of those kings a seedling.

When my parents first learned I was a Tree, they did not
react how a child might hope they would. I was lost to the
meaning and did not know it was something to be properly
hidden. I simply made a habit of passing by the bakery on my
way home from the school. The bakery was what my parents
and their friends called the building, though there was never
any baking done in that place. It was a roofless building with
decayed walls made of rubble and mud. My parents always said
people would go there to buy sweet breads, but I had never
tasted bread that was anything but sour and coarse, so I liked
to pause there and imagine what it must have been like.

I also made the habit of humming as I went along and I
noticed one turn that if I hummed just right at the back of
my throat, a particular little weed would wave its leaves at me.
There were very few weeds in the Neighboring Lands, but this
one, just an inch or two in height, grew pressed against a stone
in secret. This amused me, and so I would stop there every
turn, just long enough to imagine sweet bread and to hum a
note or two.

It was not until I was walking one afternoon with my
brother, my hand squeezed too tightly in his, that I was found
out. He yanked my arm, leading me home much faster than
my legs could consent to, and pushed my shoulders into the
wall of our shared little closet of a room.

"Never do that again," he said, hissing his words into my face.

"I do not know what I did!" I confessed. "But I will not do
it again."

"You must never even *look* at another green thing again, Aia," he said. "Never ever. Never. Do not think about them or look at them or speak to them." And then to make sure I understood, he drove his fist into my small face until I cried out.

He insisted that I never tell my parents, but they questioned me about the bruises until I confessed. It was a beating for both of us then, and more yelling about how I could 'never ever *never* do such a thing again'.

After that, I walked by the bakery and watched as the little weed, once grown bigger and healthier, its green, waxy leaves facing up, began to shrink and shrivel in the blanching sun of the Neighboring Lands. It shrank into nothing, and so did I beneath the eyes of my protectors.

Yet somehow, I found myself no longer safe beneath their strict gazes. With my parents dead, and after my brother sold my secret, I was, no doubt, on my way to the Palace. Whatever destined happenings were meant for Trees that made it so dreadful to be one...that was now my fate.

And so far, my fate was indeed dreadful. I squeezed my knees together, trying to forget the wretch of a little old man and how he had invaded me for his own speculations, trying to ignore the blood that flowed along my upper thigh and down the length of my leg. I closed my eyes and tried to imagine I was not in some strange carriage shackled to the floor and jostling about with no way to escape.

Over many turns, we stopped only long enough for the old man to bring other girls into the carriage. Some were wailing, their bright faces covered in filth and their noses bloodied from resistance. Others were dignified, their complexions of regal brown serving as mirrors for their composure in the face of this new future. Perhaps they always knew it was their destiny—to be a Tree.

In the evenings, the old man threw us chunks of bread and put out a bowl or two of water. As the number of girls grew, the fight for the bread became more ferocious. Most evenings, I chewed the only morsels I could attain and marveled at how dreadfully bitter and coarse, how very unsweet all bread seemed to be. Maybe my parents were liars. I wished they were, for then perhaps I was not going to where they always told me I would go if ever my secret was shared.

We slept wherever we sat. Some girls huddled for warmth while others bared their teeth if another came close. I assumed they stored bread in the linings of their dresses. We did not speak to each other. It seemed that was understood. We would not be friends. Perhaps we would be rivals.

Finally, we arrived at some destination in the very deadest part of night. I had no directional sense and no directional education. I hardly made it to age nine in school before my parents removed me for my own safety, for the weeds rejoiced when they saw me, whether I hummed at them or not. Because of this, I could hardly read or write and did not know which way I would have to go to get from the Neighboring Lands to the Pride Places or the Stolen Worlds.

The old man was the first person we saw upon arriving at our destination. He opened the carriage doors and made a sort of satisfied grunt with one of his curt nods.

"Well," he said, "it seems none of you have succumbed to death. Very good. Perhaps we have a promising lot. Heaven could only hope so." Then he put his hand on the carriage door. "Down you go then." And as he shut the door, the carriage floor gave way, and we plunged into what had to be an abyss—still shackled, and all screams.

I fell for so long that I was sure I would die. *What a cruel trick. So this is what is done with Trees. We are disposed of swiftly and without ceremony, like discarded objects collected in heaping piles of refuse.*

But when I thought for sure that my end would be met with my bones crushed into powder at the bottom of some dungeon cell, I felt the silky embrace of some other reality.

I yelped as I was snapped upwards and thrown sideways into what must have been a stone wall. I could not see what lay beneath me as I hovered, suspended in the air, a twisting vine around my waist and trailing along the wall, but I could hear. The crunch of bone as it struck a hard surface. The end of a scream as life was forced out of the body of a young woman. Then another. And another.

I gasped, my hands trembling as I clutched the vines that had sprung to life to support me. Not only did many of the girls I'd traveled with meet their end beneath me, but I had some plant in my grasp—or perhaps I was in the grasp of some plant. What Aman feared most for me I had brought upon myself. I was indeed a Tree and I could not deny it now.

With another snap, the vine around me broke off, and I dropped the rest of the way to the ground, landing on some-thing soft which I realized with a shriek was very recently a living human.

"This way," the old man's voice called in the echo of darkness.

I did not want to follow him, but as I led with my hands, feeling for a way out in the black madness, I realized that I was in an enclosed area. Perhaps a deep, wide well of some kind.

And some fear gripped me that perhaps there was a door or bars that would shut and trap me in. So I hurried after the old man, tripping over the fallen until I was through an opening.

And once through it, I appeared to be in a truly contradictory setting. It was a vast and glistening hall, with walls so high and shining like pearls and a ceiling domed with gold etchings of various shapes and sizes.

The old man stood before us and, with a tap of his cane on the gleaming floor, was no longer an old man, but a tall and refined woman, well in her circles, her purple dress modest but sewn of rich velvet, her hair grayed at the temples.

"Welcome, my Trees, to the place where you belong. If you are alive in this moment, it is because a destiny awaits you within these halls. If you are the last Tree living, a destiny awaits you far beyond any halls and far above any ceilings. Now we—"

The woman was interrupted by the slamming sound of doors opening and the murmuring of servants in plain tan clothing bustling about as if a fire were starting. I stood as I was, next to the girls who had also stumbled out of the dark place alive. One shook and cried silently. Another sat full on the floor, for it seemed her leg had broken in the fall. Others remained quiet and poised, their hands clasped before them. Regardless of our various states, we all craned our necks to see what could be the commotion. I noticed as well that the woman in purple paled and clutched her cane more tightly when she realized what was happening.

"Come, come!" a large man bellowed, "I was told that they would be here, and if they are, I will see them at once! Why should I be made to wait?"

The woman, who once was a very old man, angled herself to intercept the large man. "High Prince," she said, her voice wavering as she bowed deeply. "High Prince, the Trees are not ready for your observance. Truly they have only just arrived. They must be groomed, schooled, sampled, pruned—"

But the large man reached out a strong arm and batted the woman aside so firmly that she stumbled several steps before catching herself with her cane.

It was only the man then, standing before us. And of course, the crowd of servants picking lint off his shoulders and bumping into each other as they anticipated his needs. He was a giant of a young man. Broad shoulders and a strong dimpled chin. Pale blue eyes and fair hair. His clothes were as grand as he was, with a white bear coat bigger than five of my frocks put together. Each of his fingers were jeweled with gems larger than grapes. He put a hand on his hips and pursed his lips, his eyes darting between each of us girls.

"They look *dreadful*," he said, still eyeing us. He shifted his weight, as if this would make us appear more satisfactory. "Oh, they are *horrid*. Why have you even bothered to collect these, Clorente?" He waved a glistening hand. "Do away with these. Go out and try again."

The woman, Clorente, paused before she spoke. "These...are the last, High Prince."

The man whipped his head sharply at this news. "The last? The last what?"

"The last Trees."

"The last Trees in all the Realm? *These*? I will not accept this assessment of our predicament. Go out again. Search harder."

With a bowed head, "I have searched for circles with every method under my employ. I have even broken many rules of conduct to collect our Trees. Some of these you see before you were not willingly brought here, High Prince, yet I brought them at my own risk. For you."

"Well *plant new ones*, Clorente! I will not have some sniveling, shivering sapling producing my Seed! It simply will not do!"

"Trees are not planted; they are...made. It would take circles, perhaps an entire generation or two, for more young to be discovered and grown to maturity for you, High Prince. I fear it would be too late for you to find your Seed."

"And there are none who are slightly...*less* mature? But better looking and better smelling than these?" He wrinkled his nose as his eyes passed over me. "I can hardly stand to be in the same hall as them."

Clorente shook her head and audibly swallowed. "These are all. These are the last. If your Tree is not here, I fear...there is no Tree for you, High Prince."

The man gave a sigh as big as he was. "Fine. Fine. But we will find the *best* one for me. And she will match, Clorente. She will match, do you hear me? No more waiting. No more guessing. I am tired of bedding Trees and then converting them into kindling." He turned to leave. "And do not tell my father I have come here to see them. Promise me."

Clorente bowed in response.

But before he left, the High Prince turned back around and pointed at a thin, short, hook-nosed girl who was crying with violently shaking shoulders and, from the smell of it, had soiled herself somewhere between her home and the halls. "You can just go on and get rid of that one right off, Clorente. It offends me that you even considered her for me."

He flapped his hand, and Clorente nodded so that the girl was dragged by two servants, her heels scraping along the floor as she screeched.

I wanted to ask what they would do with her, but I knew the look on Clorente's face. It was one Aman would wear when his meetings with guests went particularly poorly. It meant I should be very quiet and make myself very small. If I could have locked myself in the cellar and hidden among the shriveled beets at that moment, I would have.

We were taken to a room, and the door swiftly closed behind us. The girl who had broken her leg found it very difficult to keep up, using the wall to pull herself forwards, and once we had all arrived, she lay face down on the floor and began to cry.

Our room was absolutely bare but large enough for us all to have space on the floor for sleeping. And at least we were not shackled. The shiny floor would be harder on my bones than the dirt of the cellar, but it was much cleaner than my home or the carriage or the hole we were plunged into moments before.

Finally, one girl broke into a gasping sob. "What is *happening?*" she asked, tears streaming from her round eyes. "Why are we here? *What is happening?*"

"Do not be so loud," another girl whispered with coarse condescension, "or they will come in here and take some of us away. If we are quiet, they will forget about us."

"No," another girl spat out, "why would they travel all over the Realm to collect Trees and then forget about us in a room? Were you not listening to the High Prince? We are coveted and desired by the Monarchs. The High Prince could not even *wait* to see us. I, for one, believe I have caught his eye." The brown girl nodded her own affirmation, her thick, tight curls bobbing as she did so. And for a moment, I swore I heard a faint rustling sound, like what I'd always imagined leaves to sound like as they moved across the ground. "I will be his True Tree. I will give him the Seed every Monarch desires. And our Realm will ascend to great renown because of me. It is my destiny."

She said the last word, 'destiny', as if it were some sort of incantation.

"Seed? *What Seed?*" The round-eyed girl could not stop crying. "What Seed?"

The brown girl sighed. "Stupid Tree. If you even are one. We are the very spirits of nature, are we not? Descendants of the first trees given to humankind. And as such, mating with one of us would produce a seed for a Monarch. An heir not to the crown, but to nature itself. But first we must be the match for that Monarch. And so far, no Monarch has found a matching Tree in many generations."

The round-eyed girl still shook her head. "But I've never even *seen* a tree! There are no trees in the Neighboring Lands! Those are only left in children's stories!"

"All the more reason why you will not be chosen for the High Prince," the brown girl said with a little smile. "We still have trees in the Pride Places. I can already feel our future Seed coming to life within me." She sighed. "The High Prince is everything I dreamed of. He is so commanding. So...strong."

Just then, the girl with the broken leg let out a little groan and sort of...deflated where she lay facedown in the center of the room.

"Oh heavens," said the brown girl. "Did she just...die?"

I crawled over to the one with the broken leg. Upon a simple touch, I realized that she was quite feverish. Burning much hotter than anyone ever should. The girl would in fact die if no one tended to her. *What if no one comes for some time?*

I tried to reason with myself. Many girls had already died. They were weeded out, really. And what was one more? And if I spoke up on this girl's behalf, she would probably die anyways, and then there would be two deaths on her account because I would be killed as well.

But the broken-legged girl refused to stop groaning, and after some time I could not stand it anymore. I stood up and tried the door handle. To my great surprise, it opened.

"Are we not locked in here?" the round-eyed girl marveled. But then she shook her head. "Still, I would not go if I were you, strange girl. It is probably a test of some sort."

Strange girl? What does that mean? Was I more strange than any of the others who sat or lay curled up on the floor of some foreign room, awaiting torture or death?

I ignored Round Eyes and slipped out of the cracked door.

I was always very good at sneaking. Aman would complain that my footsteps made no sound. That I could light from one room to another as if I were hovering over the ground, invisible. So I tiptoed through the many corridors, looking for someone who could help me with the girl who lay fevered and dying in our room. I hoped they would not be too angry that I came for help, seeing as the loud Prince was very concerned about an apparent shortage of Trees and would not want one of us to die for no reason.

Most of the rooms were completely empty and chilled, no fires in their hearths. But finally, I peeked into a room with a door half-closed and when I noticed how warm and inviting the place was, I slipped inside, careful not to make a sound. There was a man there, tall, though he leaned back against a large wooden desk surrounded by shelves and shelves of massive books. He held one of those books in his hands, his head bent and his eyes trained on the words. He flipped the pages often, as if the book had very few words on it. But I could see from where I stood near the door that there were a great many words on each page. I could read none of them, while he devoured them with such ease.

"It is impolite to stare." The man said this without looking up, and I wondered at first if he referenced someone else. But upon glancing around, I realized he must have been speaking to me, for no one else was present, and somehow, without my noticing, I had left my hidden corner and ventured into the center of the room.

I wanted to speak to him, then, if he had already gone and noticed me, but it was suddenly very difficult to find words.

The man closed the book and straightened up, moving closer to me. His dark hair reminded me of smoke and soot, and as he approached, I saw his eyes were a deep, stormy blue, clouds of gray passing across them as if someone were stirring a great sea.

"Are you lost?" he asked. "Or simply too nosy to bother with manners?"

I was neither. *Speak, Aia. Tell him why you came.*

The man tilted his head at me. "You are not dressed as a servant but are too filthy to be a dignitary. Are you here to take my life then? Is this a coup? This happens from time to time. Someone creeping past the guards to finish me off." A smile played at the corner of his mouth. "Did my brother hire you? He is getting desperate."

I swallowed and brought words to my lips. "Someone is dying."

He blinked, shocked. "You *are* attempting to kill me? Could you even manage it? You look half starved!"

"No." I shook my head, making fists out of my sweaty hands. "No, someone has a fever. One of the girls. I came looking for help."

"Girls?"

I nodded. "Yes."

"You will have to be more descriptive. There are many, many girls in this Palace."

"One of the Trees."

The man paused, studying me. "I thought, by the look of you, that perhaps you were one. But I did not want to assume. Safer to believe you were a killer." His face became stern, his jaw tightening. "I will send someone to help her. Now go back to your room before it is found out that you came here. And never do something like this again...wandering off to help someone else. It will only get you killed before your time, Little Tree."

I looked over my shoulder to where I had come from. "But the door to our room. It was open...."

"An open door is always either an invitation or a trap," he said in a tone too solemn. "Sometimes it is both."

"But your door was open as well...." I swallowed, wondering why I had said such a thing to a strange man who was obviously much more important than I, who could read books in mere moments, and who had the authority to send for help when it was needed.

"So you should listen to my advice on doors then, Little Tree, and leave this one as quietly as you entered through it."

I turned to go, but even as I walked back to the other girls retracing my silent steps, I remembered the feeling of the man's eyes on me, searching me, pondering. Eyes that were stormy blue and wildly gray. Calculating. Fierce. And filled with unspoken sadness.

Without knowing why, I thought to myself...*I will get those eyes to see me again*. I kept this thought tucked in my heart, for I was afraid to even acknowledge its existence.

Ep 5

Silence is the Pride of Every Tree

I slipped back into our small room and found a spot on the floor. Quite accustomed to making myself comfortable in various spots on floors, I waited for someone to come help the fevered girl with the broken leg. I fell asleep, my head leaning on the bare wall, and dreamed of falling down a deep, dark hole until my whole self was planted in the soil, buried in the depths of the dirt. The High Prince stomped his heel into the ground above me, sealing me in until the soil filled my mouth and eyes and nose.

I awoke with a gasp, a cold cane smacking the bottom of my worn shoe.

"Open your eyes. There is no time for sleeping." Clorente loomed over me, a scowl painted on her elegant, tired face. "We have work to do and no time in which to do it."

She drove her cane into the ground over and over, shaking the very walls of the room until all the girls stirred. I looked for the one with the broken leg, but she was no longer with us. I wondered with a sinking heart if she had died or if anyone had ever come to tend to her. Had the man with the book done as he said he would and sent for help?

Clorente pulled my attention back to her. "Our first course of action is traditionally to prepare you for work, but because of the eagerness of the High Prince, which was on full display for you all yesterturn, we will change our usual programme and begin with appearance. If he sees you again in such slovenly states, the High Prince might just toss the whole lot of you out. And that will not do."

Clorente moved to the center of the room, the train of her violet dress following behind her in ripples that made me dizzy, and lifted her cane high into the air. She brought it down, but I never heard it connect with the floor, for the moment it should have done so, I was submerged in a flood of water.

I held my breath, telling myself not to inhale from the shock, an action that might have filled my lungs with water. Instead, I reached my hands out to feel my surroundings, for I could see nothing but blue at first. Was I in a body of natural water? A river or a lake? Or had I been plunged into another well or a pool? My palms pressed against an invisible barrier— possibly glass.

I focused my eyes to see through the cyan water and found the other girls, each in their own water baths, fully submerged, their hair dancing around their heads like strange sea-bound flowers. Some girls, like Round Eyes, panicked, running their noses into the glass in vain. Others tried swimming upwards, though it was clear to me that they were not moving one measure no matter how hard they swam.

I looked over to the beautiful brown girl, who noticed me as well. She was not striving, but rather floated with both her hands on the glass, bubbles leaving her mouth and nose and traveling up to some surface we could not see.

After a few more moments, when my lungs burned beyond belief and my mind told me surely I would die, I inhaled without meaning to. The water trickled into my lungs and forced me to cough, and when I did so, I swallowed even more water. The more I swallowed, the heavier I became until I began to sink to the bottom of the containment. I wanted to thrash violently, but I saw no point to it. My brother had already sold me to my demise, and thrashing had not saved me then. If this was it...this was it.

When I felt I was more water than girl and had sunk further than I thought possible, I was spit out onto the floor, landing back in the room where I had started. I did not cough or hack, only took in a powerfully long breath, the air entering me like a sharp knife. I observed in awe as the water I'd swallowed gushed out of my pores like a thousand little waterfalls.

Clorente frowned, still in the center of the room, as girls appeared, seemingly out of nowhere, soaking wet and gasping for life.

There were only so many Trees remaining. Nine of us. Some did not return from the water. I thought we'd lost Round Eyes, but she collapsed onto the ground at the very last moment, gagging and expelling water from her stomach through her mouth. That made ten.

"Oh dear," Clorente huffed. "Are none of you even partly prepared for this?" She pressed a hand to her temple. "Attendants," Clorente called out loud to no one. "The grooming may begin."

The door burst open, and many plain-clothed servants cluttered the room, each carrying a cloth bag half as large as they were.

One of them came to me, circled around to my back, and began tugging through my pale hair with a wide comb while I was still on my knees. She murmured at the back of her throat every time she hit a particularly nasty snag, but I tried not to complain or pull away. Instead, I studied the other girls, for they were so varied in appearance and reaction.

Round Eyes had straight brown hair cut off at just below her chin, with another layer in front cut right at her eyebrows. Her servant clipped her hair shorter with a small pair of scissors so that it only reached down to her cheekbones. Then, the groomer tilted her head back with a rough tug and began applying a thick white cream to her cheeks and nose. Round Eyes whimpered and tried to pull away, but the servant was not gentle and did not permit it. After a while, Round Eyes resisted more aggressively. "It burns!" she shouted. "Oh, it burns!" But the servant pretended not to hear her, coating her arms and legs in the same cream.

"Do not resist," Clorente instructed, pacing and overseeing, her hands clasped behind her back. "Practice stillness. Practice quiet. Submit, submit."

Another girl, with thick wavy hair so red it outshone the tomatoes I'd sliced for Aman's meetings, wept as the servant dipped her hands into bowls of pink liquid.

The Brown Beauty kept her eyes closed as her servant combed through her crown of black and gold curls. For some reason I could not fathom, smoke billowed up from the back of her head. I wondered if her servant was singeing her hair or her scalp. When a silent tear slid down her noble nose, I decided it was the latter.

As for me, the servant opened a basket of what looked like powder. She took a soft brush and began to dust it on the tops of my shoulders, my forehead, my nose. Even my hair. At first the powder tingled, like little cinders lighting on my skin. But after a few moments, the tingling was more like the lightning I'd seen through the window slits of our home. Because the slits were always either angled to the sky or to the ground, I could see very little of my surroundings. So when lightning lit the heavens, I enjoyed the thrill so terribly much, for the changing lights were not lost on me.

But that thrill was not so enjoyable as the powder bit through my skin. I wanted to scream, but I had not screamed when I was falling to my death in a dark well or when I was trapped in a watery prison, so I did not scream then.

"Open your eyes please, Lady Tree," the servant said in her timid murmur, moving so she was facing me. I realized then that she was just a girl, no older than fifteen or sixteen.

She pinched my eyes open and dripped what looked like oil into them. A flashing, blinding blast of white heat followed by ice. A sound left my mouth, released out of sheer terror, and after that, I bit my lips, pressing my palms into my knees. *No more, no more of this.*

"It will not last forever," the servant girl whispered. "I'm almost through, Lady Tree. I promise."

She poured a honey in my hair that made me lose all feeling down my back and shoulders.

Then followed water that smelled of something...different. I had never experienced such a thing before. The scent of starting over, of persisting through many circles, of coming alive even after dying. She poured the water over my whole body, rinsing the powder, the oil, and the honey away and ridding my body of any recollection of pain. This last part was so pleasant that I could not stop the tears from leaving me.

"There," my servant said. "We are finished for this turn."

She gathered all of her odds and ends into her enormous cloth bag, hauled it over her thin shoulder, and left, straining to fit through the door.

"Now we will clothe you," Clorente said with another tap of her cane.

I braced myself, closing my eyes for whatever horrid ordeal was about to ensue. *Will she stitch the clothes right onto my body? Will I be forced to walk around the Palace naked?* But when I opened my eyes, all the girls were in matching green dresses—such a light green that it might have been sage. They were ordinary, but they flattered each of the girls' shapes nicely. A low neckline for Round Eyes, one that revealed all of Brown Beauty's shoulders, and so on.

"Follow me," Clorente said, snapping her ankles as she made a sharp turn and headed to the door. "It is time to teach you how a Tree must eat. Quickly now. We have so little time."

Brown Beauty was first, lining up behind Clorente as she exited the room. I watched as the other girls found their way into that line, and I too fell into place, dead last. I preferred this, for I planned to take in my surroundings as we walked, and being boxed in by girls on both sides would only make me nervous.

The Palace was extraordinary. Servants hustled through the grand open foyers and slipped quietly through the wide gallant corridors. The ceilings were gilded with gold and the floors shimmered and gleamed as if soaked with water. We walked past the room I had ventured into the night before, and I dared to peer inside as we hurried by. The door was still open, but no brooding man could be seen among its books.

I wanted to leave the group and lose myself in that room in case he returned so I could ask about the broken-legged Tree, but I kept with the group. *Better not end up wherever the poor girl with the broken leg is now.*

Into a dining area, a long table was set with the finest linen and the most elegant placements. The spoons shone a blinding gold. The glasses glinted like they were carved from diamond.

"Sit, sit," Clorente said.

We all took a seat and waited. But no one brought out any food. No servants dared to move.

"Umm...excuse me, Miss...Lady...um...." A girl with short, pretty brown curls raised her hand. "Will food not be served?"

Clorente narrowed her eyes at the girl. "Have you never heard that silence is the pride of every Tree?"

The girl's eyes went wide. "Silence?"

"*Silence.*"

She clamped her mouth shut and turned a reddened face back to her empty plate.

Finally, Clorente cleared her throat. "Very well. Off we go"— a servant interrupted her, whispering into her ear until both she and the servant wore matching strained expressions.

"We are being called out of doors at the High Prince's command and we cannot deny him nor keep him waiting so...up. Up! Quickly! I will speak of him as we go so you may fill your empty heads and perhaps not be thrown into the fire on your first full turn." She sighed, leading the way. "High Prince Theor. He has twenty circles. This spring will mark his twenty-first, and he will need his Seed by then. His father, High King Harrod, did not receive his Seed in time. And neither has any High King in the Royal line for many generations. So one of you must provide the Seed for the High Prince. You simply must. Here are some things about him you ought to keep in mind so as to not turn his wrath upon you. First...."

At the back of the line, I could hardly hear Clorente. This did not trouble me so much, for I found an object that much better held my attention. In the walkway, on an elaborate little table, was a glass with water in it. And in the water floated a plant. Not just any plant, but one so beautiful, it took all my focus not to touch it.

I stared at it, noticing the subtle way its pink little leaves unfurled as I watched.

"Would you like it?"

"Very much so."

"Well then, it's yours."

"Mine?" Very few things in my life had ever been mine. I honestly could think of nothing I owned except the clothes Aman found for me, and even those were his to give or take. "What do you mean?"

When I asked the question, I realized I was not having a discussion in my own mind, but was indeed speaking to someone. I shook my head, turning to see who it was.

The stormy one did not smile at me. His face was solemn, his eyes more violent and overcast than they had been the night before.

He cleared his throat, as if trying to communicate something to me, but I did not catch his meaning, so I ended up only staring at him, lost.

This did make the corner of his mouth ease upwards. It was a beautiful mouth, perfectly carved into a handsome face. I wanted to touch it as much as I longed to hold the plant. But I kept my hands where they were.

The man nodded at the plant. "You have made it bloom. Are you well practiced?"

"Practiced?"

"You appear to be skilled. You influenced the flower without even touching it."

I turned back to the pink-leaved plant. "Flower? That's what it's called."

"A leona flower, to be specific. I am surprised you do not know of this...."

"I know very few things, I'm afraid."

"I doubt that." He stepped forward, plucking the flower from its home in the glass and offering it to me.

I could feel the water in the flower immediately begin to decrease as he held it in the air. "No," I said. "Please put it back. It prefers the water, I think."

He plunged it back in the glass, placing his hands behind him. "Very well. As you please."

Then, as if startling himself, he looked around, his cheeks going red. "What in heaven's name am I thinking, talking to you in the middle of a walkway like this. You must forgive me; it's not proper of me at all."

I blushed on his behalf. "It was only talking."

"I should not...." He bowed to me. "Goodbye, Little Tree. Do not lose Clorente, or she will find out you and I have been speaking. Go on and catch up with the others."

I had forgotten all about Clorente and the others. I hurried after them, lifting my skirts as I ran.

I met them on the stairs that led out of doors, and when I looked up, I almost slipped and fell all the way to the bottom, for the sight I beheld made me shriek.

Plants. So many. And so big and tall they towered well over any man. Maybe a hundred times the height of a carriage.

I did not know I was running until someone caught me—a servant's arm across my belly, holding me still—and forced me to stop. It was as if a madness had taken over me, a desire to be where those plants were, in the heart of them, touching them, knowing them.

"You must practice stillness," Clorente said, her voice attempting to cut through my complete lack of thoughts. I felt as if I were made of instinct. As if the buzz of the plants had replaced my mind.

Clorente came to me and put her hands on my shoulders so she could shake me. When that did not work, she slapped my cheek. The sting only made me want to run to the plants more. Finally, she held my face, blocking my vision of them.

"Child, come now. You must calm yourself."

I wanted to answer her but could only mumble nonsense.

"What you see there is a tree. Perhaps your first tree. But you cannot go to it yet. They will be there, *waiting*, when it is time. For now, you must embody that tree you see. You are the Tree, child. Now come. Stand up straight, with dignity."

She tucked some loose strands of my hair and straightened the straps of my sage dress.

It was still so difficult to pay attention to her, but I tried. I did not want to die until I had touched one of those trees. So I would obey.

"Here he comes," Clorente said, smoothing her skirts. "Remember what I taught you."

Taught me? Oh, I was not present for her lecture. What was his name? The High Prince?

The fair-headed giant of a man rode up on horseback, dismounted with no care as to who would take his horse, and strode up to us, slapping his black gloves against the chest of the servant who had stopped me from running into the trees.

"Well now, Clorente, a much better looking crop than yester-turn's," he said, his light blue eyes glossing over our bodies.

"These are the same Trees, High Prince," Clorente said carefully. "Only now they are more prepared to see you."

"They still seem a bit plain," he said with a shrug. "Shall I pick one now and take her inside?"

My being involuntarily stiffened, and suddenly, I wished I were crouched in my dark cellar.

High Prince Theor continued. "I don't see why I cannot simply bed them all and see which gives me a Seed."

Clorente paled. "Most esteemed High Prince, doing so would only assure that you have no Seed at all. A Seed is to be granted only when there is a match made. You must be compatible, and the Tree must be...willing."

"So...*make* one of them compatible with me."

Clorente bowed. "I will do my very best, Prince. What will be the most helpful in this process is for you to guide us. For us to know what you desire in a Tree. If you would take the time to share with us—"

"Light," Theor snapped. "Should they not sparkle or gleam? The histories say they must. But these...they look like blocks of wood standing here before me. And we have the ball coming soon, at which I would like to show them. They should sparkle at my ball."

Clorente nodded. "Yes, but Prince, what do you desire...personally?"

He frowned. "I like a good breast. Two of them, to be more specific."

A couple of the girls gasped. Clorente could not have paled further. "That is not what I—"

"You know who would be better at this?" Theor said, switching which hip he had cocked out. He motioned to someone walking very far away across the lush green of the courtyard. I tried not to run and dive into that green, keeping my feet planted as Clorente expected while the faraway figure drew near.

"Heavens, could you not walk any slower, Willen?" Theor said.

Stormy eyes peered at us in the morning sun. I felt my heart squeeze tightly in my chest as those eyes passed over me, pausing briefly as if in acknowledgment.

Theor gripped the shoulder of the man he'd called over. "I need you to tell the Trees what I like."

The man frowned deeper than he already was. "What you...like?"

"Yes. What interests me, or something. Besides breasts. And sparkling. Clorente already knows those two."

The man—Willen, the High Prince had called him—put a hand to his temple. "Why do *you* not simply tell them your preferences, Theor?"

"Because I can't be bothered. And you know me better than anyone, wouldn't you say?"

Willen shook his head. "I am to have lunch with the ambassador of—"

"Lunches can be rescheduled."

"I have to prepare so many documents this turn. The High King has demanded—"

"There is nothing more important to our father than my finding the right Tree, is there, Willen?"

With that, the High Prince kissed Willen's face and left, yelling at a servant as he ascended the stairs.

Willen sighed, letting his arms fall to his side and facing us. "Good morning, then, I suppose," he said, his voice subdued as if his thoughts had not settled. "I am..." he sighed, then snapped out of it, "...I am Willen Vedan, Second Prince of the Realm, and I will...*quickly*...explain my brother's preferences. Heaven help us all."

I must have imagined that he glanced at me before he began. It was easy to fabricate such a thing because I was relentlessly staring at him. Realizing this made my cheeks burn, but I still could not stop from looking.

Of course you are looking, I told myself. *He is the only one speaking. Where else would you look?*

"My brother enjoys many physical exploits, including riding, wrestling, boxing, and swordplay. But he likes these things because he enjoys being complimented and admired, even more than he likes winning. He also prefers women who put up just enough resistance to his...charm. Good luck with finding the balance there.

"He despises duck but loves pheasant. He desires to be the loudest in the room at all times. Tell him he has a strong neck, and he will melt in your hands. He hates to read but loves to appear well read. Therefore, he misquotes many books. Never correct him. He knows nothing of politics except for how to make a mess of them. A decent grasp of politics yourself would help you to keep him from starting a war, particularly from starting one in your name.

"He likes things that sparkle. He likes women who dance for him. And he belches unforgivably once the hour has reached past nine."

Willen turned to Clorente. "Is that enough, Clorente? I really do need to be off."

Clorente bowed deeply. "You have been most helpful, Second Prince, as always you prove to be."

"Oh yes," he said, scowling, "so much *help* am I." He was about to leave but he held up a finger. "I almost forgot. The last thing you should know about Theor is that he has attempted to have me killed at least thrice every circle since we were children. He cannot do it himself, of course, what with the Royal laws, but heaven help if he doesn't find a way for someone to slip on a wet floor while holding a poisoned knife aimed at my stony heart." He nodded. "Good turn and good luck, Honorable Trees. I do not envy your plight, nor should you envy my complete lack of one."

I watched him leave, his back erect, the nape of his neck lit with the sun, and his ashen hair disappearing from my sight the further he got.

I turned my attention back to Clorente just in time for her to say these words, "...and you will need to read the *Tree Of Light* manuscripts, specifically the passage on glowing, before the ball. The books will be waiting in your room."

I could hardly lift my feet off the ground as we left the sight of the trees and the glow of the sun. What a feeling, having light on my skin and pouring into my eyes at last. And what a feeling, to know that not only would I have to learn how to glow in one night if I would live to see the next turn, but that I would also have to learn how to read.

Ep 6

What Nightmares Do You Mean?

Tree Of Light. A heavy book with a leather cover. Well worn and with a grand, sprawling tree etched onto the front. I traced my fingers along the engraving, imagining that the brown markings were truly leaves, singing with life in their veins and pretending that the twisting roots along the bottom of the cover could reach their tendrils down to the soil and drink like the little plant at the bakery near my home. I ought to have been reading the manuscript but I had not even attempted to open it.

Brown Beauty sighed, shutting her copy of the book with a snap. "This is pointless," she muttered, leaning back on the wall of our small room, her long legs crossed on the floor. "I have already memorized most of this text. My education as a Tree was very thorough. The nobles of the Pride Places took great pains to make sure I had unlimited access to all the ancient texts."

Round Eyes sniffled, though there were no tears in her eyes. "We don't have nobles in the Neighboring Lands. Or access to ancient texts." She held the book up, revealing that the knuckles of her left hand were calloused and marred from what must have been circles of hard work. "This book might as well be written in another language. I can't make any sense of it. Maybe you could translate...?"

Brown Beauty barked out a laugh, her white teeth gleaming. "Why would I aid my competition? On the contrary, I hope you become more and more confused the longer you read! Stupid Tree. Now I know your weakness, though I suspected it from the beginning. Why would you share it with me? I will use it against you, don't you know? The High Prince will be mine, and to ensure this, I will make certain he is not yours."

Round Eyes blinked, her mouth agape. "I do not want the High Prince! I also do not want to die here in this Palace. And speaking of dying...will we make no mention of the nightmares we have endured?"

She looked around, but most of the girls pretended they were reading and could not hear her at all.

Brown Beauty sneered. "Pray tell, what nightmares do you mean?"

"Are you making a joke? We were taken from our homes in chains. And then dropped into a literal hell hole. And then drowned almost to death. And then servants came and burned and poisoned us. We have not been fed since the chains in the carriage, and even then it was only bread and water if we were lucky enough to snatch some before anyone else could get to it."

Brown Beauty shrugged. "First of all, I still have bread in my dress."

Round Eyes gasped, moving to her hands and knees in her excitement. "How? Clorente changed our clothes!"

"I brought it with me, Stupid Tree." Brown Beauty sighed, as if being bothered, though she seemed more than glad to be caught up in conversation. "Do you truly know nothing? And the bread was only first of all. Second of all, these trials are not nightmares. They are hardly even trials. They are rites of passage and are meant to prepare us, body, mind, and heart, to be True Trees for the future High King. For the realm. Trees are constrained to keep them erect as they grow. Hence the chains. And their seeds are planted deep in the earth, hence the dark shaft. We must be watered, so the water bath makes perfect sense. They are taking care of us, not torturing us. And the hardships are merely symbolic."

Symbolic? I rubbed the place on my wrist where the chains had worn on me and caused pain. The events seemed rather realistic to me.

Round Eyes paused, licking her chapped lips and staring at the book in her hands. "So...you will not help with the book? You know it so well—"

"I will not help you. And no one else will either. Because I have my eye on all of you, and if you try to form an alliance against me, I will destroy you with great ease."

One of the other girls giggled. "Destroy us? No need to be so dramatic."

Brown Beauty narrowed her eyes at the giggler and remained glaring at her for some time until she began to scream. Thin dark green vines curled out of her nose, slowly at first and then more quickly, twisting as they went.

Brown Beauty grinned in response, willing the vines to curl further and, I was certain, forcing the plant to take root in the girl's brain or perhaps down her throat.

"Enough," I said. I was amazed, first off, that I spoke this out loud. I was also quite surprised that my voice was so clear and deep, filling up the whole room. The sound of it made the skin on my arms tingle.

Brown Beauty tossed her head toward me. "Oh, the saintly Tree will come to the rescue of the arrogant one, now will she?"

"No," I said, still cool. "If you do not stop, it will be you who needs rescuing." *It will be? Heavens, what am I saying?*

Brown Beauty sneered. "Your empty threats fall at my feet like dead leaves."

The girl, whose only mistake was to giggle at the wrong time at the wrong Tree, flung herself onto the floor, arching her back and clutching at her face, trying in vain to pull the plant out.

Brown Beauty eyed me. "What will you do?"

I did not know what to do. I did not know how to stop Beauty. But people—or Trees rather—were not playthings. There was no purpose to this abuse, and so it needed to end. But since I could not think of what to do besides glaring back at Brown Beauty, I was quite useless.

Finally, the white-toothed Beauty chuckled, releasing the giggler from her misery, the vines retreating back where they came from. "I will leave the seed where it is, just in case you decide to mock me again," Beauty said, scooting back against the wall and spreading her book open in her lap. "And take note, Trees, that I have put one in all of you while you slept, but you will have no idea in what location it has been buried." She reached her hand into the bodice of her dress and pulled out a chunk of bread, nibbling on it and humming a tune.

I heaved a sigh marbled with frustration and relief and I returned to my book as well, cracking it open for the first time. The shapes and figures meant nothing to me. I could hardly recall the ones that marked out the spelling of my own name. I tried to make sense of it, turning the pages at the same pace as the other girls so it seemed I was making some realistic progress of my own.

When at last it became too dark to see and the gentle snoring of the girls rose and fell around me, I stood and tiptoed to the door. Yet again, it remained unlocked.

Do not go the same way you went last time, I told myself. *You must not be a bother. You must not harass a Second Prince more than once. It is a wonder you survived doing so the first time!*

I turned the opposite direction, keeping close to the walls in case I ran into anyone who could punish me for wandering in places I was not permitted to wander. The walls were smooth and bright compared to my childhood home, with its dilapidated, insect-ravaged wood paneling and cracked, warped floors. I could hear no pipes leaking in the Palace and no floorboards groaning with my steps. The glistening material beneath my feet danced under the many chandeliers dangling like clouds in the sky.

Eventually, after meeting many closed doors, I came to one that was partly open, warm golden light filtering through the hazy air. The sound of rustling papers and a scratching quill tickled my ears. I peeked past the door to see an ashen head bent over mounds of scrolls, scribbling onto many pages.

How did I arrive here when I set my intention to go the opposite way, to avoid this very scenario? I studied him for a while longer. The slight downward curve of his fine mouth. The way he brought his hand to his brow when he paused to think. *What dense work he must be doing.*

After some time, I scolded myself. *Go back to your room, Aia, or he will catch you.*

Just then, he set his quill back in its inkwell. "May I help you?"

I gasped, dropping a book onto the floor, quite nearly on my own toes. Too many realizations flooded me then, and all of them were curiosities. *Where are my shoes?* I was completely barefoot and could not remember taking off the sturdy green footwear Clorente had magically placed me in. *How did this book appear in my hand?* For I had not planned to bring it with me. Why would I have, when I certainly could not read it? And finally, *Why—how in heaven—did I stray to the center of the room, yet again, when I firmly decided to remain hidden behind the door?*

"You dropped your book," the Second Prince said with a smirk. "Did you do that on purpose, Little Tree?" He folded his ink-stained hands together in front of him, his elbows on the desk.

I bent and snatched the book up, clutching it to my chest. "Why would I drop a book on purpose?"

He tilted his head. "To appear helpless."

"Why would I put so much effort into feigning a state to which I have already fallen victim?"

His eyebrows raised, his stormy eyes lightening for a moment. "You are a victim to helplessness?"

"Well, I am here in this Palace against my will. And I cannot help myself except to accelerate my own demise if I so choose, which I do not. So yes, I would say I am quite helpless. And so, if I drop a book, it is not some strategy. I am merely nervous. And now you have made fun of me for it."

"Hmm...." He picked up his quill after studying me for just a bit and made as if he would write again. But before he touched it to his paper, he looked back up at me, surprised that I still stood before him. "Will you not...*go*, then, since I have made you so nervous?"

I knew how ferociously I blushed, and how my heart squeezed almost to the point beyond beating in my chest, and how my hands gripped the book too tightly. But I could not, for any reason or after any amount of urging myself, convince my feet to move.

The Second Prince laughed, but not the happy sort, and stood up from his seat. He approached me, his white shirt unbuttoned at the top and his brown breeches nicely cut and perfectly hemmed. When he was very close to me, he reached out to take the book from my hands.

I let him do this, of course, because he was a Monarch of the Realm, and who was I to deny him? Except when I looked down at my arms, the book was still pressed against my bosom, and his hand had retreated, for I had dodged its advance with the slightest deflection.

He was very surprised then, as was I, and his dark blue eyes glittered with amusement. "May I see your book please, Honorable Tree?"

I bit my lip as I handed it to him. And then, because I did not know what to do with my empty hands, I clenched the formerly smooth fabric along the sides of my sage green dress.

The Prince traced his fingers across the leather cover of the book, and I felt my chest burn. I gasped at this response, for it was not allowable for me to think about his fingers or the way they moved so lightly over the brown leather. I was not meant to wonder what those same hands would feel like wandering over my skin.

His eyes flicked up at me when I gasped, but then, when he saw I had nothing to say, he continued with his examination of the book.

"*Tree Of Light*. One of the primary ancient texts. I am assuming Clorente will have you read a passage?" He flipped through the pages, devouring the words with great ease.

"Yes, we must be prepared by tomorrow. She expects us to...glow...at the ball."

"I see. And you are wandering the halls because you have finished with your studies?"

I shook my head, swallowing so the words might come out. "No, I am wandering because I am not entirely sure what a ball is or what it means to glow during one."

He kept his gaze on the turning pages. "A ball is a faux-elegant, loud, tasteless party where women are put on display and men must publicly pretend they cannot have them. They are both gaudy and tiresome affairs and largely mandatory for Monarchs." He held the open book up in one hand. "And as for the glowing, I believe you were to have learned how to do so by reading the instructions in the text."

I sighed. Very heavily.

He narrowed his eyes, snapping the book closed and passing it back to me. "Too much work for you?"

"I am a *very* hard worker." When I tilted my chin up as I said this, I almost fell over. *What boldness has overtaken me?*

"Oh, so you simply do not *care* to read?"

"No, I simply cannot read at all."

A short laugh of disbelief. "Everyone in the Realm can read. It is the law. Has been for centuries. My great grandfather put it into place."

"Forgive me, Second Prince, I am sure your great grandfather was a noble High King with virtuous intentions, but he was not present to enforce such a decree in my home, and thus, I stand before you dull as a ditch."

"Where are you from exactly?"

"The Neighboring Lands."

"Yes, I can tell that much by your demeanor and manner of speaking, but where in the Neighboring Lands? Which region?"

"I know not."

"Well, which district?"

"I do not know."

"Surely you know the street you lived on?"

I inhaled, trying my hardest to remember. Aman had made a point not to mention it to me so as to discourage me from running away. At least this was his explanation every time I inquired. "I think...Radford? Redford? Something like that."

He paused, thinking while he watched me. "And you did not learn reading in school?"

"I did not attend school. Well...not after age six or seven. I cannot recall the circle, I'm afraid."

He balked at that, but his voice softened. "Little Tree, why did you not attend? Were you ill?"

"No, I was healthy. I"—*Goodness, I do not know what to say to this man.* How to explain my life and how immeasurably different it was to the life he knew. "I was not allowed."

57

"Hmm." And he said something I could not have predicted, not even with the trees themselves whistling in my ear. "Will you look at me for a moment, Little Tree? If you do not mind."

Oh, heaven help me. And how I wanted to look. I did. Truly. How the desire to please him swelled in me, nearly lifting me from the very ground itself. But raging in battle against the will to please him was the panic of having to stare directly into the eyes of the Second Prince Of All The Realm.

He released me of this tension at last. "Alright then, a command instead. Read the passage on the forty seventh page of your book. Aloud. So I may hear it."

"I...."

"Go on. I insist."

My hands sweating on the cover, I wondered what possessed me to come to this room in the dead of night yet again. I parted the pages and stared at the markings.

"Read it."

I shook my head, refusing to cry. "I cannot. I do not know how."

"I don't believe you, Tree."

"If belief is what makes it so people can read, then perhaps your believing I can read will change the fact that I certainly cannot."

He sighed, running a hand through his dark hair. "Well, I cannot aid you in studying, that much I know for sure. You will be eliminated. Grandly eliminated. But...."

He circled around to his desk. "Come. Come over here."

I was too afraid to move, but there my legs went, taking certain steps across the room to join him where he stood waiting.

Even worse, those legs of mine did not stop moving me until I was far too near him, my shoulder practically grazing his chest.

He noticed this proximity, to my absolute terror, and I dared not look up to see his expression, though I could feel the intensity of his gaze on the side of my face. He reached down and took his quill, flipping through scrolls until he liberated a book buried beneath the parchment and opened to a blank page.

"Do you know how to spell your name?"

I swallowed. "There is an 'A' in it. Two of them. But that is all I remember."

"Why don't you pronounce it for me. I can deduce the spelling."

I cleared my throat. "Aia."

He paused, a smile playing at his mouth. "Aia," he repeated. "Do you know what that means?"

"It has a meaning?"

"Yes. It means 'miracle'." Then, he swooped an 'A' onto the page. Perhaps the only letter I could recognize. Another squiggle, and then an additional 'a'. "Each symbol is a letter with its own sound. The sounds string together to form words. And the words represent meanings."

"So if I learn all the symbols and sounds, I might read the book and learn how to glow in time?"

He sighed. "There are forty letters, each with a new sound. And many large and old words to which you might not know the meanings."

I nodded, reaching out to the shape of my name on the paper. Touching it resulted in ink marks on my fingertips, but it was all worth it to feel my name spelled out by his hand.

"But there is hope," I said. "I could try."

"Aia...."

A tingle—or more like a jolt—strung up my spine when he said my name once more. I had to work very hard to listen to him after that.

"...but yes. You could try. Here, I will write the letters for you and tell you the sounds."

My cheeks ran crimson. "I could not ask you to labor on my behalf."

"It's hardly labor. A few letters will do no harm." He scribbled as he spoke and then sounded out each symbol for me."

When he was finished, he blew on the page and tore it from the book. "Press it in your book," he instructed. "And tell no one I gave it to you. They must not know we have been speaking."

I nodded. "It is against the rules?"

His eyes flashed, a storm brewing once again. "It is not Clorente and her rules we have to fear. My brother is...jealous. It will go poorly for both of us if he finds we spoke."

"What would he do? Try to...hurt you, as you said before?"

"Theor cannot kill me with his own hands. The Royal Laws forbid it. By this, I mean literally. He cannot lift his hand to take my life. But he can orchestrate my death and regularly attempts this. And so we should not unsettle him."

"Would not your father...mind...if your brother had you killed?"

With that question, the Second Prince picked back up his quill, his jaw clenched, his breath held. "I must return to my work. And you must go and try to make a miracle out of forty letters and a bit of hope. Good fortune to you, Little Tree."

And he returned to work.

I took my book back to our room, sitting outside the door so I could use the chandeliers for light. I traced each dried letter, wishing they still left ink on me, and imagined the gritty, dark voice of Willen Vedan making the sounds out for me, his chest brushing against my shoulder and his gaze against my cheek.

I crawled to my spot near the wall just as the servants began to bustle. Clorente seemed to fill the whole Palace with her purple gown as she entered, her cane clanging against the floor. "Arise, arise! And spread your branches. This morning, you glow; this afternoon, you prepare; and this evening, you dance! Come now, and we will have our breakfast. Then, we see how you did with your reading, Trees!"

We followed Clorente through the Palace, which seemed to have changed overnight. The corridors had moved, the floors in new and varying colors, and the windows different shapes and heights. It would have been one thing for the servants to have changed the drapes or the table cloths, *but how did they manage to alter the very depths of the walls and heights of the ceilings?*

We made it to another immaculately set table, the porcelain dishes gleaming, the silverware pure gold and polished to perfection. There was not one morsel of food on the plates or in the bowls and not one drop of water or wine in the glasses.

The curly-haired girl made an audible groan of sorts, her spine slumping. Clorente shot an icy look at her until she straightened back up. We sat silently until the older woman snapped her cane against the floor. "And onward then. We shall go to the smaller performance hall so you may read aloud the passage you preferred to study."

Read aloud? I tried not to trip over the heels of the only girl in front of me in line, for panic and grace are not known to coexist.

The performance hall, as Clorente called it, was a large space with a raised stage and heavy scarlet curtains. Clorente directed each girl to stand upon the stage, open the book, and read whatever passage they wished aloud, but not to demonstrate what they had learned until the ball, where the High Prince might see and take pleasure.

Round Eyes read a bit about the sun. It was lovely, though she stumbled in one section and lost her place, coming almost to tears.

Brown Beauty recited hers, no book needed, her nose pointed in the air and her arms poised just so before her.

The other girls went, some trembling, some blank and droll. When it was my turn...well, I did not want it to be my turn at all. I closed my eyes and imagined I was safely in my cellar or underneath the floorboards beneath the wash basin, Aman aiding some guest and me being careful not to breathe too loudly. All preferable to this.

But alas, I rose without meaning to and found myself center stage. I raised the book and immediately dropped it on my toes. *Heavens, Aia, can you not even hold the thing?* It was then, with a great lurch of my heart, that I realized the Second Prince had taken a seat far in the back of the hall, his elbow propped on the arm rest and his knuckles beneath his chin.

His eyes, though so far away, I could feel burning me up.

I retrieved my book and opened it to my chosen passage. "H—how d...does th-the Tree mmmmake her...." A great pause, for I kept forgetting the sound of the middle letter. "Light? She makes it by...by...."

Clorente clapped her hands once. "Alright then, we will be petrified into stone if we wait until the end of this one. We cannot all shine bright, I suppose. Who is next?"

By the time I left the stage, the Second Prince was gone.

Ep 7

The Beauty is Yours

"What is a tree without its fruit? Without its leaves? Its branches must not droop. They must not bow. It must be erect, noble, dignified, and unshakeable."

The servant girl assigned to me bit her lip and put one foot on my hip as she tugged the corset that wrapped around my torso.

Clorente circled the room, examining the progress of each girl while smacking her cane into the floor as if keeping count to a song only she could hear.

"Tighter. Tighter!" She chided Brown Beauty's servant, who was nigh to bursting a blood vessel from the effort she was putting into tightening the torture device apparently worn by stately ladies.

I could hardly breathe, my lungs squashed beneath the bones and fabric, my skin pinched and squeezed between the clasps and lacings. Before this, however, a stinging cream had been applied to my eyes, and my skin had been bathed in something thin and slippery which still burned on my arms, neck, and chest.

"Her hair must make a statement," Clorente said far too loudly. "Her fruit must appear appetizing!"

I glanced around the room at the other Trees. They all wore magnanimous hairstyles, with curls and tresses piled on their heads. Except for Round Eyes, who kept her short cut, though her eyebrows had been incredulously enlarged on her petite face.

"Etiquette is everything at the Palace. You must not forget...." Clorente continued on, her voice filling the room, yet drowned out by my wandering thoughts. I pictured myself on that small stage, stumbling through the words of my selected passage in the *Tree Of Light*. I imagined the Second Prince sitting at the back of the room, enduring my displayed ignorance. Was he appalled at how I stuttered? Was he distressed by my lack of schooling? I could not tell from his expression—always so clouded and brooding. But I wanted to know what he thought. I wanted to have the ability to discern his emotions, predict his preferences. I wanted him to become...familiar to me.

"...so you must not forget this, no matter if you forget everything else I have taught you thus far." Clorente concluded with a clip in her tone.

Of course, I had missed whatever life-saving information she'd imparted. I glanced at the other girls, wondering if they would be gracious and tell me what I had not heard, but decided that revealing my ignorance would make me seem more prey than partner.

"And now, for final touches. You must pray, Trees, that your designers know the High Prince's desires better than you do. For you are in their hands. And the next time we meet, you will be presented at the ball. Good luck. For certainly, we need it."

With that, Clorente tapped her cane, and we were no longer in our small room altogether. Instead, I was in a rather large area, with light streaming in through big glass windows. From the walls hung reels of fabrics—every color and texture I could dream of. Ribbons draped down from the ceiling. Shoes filled every corner, the racks of them stretching higher and higher the longer I looked.

"Well then, we are alone at last, Lady Tree," my young servant said, placing her hand on her hip.

"We are?"

"We are. And we may speak freely here. I am Glenne, your designer, and dare I say the best the Realm has to offer." She leaned forward, winking at me. "Though all the designers will say this to their Trees, they will all be exaggerating. I, on the other hand, am the only one telling the truth."

I smiled. Glenne was feistier than she appeared to be when she dressed me in front of the other girls and Clorente. "Pleased to meet you, Glenne. And thank you for helping me. What makes the best designer the best?"

She grinned. "Good question. I *should* believe that telling you my secret would be a risk, for you might share it with the other designers. But...even if you shared it, they would not listen. For my secret in itself is too daring, and they are all cowards. They would not even try it."

Genuine curiosity tickled me. "I will not tell."

Glenne nodded. "Alright then. The secret is this. While the others design their Trees to match what they think the High Prince desires, I will not. I will design my Tree to reflect what *she* desires."

I felt my eyes go wide. "Why would you do that? It seems risky indeed."

"Because"—she spread her fingers and widened her eyes, looking a bit like a mad woman about to scoop me up into a storm—"Lady Tree, the beauty is yours, not his. And I am meant to display *your* beauty. So I will."

She put her hand under her chin. "Now, we haven't much time. These things are always rushed, though never for the life of me will I understand why they do not simply schedule the time we need. You must choose a fabric, Lady Tree."

"Please, call me Aia."

She bowed. "As you wish. Now go on. Quickly."

I shook my head. "I have only ever been given the clothes I wear, and there were never options. I have not so much as chosen what I will eat. Not even once. I'm afraid I cannot select from so many lovely options, Glenne. It is too overwhelming."

"Alright then. I will make three selections, and you will pick your favorite. That way it remains simple for you."

She twirled off and returned in less than a moment, holding three fabrics in her arms that seemed to stretch on forever, rippling behind her until I could no longer see them. When I squinted, I realized I could not actually make out the walls of the room. They too seemed always to be some distance away.

Of the three fabrics, one was a deep green, lush and mysterious. Another, a red material that seemed so thick and soft. And the third was a pale number. So pale that I could not identify what color it truly was. A hint of green, a swirl of blue, a whisper of pink.

It was then that I needed to close my eyes a moment, for I realized that I had spent most of my life in a place devoid of vivid color. The tans of the table top, the brown of the floor-boards. The gray of the walls. The darkness of the cellar. And from the slits I was permitted to gaze out of, there was little color in the streets. No flowering trees. No dyed dresses and shirts—how could there be with no flowers or fruit to give them their radiance? And so the newness and the vibrancy of it all overwhelmed me.

"Are you alright?" Glenne asked. I could hear her smile begin to fade. "Are you unhappy with these fabrics? I can always choose another three...."

I rubbed my eyes so I could bear to open them again. "No, no, they are beautiful, Glenne, truly. I only became a bit tired, is all. I am alright. And I certainly like this one the best." I touched the pale fabric. It was soft, like a gentle breeze. *A breeze would feel wonderful against my skin right now.*

"Hmm...." Glenne tossed the other two fabrics over her shoulder, and they disappeared. She studied the one I chose as she spoke, holding it up to the light, which changed for her, shining directly on the fabric. "Tell me how else you are feeling, Lady Tree."

"Aia," I corrected her.

"Oh, yes. Aia. Apologies."

"No need to apologize." I wrung my hands together as I watched the girl manipulate the light as she moved the fabric this way and that, calling out the subtle purples and yellows of the cloth. This amazed me, for the light source seemed to be coming from outside the windows. *Can designers change the direction of the sun? And if so, why are the Royal family not seeking them out instead of us?* They seemed much more useful.

"Go on," Glenne encouraged.

"I am feeling...confused." *And nervous.* No one had ever asked me how I was feeling. It was simply not something my family was concerned with. The questions I received were regarding whether anyone had seen me or whether I had made myself useful enough. "Also worried. Tired."

"You already said that one." She tilted her head as she looked to me with a frown. "How about...tell me how you wish to feel. What would make you feel better?"

"Oh." I thought about this for a moment. "I would like to sit, I suppose. That would be nice."

Just like that, a plush chair appeared before me. Glenne gestured to it, and I circled and perched on the edge. But oh, it was the most comfortable chair I had ever encountered, and soon, I sank back into it, my limbs groaning with relief.

"More," Glenne said.

"I like that the fabric seems breezy. It sounds so soothing to me. And...perhaps this might sound strange, but I miss the dim lighting of my home. I was often kept in the dark, and while all this glimmering and shimmering is beautiful, I am not accustomed to it. I would like for things to be less...harsh."

Glenne hopped up and down with a squeal, clutching the fabric to her chest. "I know! I know! Alright, this will be perfect, Lady Tree. The theme of the night will be...subtlety." She motioned with her hands as if revealing a secret plot.

I was too comfortable to correct her for forgetting to use my name. Instead, I nodded. "That sounds lovely, Glenne."

She grinned at me. "You're nice."

"I am?"

"Very much so. I am glad I did not get one of the other Trees. Some of them seem terrifying."

"Some of them *are* terrifying."

Glenne waved her hand at me. "Don't think of them, Lady Tree. Instead, why don't you take a rest while I prepare your designs. I think you will be pleased when you awake."

I did sleep, as Glenne suggested, and dreamed that the winter darkness had overtaken me, plunging me into nothingness for all eternity. I awoke with a pounding in my head and Glenne beaming before me.

"It's time," she said, holding out her hands to me.

I took them and rose to my feet, feeling at least rested if not disturbed by my dream.

"I took the liberty of designing your hair and skin while you slept. But I need you awake for the next part. You must put on your dress and shoes. I do hope you like them."

She waved her hand, and the dress appeared before me, floating on nothing. Though float it did, for it seemed to be made of nothing but air. Like a mist had been caught and sewn into a gown. When Glenne moved the fabric, it shifted the light, glowing a gentle array of colors.

"Oh Glenne...it is the most beautiful thing I have ever beheld. In all my life. I swear it."

Glenne's eyes welled with tears as she peeked out from behind the dress. "Really?"

I nodded, my hands on my cheeks. "I fear it is too beautiful to wear."

"Oh but you must wear it. And quickly or you will be late. A little late is fine, but not very late. You will upset Clorente." She snapped her fingers and darted away. "I almost forgot the shoes!"

The shoes. They were clouds themselves. Shifting and moving, fluttering in a breeze I could not see.

"How...how did you—?"

She giggled. "I told you, Lady Tree. I am the best! Actually the best, not pretend the best."

She motioned for me to remove my dress. "I cannot remove it for you," she explained. "Clorente's Wonder-working is much, much stronger than mine. If she puts a dress on you, I cannot remove it even if I used all my Wonder for the task."

"Wonder?" I asked as Glenne helped me slip out of my dress.

"You have no schooling in Wonder, Lady Tree?" Glenne seemed genuinely startled. "How in heaven have you made it this far?"

"I don't even know what that is, Glenne. I was not taught to read, much less given an education in making magical dresses appear out of nowhere."

Glenne nodded down at the shoes. "I made those using Wonder. It is how Wonderful things are done, you see."

"Is that how the Palace changes its shape in the mornings? And how Clorente can tap her cane and drown me in a bath?"

"Yes. Exactly. But I cannot teach you Wondering, Lady Tree. It's not allowed. Well, I mean it's allowed to be taught, in general, but as your designer, I am forbidden to help you with those sorts of things."

"I wouldn't ask you to break the rules, Glenne. I don't want you to get hurt."

She touched my chin. "See? You are nice." She held the glorious dress up to me, and I stepped into it. "Not all Wonder is light and beautiful, Lady Tree. Sometimes it is terrible and frightening."

"Like the deep hole we were dropped in when I first arrived."
I began to be swept back toward that night—the fear, the confusion. But the memories of darkness were obliterated once I
felt the sensation of the fabric on my skin.

"Is it good? I wanted it to feel like standing naked on a seaside
cliff, with the sun setting and the light not too sharp in your
eyes. Just the wind teasing you and no worries left."

Tears began to well in my eyes. "Glenne. This is so unbeliev-
ably kind. And perfect." I placed my feet into the shoes and
giggled. "Look! I am walking on clouds!"

"Yes. You are not too ticklish, I hope."

I shook my head. "It makes me smile."

"Good. That is what I had hoped. And now for the final test.
Do you feel beautiful, Lady Tree?"

I ran my hands over the ripples of the full-length gown,
raising goosebumps of pleasure on my arms and legs. "I have
never felt so wholly mesmerized in all my life. I did not even
know such a feeling was possible."

Glenne sighed and placed her hands on her hips. "Then off
you go. Don't fall on the High Prince's bad side, Lady Tree,
or we will both be ruined." She grinned. "But you shouldn't
worry too much. Tonight, you will be impossible to resist."

One more nod from Glenne and I was no longer in the
designer's studio. I was in the loudest place I ever had the dis-
pleasure of occupying. There was a tremendous wave of
voices—laughing, cackling, humming, squealing, singing.

I stood alone in a room full of people. They hardly noticed
my bizarre entrance, their fancy glasses filled with many colors
of drinks. In the corner, some musician played a stringed thing
very furiously, trying to be heard above the clamor. But the

clamor was too great for him, and not all the forehead perspiration in the Realm could convince the occupants of the large room that his music mattered. No one paid him any mind.

"There you are!" Clorente said, snatching me by the elbow. "You're late!"

Clorente looked fabulous. Her dark purple gown glittered with flecks of black that reflected the light in dozens of directions as she moved. As usual, her hair was woven tightly behind her head, her steely eyes surveying the crowd as we maneuvered through.

Once we were free of the room, the noise grew even louder. Hundreds of people, all dressed in their finest. They wore piles of hair on their heads and red tint on their cheeks and lips. Jewels glittered on their fingers and around their necks. The women wore form-crushing bodices and enormous, billowing skirts. The men wore tight pants and even tighter coats, frilly kerchiefs piled up to their chins.

"That must be one of them. There, with Clorente," someone murmured, though the volume was more of a shout to be heard over the chaos.

A group of musicians played in the grand open hall, a different song in a different key, it seemed. I did not know much about music except that I greatly disliked everything I'd experienced of it at the ball thus far.

"Here, with the others," Clorente said, leading me to a smaller room.

I exhaled with relief, for it was more quiet there. The red carpeting absorbed some of the sound, and there were no musicians present. No guests with their piles and piles of hair. Just ten Trees and Clorente.

"Of course she is the last to arrive," Brown Beauty muttered with a scowl.

"Jealousy is an ugly color, Gretaline," Clorente chided. "You do not have to be friends, but making enemies out of your sister Trees will not end well for any of you."

Too late for that. To mark my thought, Gretaline glared at me as soon as Clorente turned her back on us.

"So then," Clorente explained, "this is your first ball, and the Palace court shall meet you for the first time. There will be many judgments and opinions cast, but remember whose matters. The High Prince is the only one you need impress. Though any admirers in the court will no doubt whisper in his ear on your behalf. Mind your manners, as I have taught you, and do as the High Prince has requested. Glow brightly for him, my Trees. I hope the passages you chose to study will aid you in this, for I cannot. Now...go on. Make yourself seen and known. And above all else...be like a Tree."

Clorente and the girls all filed out of the room, leaving behind Round Eyes and myself. The pretty girl swallowed, staring at the open door from across the room. She had feathers on the tips of her lashes, and her dress poofed at the waist so high that she could not lower her arms properly. It shone such a brilliant blue that I could not look directly at it without my eyes watering.

Round Eyes clasped her hands together. Even her fingernails were blue and feathered. "I've never seen anything like this in the Neighboring Lands. Have you?"

I'd hardly seen anything at all in the Neighboring Lands. "No. Nothing quite like this."

"I'm...I'm terrified. And confused. I fear I will be confused for the rest of my life. And that the rest of my life might be over at any moment."

"I know how you feel."

"You do? And you're not afraid?"

"Me? Well...I suppose I am."

Round Eyes blinked at me. "You don't *look* afraid."

"I don't? Then...how do I look?"

Round Eyes inhaled as she met my eyes. "*Beautiful.* And clever."

"*I* look *clever*?"

"You do." She pointed two fingers at her own eyes. "It's in here. The cleverness. And I don't mind it too much. It intimidates the Mean One."

I chuckled. "You mean Brown Beauty? That's what I call her in my head."

Round Eyes scoffed. "That's too nice a name for someone so dreadful. Though I suppose Mean One is too...on the nose. We must come up with something better. Something that reflects her acute and particular flavor of awful."

"How about...Gretaline?"

Round Eyes snorted and slapped her knee. "See! Ha! I knew it! *Clever.*" Then she sobered, looking out again through the door frame at the swelling mass of fancy bodies. "I shall be killed after this part. I can feel it."

Without realizing it, I crossed the room and took the Tree's hand in my own and squeezed. "I'm Aia."

She gave me a watery smile. "I'm Shrane."

I nodded. "And what name did you have for *me*, Shrane, before you knew what I was actually called?"

She sighed. "Must I tell you?"

"Yes, you must."

"Fine." After a groan came her confession. "I called you My Competition."

I laughed out loud at that. What a ridiculous notion. That I could compete against Shrane. That I could compete against anyone! "I called you Round Eyes."

She squeezed my hand back. "I quite like that actually."

"Oh? Well, good. And now, we must stop delaying and walk around as we were told. Or your feeling will come true, and we will both be dead by tomorrow."

With that, I stepped into the light of my first Royal ball, a trembling new friend in hand and no idea how I planned to survive the night ahead of me.

Ep 8

Death Would Be Mine

"I earnestly hope we are not meant to dance," Shrane squeaked, squeezing my hand so tight she pinched my fingers. "I don't remember Clorente saying anything about dancing."

I did not remember Clorente saying almost anything at all. *You must pay more attention, Aia,* I scolded myself. But I hardly paid mind to that either. For around us were dancers swirling golden and pink ribbons in their hands, their clothing flapping and billowing as they whirled around the room, somehow evading all the revelers gorging on food and drink. Above us were people wearing nothing, it seemed, but colorful glitter, swinging from big swaths of fabric without colliding or falling to their deaths.

"Watch where you are going!" Someone was quite unhappy that I had bumped into them. His floppy face shook with red anger. "You nearly ruined my ensemble, foolish girl."

I sidestepped the man, and he forgot me just as quickly as he'd been overcome with rage. I realized, however, that I had lost my partner, for my hand was empty once more.

"Well, hello, Lady Tree. I don't think we've had the pleasure of meeting." Some flax-headed man bowed and smiled all too warm at me, his eyes cold and hard. "You are not as...shiny as the others. But I suppose any Tree is nice to look at."

I blinked, trying to understand what this complete stranger wanted with me. But understand, I could not. Until he outstretched his hand.

"Will you dance with me? It's only proper to accept my invitation, after all."

I had no idea whether it was proper or not, but before I could think of taking his hand, it was slapped away. "Go off, Petrus. No dancing with Trees tonight."

The flax-headed man scowled. "You're not in charge of me, Beralt."

"No, but I should be. Very well *could* be. Go off." The short, gruff man pointed a stubby finger at Petrus. "Go off."

Petrus gave one final look at me with those cold eyes and then turned on his heel, snatching a drink just as a servant was offering it to someone else. He disappeared into the throng.

"Don't mind him, Miss Tree. Or me for that matter. We are of no consequence to you," Beralt said, his voice sporting a strange lilt. He was a short man, only reaching my shoulders, but his chest was barreled and his muscles taut and plenty. He even wore a braided beard, which I noticed no other men at the Palace seemed to wear.

"Thank you for saving me from dancing," I said.

The man blushed bright pink, the color spreading up from his beard to his nose. "Oh no. Think nothing of it. He is one of Theor's companions, and those lot...they do not always have the best intentions. Certainly not known for their inhibitions with women. But, Miss Tree, you must know, Theor would not have liked you dancing with his friend. By this I mean... Petrus did not have your wellness in mind when he offered you his hand."

I nodded. "I see. But why would he mean me harm? He does not even know me."

"He does not mean you harm. Only means to cause trouble. You would have been merely a casualty of that trouble."

"I am beginning to see that very little of what goes on here is actually about Trees."

Beralt released a laugh as short and vibrant as he. "You are a clever one!"

"Are you also one of the High Prince's friends?"

"All reverence to the High Prince, but I do not think he would consider me his friend, no. I am well acquainted with the Second Prince and lucky to be so. Beralt The Merciful. But Beralt will do just fine." He bowed deeply, revealing a bald spot at the back of his bushy head.

"I am Aia," I said.

Beralt blushed again. "I will call you by your title, Miss Tree, as you greatly outrank an old warrior like me."

"It's *Lady* Tree." Gretaline appeared out of nowhere, slipping her arm into mine and turning her nose up as she led me away. To me, she whispered, "You must not waste all your time cavorting with Dwarves. Trees have reputations to keep, and you sullying mine with the company you keep simply will not do."

"He seems nice," I explained.

"It doesn't matter how he *seems*. It only matters what he *is*. And who he is suited to speak with. The answer to that is not *us*."

I wanted Gretaline to release my arm, but she only clutched it tighter. "Come," she said. "You and I will speak with the High Prince. You must accompany me because your designer has made you look so ridiculously plain that I will surely sparkle when compared side by side with you."

I yanked my arm away from Gretaline, only to smash into a tray of drinks behind me. Quickly, I reached to grab them before they shattered and, to my surprise, caught none of them. No matter, though, for the servant managed to slip his tray beneath the glasses before they even touched the ground.

I wanted to ask him how he managed to do this, but Gretaline was already introducing us to the only person in all the Realm who had the power to spare my life.

"High Prince, your greatness precedes you," she said, bowing deeply. "I am Gretaline, one of your most glorious Trees. I am so pleased to shine for you later tonight—"

Before she could introduce me, I ducked under the arm of the servant who had resumed passing out drinks to dozens of snatching, jeweled hands. I weaved through the crowd, on my way to anywhere but before the High Prince. A few perfumed guests thought my attempt to flee was a wish to dance, and they scooped me up and spun me a few times until I could escape them as well.

Utterly breathless, I spotted a staircase and attempted to circle around it. Perhaps there would be some safe haven offered in the dark spot beneath the stairs. Some place that more resembled the dim lighting of my home or the utter darkness of the cellar. But alas, behind the staircase were only couples engrossed in passionate kissing and groping, the likes of which I had never imagined.

I rushed backwards, without turning around to see where I was going, and ran very fully into yet another person.

"Slow down, slow down," he said.

Of course, I recognized his voice in an instant. Maybe even less than an instant. It was careful and low, each word placed just so. The sound of it made a shiver run the length of my body, which only made me all the more nervous.

"Are you alright?" he asked.

I had not turned around to face him and I did not know why I hadn't. "No."

No, Aia? Have you never learned how to lie? It is not the time to be flippantly honest. It is the time to put on your nicest disguise and fake it. "I...." *And now words fail me.*

"Are you ill? Do you feel unwell?"

"No." *Give more detail, Aia. You are hardly believable.*

Willen paused. Perhaps he was studying me, observing me. Or passing judgment. I could not tell, for still I had not turned around.

"What can I do to make it alright, then?"

"I want to go home." Again, the words left me with little permission.

He waited. And then he spoke. "I asked what I *can* do, Lady Tree. I cannot do that. Is there nothing else?"

"I would like this awful ball to be over."

He chuckled. "You and me both, then. Oh here, this might help, actually. I have something for you." Then he chuckled again. "Well, you would have to bear looking at me to receive it, I would think."

"No...no thank you."

"No? Why not? Am I that dreadful to behold?"

"No, you're very beautiful." I waited for my heart to collapse in on itself, for I had just said those words out loud to a High Royal member of the Realm. "I simply do not wish to look upon any more overwhelming sights this evening."

"Oh."

It was then that I realized not only did I have my back turned to the Second Prince, but I had my eyes entirely shut. No wonder the Prince questioned whether I was alright. Clearly, I had lost my mind.

"I do not mean to offend," I explained.

"I'm not offended. Not at all. Actually, I rather appreciate your honesty. It is most refreshing. Hardly anyone at court is ever truthful."

I could feel him draw closer to me. It was what I imagined an eclipse to be like. Only I was the moon and he was the sun. Surely, the entire ballroom would notice that the light had shifted. He placed something into my palm. "I thought you might like that, now that you've mastered reading."

I clenched my fist around it. "Are you teasing me?" I asked with a gasp.

"I am not. I am simply impressed. And that is a state I rarely experience, I promise you."

"But...I did so terribly when I read for Clorente."

"Clorente does not know anything about you, Lady Tree. She cannot be impressed by what she has not seen."

I blushed then and was very embarrassed to be doing so. "I must thank you for the gift."

"It is literally nothing. A simple gesture. But I do hope your night improves, Lady Tree."

I wondered why he did not call me by my name, seeing as he knew what it was already, but perhaps he had forgotten it. I was sure the Second Prince had a great many important things to remember.

"It's time, it's time," Shrane said, whizzing by me and grabbing my hand once more. "I thought I lost you, Aia, but I found you with not a moment to spare."

"Time?"

"Time for us to shine, whatever that means. Clorente has asked to come to the center of the entire ballroom. Hurry, hurry."

When we reached the center of the enormous room, Clorente had us form a circle, all facing her. She seemed so confident, so regal, yet I could tell her voice had the slightest warble to it when she spoke. "Ladies and gentlefellows of the court of our most tremendous High King, Harrod Vedan, I present to you the Trees of our most plentiful Realm, one of whom will, undoubtedly, prove to be a match for our esteemed High Prince Theor."

Clorente bowed deeply as Theor entered the circle, moving slow and grand, his thumb tucked into his waistband. It struck me that he was attempting to appear relaxed, but secretly was quite anxious.

Beyond him, half-buried by the swarm of faces pressing in for the spectacle, I saw the Second Prince, his eyes more storm than blue. He watched with intent, as if he was preparing for some danger to ensue. And I still could not shake the notion that his eyes were mostly settled on me.

Theor spoke up, his voice booming from within the circle. "And what lovely Trees they are! Tonight, I have asked them to shine for me. We will see what this crop of Trees can do!"

He crossed his arms and waited.

"Begin, my Trees, for the eyes of the Realm, and of your High Prince, are upon you," Clorente said.

I tried to not to ball my hands into fists out of sheer terror. For I had not even a visual example of what glowing should look like. I glanced around our circle to see Brown Beauty with her chin tilted back, her curly updo at an angle as she looked to the ceiling. She opened her palms, and...I shut my eyes once again.

I wished I had some voice in my mind that guided me, that told me what to do or how. But there was nothing but silence in my mind. That and the echo of my nightmare becoming real. The fear of death—uncertain and uncalled for. The fear of success—of being a match for a Prince I did not know and perhaps could never please.

I closed my eyes and imagined I was in the deep, thick darkness of my cellar. Aman was busy entertaining his guests, the smell of the food filling the dry space around me. And I was silent. A little sad, yes, but satisfied with my place. Suited for it, really. But then, my imagination led me to the moment Aman sat beside me and told me he had sold my secret. That someone had arrived to take me away forever. I felt my hands begin to shake as I re-envisioned the struggle between Aman and myself....

And then I chose a different image. A better one. The vision of a man with ink-smeared hands, forming the letters of my name on parchment. Patient. And diligent. I could hear his voice as he sounded the letters. I recalled the words I read that night, remembering his voice as I stumbled over them again and again. I knew them by heart at that point in time. *How does a Tree make her light? She makes it by wishing light made.*

"Enough." Clorente tapped her cane on the floor as I peeled my eyes open. She turned to Theor and waited for his response.

"Hmm...." He switched sides so his hip cocked out in another direction. His fair hair had been slicked back, though a bit had slipped from its coif and shadowed his left eye. "I do say some of them shone more brightly than I thought they would. Others were underwhelming. And a few did not shine at all. Clearly unworthy, those few, Clorente, wouldn't you say?"

Clorente's lip thinned, but she nodded her head. "I would never argue with the High Prince."

"Well then...." He looked around, surveying his audience, who had begun to murmur at what the Prince was suggesting. "Such is the nature of this thing, Clorente. It brings me no joy...but those who cannot shine clearly must be...sifted."

Clorente did not waste time. "Wise words, High Prince Theor. My apologies for those Trees who could not shine for you. I am sure they greatly wished to possess the ability to please you."

Another glance over at the Second Prince because I could not seem to help myself. There was no mistake this time that he was staring directly at me. In fact, he wore an expression I had not seen on another human before. His lips were just barely parted, his eyebrows slightly raised, his eyes wide and unflinching. Perhaps it was a trick of the light that made it seem as though his clouded eyes were brimming with unshed tears. Just then, Beralt grabbed on to his shoulder and pulled him aside so he was not gazing into my eyes any longer.

Willen seemed startled by this and a bit off-put. It seemed the short man was questioning him and the Royal was attempting to answer.

"I am fine," he told Beralt. "Truly. Fine."

"You do not seem fine, my Prince. You seem...out of sorts."

He waved a firm hand, as if putting the matter to rest. "Everything is as it should be, Beralt, I assure you. All the sorts sorted. I only wish this travesty of a ball were over."

"Yes, as do I, Your Goodness."

"I hate when you call me that, Beralt."

"Well, I can't go on calling you by your first name in a public setting, Second Prince."

Willen pressed a hand to his forehead as if on the back of his neck he bore the world's heaviest load. "I hate it here."

"Come on, my Prince. Let's find you a drink or ten." And Beralt led Willen away. But not before the Second Prince turned his head to glance at me one last time.

"...and we must not," Shrane finished, her hand in mine once more. Of course, I had missed most of what was being said around me. Yet, somehow, I had managed to hear a private conversation across a packed ballroom. Or perhaps I had only imagined it. Perhaps I fabricated what I wanted the Prince to have said.

Apparently, we were to walk back to our room. No Wonderful transportation by way of Clorente this time. Good old-fashioned movement of the legs, one after the other. I was relieved at the prospect of stepping outdoors, to breathe in the sweet air I had tasted when I first saw those trees on the lawn.

"You will go now to your temporary rooms, each of you," Clorente instructed. "I have had six made up. I hope they are more comfortable."

I knew there were more than six of us Trees present at the ball. That meant some would be taken away. The ones who did not glow, of course. My hands began to perspire as I held fast to Shrane, the present Willen had given me held even faster in my other palm.

"Will you not make your choice plain, Lady Clorente?" Gretaline asked, a glint of excitement in her gorgeous dark eyes. "I am so eager to know who has made the cut."

Clorente sighed. She did not seem to be as eager as Brown Beauty. "You will know you have survived this night if indeed there is a room waiting for you. Now go. Find your place. And good luck."

"Good luck, Aia," Shrane said before releasing me and running off.

The other girls scattered as well. Some were lost to me in the swell of human faces while others took the stairs to try all the upper rooms for one that might be theirs.

As for me, I went outside. For outside would be that sweet air and less jostling. No eyes on me, either, which would be nice. *Maybe my room will be outside, beneath a tree.* Wishful thinking, of course. It would probably be no better than the bare room in which all the Trees had huddled for the past few nights. Or the mat Aman laid out for me beneath the kitchen table on cold nights.

When I thought no one was looking, I dared to open my hand and peek at the present the Second Prince had given me to congratulate my learning to read. It was not what I had expected, though I admitted to myself that I really had no expectations. It was the first gift I had received in many, many circles. Perhaps the first ever.

It was a small piece of paper. Just a scrap from one of Willen's books. And on it, in small letters, was written the word 'Flowers'.

I smiled and touched the ink with my finger. He'd written it with his own hand. *For me.* Perhaps he knew how much I liked flowers since we discussed the lovely one in that walkway once. Or perhaps flowers were a customary gift of congratulations. Regardless of the reason, I adored the gift. For it meant that someone, another human—a particular other human—had thought about me during his turn and had brought something all the way to the ball with the intention of slipping it into my hand.

I imagined that I had been brave enough to smile at him when I received it. Or to offer my hand for a kiss. But I had not been, and the moment was over and gone. Still, I would hold onto the scrap of sentiment for as long as I could.

Eventually, I wandered inside and upstairs. Wandering and wandering. When finally I grew weary enough, I decided to try a room. Any room. Perhaps it would be mine. If not, death would be mine. *I'd prefer the room.*

Of course. Of course the door I opened led to a study, warm candlelight filling the room and a fireplace roaring. But this time, no Second Prince. No quill scraping against parchment.

I eyed his parchment, musing on whether I could manage, with my clumsy hand, to write him a thank you note. I went over, running my fingers along the length of the feathered quill. And then a door slammed shut behind me.

I gasped, spinning round to see who it was and what sort of trouble I was in.

But it was the Second Prince, after all. Only he held a flower in his hand and a thunderstorm in his blue eyes.

"*You*," he said, his voice gravelly and lower than usual. "What did you *do*?"

"Me?" I moved my hand away from his quill with immediacy. "I am so sorry. I did not think you would mind—"

He approached and tossed the white flower onto his desk so hard that a few petals flew from the stem.

I winced. "Don't—"

"So you admit it?"

I was so confused that I could have cried. "What is it you think I have confessed to? I am lost, Second Prince."

"You are indeed lost. Misguided. Maybe even deranged."

I shook my head, wishing suddenly that Willen Vedan was not standing in between me and my way to the door.

"Did you or did you not place this very flower in my room this night?"

"In...your room?"

"Yes, Aia. In my *room*. Where I sleep. You do know what a room is, don't you? Even you had one of those in your lifetime." He gestured to the wilting flower. "You may have whatever madness compels you to come to my private study, Tree, but I warn you, it cannot possess you to visit my private chambers! Do you have any idea what would happen if we were caught together? Even if we were completely innocent, as we are now? If we were seen smiling at one another or chatting or touching hands, even. We cannot be this obviously *stupid*! You cannot risk it, and neither can I. Do you understand?"

I was aware that warm tears spilled from my eyes only because Willen stared at them with great conflict of heart, as if he was angry with himself and angry with me all at once.

"Please do not...do not cry—"

"Oh? Am I not permitted my own tears either?" I could not believe that the words blurted so clearly from my mouth. But then more words followed, accompanied by more tears. "If you must know—which it is clear you must, and because I cannot deny you, for you are far superior to me in every way—I did *not* locate your private chambers. You may ask anyone you so choose who may have seen me wandering through the Palace, not touching one door and certainly not entering any before entering this one. I would not even know where to *find* a flower, especially one of such elegance, the likes of which I have never seen.

"I only just read the note you left for me, and thought it would be kind to try to leave my gratitude in some written form, so you would know how much joy it brought me to receive it. For I have no memory of ever receiving any gift at all. And no, Second Prince Of All The Realm, I did not have a room as a child, save what you might imagine as a small closet I shared with my brother for a few years, and I do not know what it would be like to have a real one. Perhaps if I can locate mine, I will finally know. Either that, or I will finally die. So...." I inhaled and scrubbed the tears from my cheeks. "If you will excuse me, I will go and attempt to discover my fate. Alone." I snatched the flower from off his desk. "And I am taking this sweet flower with me. She did you no harm, but clearly you enjoy making others pay the price for your anger."

And I, Aia, a Tree—and perhaps not even a special one—left the Second Prince staring as I slammed his door behind me.

Ep 9

You Should Fear Me

The moment I left the warm and inviting study of the Second Price, I felt the unfolding of layers of overwhelming regret. And, to truly emphasize that sensation, a good measure of shock and fear as the finishing touch. For, rather than entering the corridor from which I had come, I found myself in another room entirely. Perhaps it was the room Clorente mentioned. If so, I was safe from elimination by death. Yet, that hardly seemed to matter. For within an instant, I knew where I was.

Dirt floors, rotting walls, and a few narrow slits which allowed sparse light to penetrate the utter darkness. The door closed behind me, followed by the familiar sound of the lock clicking into place.

Though I knew the cellar well, I had not expected to return to it so soon. Or rather, I had hoped I would never see it again. How quickly my mind had changed, for upon arriving to the Palace, I would have begged to return to my childhood home, to be stuffed away with the other unseen things.

Oh, how confusion and panic wove a net around my heart. Had it all been a dream? *Of course it has, Aia.* Was I so desperate to escape the cellar that I'd fallen asleep on the floor and fabricated a fantastical world? How could I have been so convinced that High Royals took interest in me and my small, hidden life? That Clorente had come guised as an old perverse man to take me away for some elaborate, Wonderful testing?

No, it made more sense that I was trapped where I had always been. I sat down in the dirt and wept hard enough for my chest to ache, for there was indeed something worse than spending a lifetime in a prison. It was to have spent a lifetime in prison and then to have imagined a future free of that cage, only to realize the dream itself was nothing but haze and dust.

I fell into a fitful sleep and awoke to the nightmarish echo of bones crunching as Trees fell into a deep, dark hole, landing in piles of death. The dream was so real, I almost screamed for Aman to open the door and let me out, when I realized that I ought to be quiet. *He might be hosting guests. I cannot disturb. I will be most useful if I am silent.*

It wasn't until my fingers brushed against something on the cellar floor that I allowed myself a glimpse of hope. I lifted the object and crouched near the bottom of the locked door so that the crack of light might shine on me and I might see what it was I held in my cold fingers.

A white flower. Beaten and fading, but truly real.

Real. It's real. He's real.

I stood to my feet with renewed vitality and tried the locked door for the first time. Since I had only heard the lock fall into place, I had not thought to test the fortitude of my imprisonment for myself. To my great bewilderment, the handle of the door simply opened beneath my touch, and the door swung outward. Strange, for the cellar door of my child-hood home had always opened inward.

I rushed through the door and right into the chest of the Second Prince as he was preparing to leave the study for the night, causing him to drop a good number of pages and his entire inkwell along with them. I did not know whether to react to the spilled ink as it stained his papers or the fact that I assaulted his person by colliding into him.

Regardless of what direction my panic chose to take, Willen put his hands on my shoulders to steady me. "Well now, Little Tree, slow down, slow down," he chuckled. "You nearly knocked the whole Realm off kilter."

But when he looked at my face, his teasing faded and his expression changed, his eyes clouding and his lips downturn-ing. "What happened? Aia, you are shaking. Tell me." When I did not answer, he shook his head. "Have I so greatly upset you? I...." Gently, he touched the flower that I held in my fist, perhaps recalling our altercation earlier that evening.

His observations were correct. I was indeed shaking. My whole body trembled, causing the petals of the wilting flower to quiver in my hand.

Finally, Willen resorted to bringing me close to him and wrapping his arms around my frame. He said nothing for quite some time. Only stood there and held me well, breath-ing slowly until my inhales and exhales matched his.

When he spoke, I could feel his voice move through his chest, reverberating within my body. "Did you have a night-mare, Little Tree?"

It was only then I realized how I gripped his back with such ferocity. I feared perhaps I was hurting him but could not bring myself to relax my grip. "I found my room," I whispered into the fabric of his shirt.

"Oh? And was it so dreadful?"

I nodded and held him with even more intensity.

"What was it like? Describe it to me. It will not seem so frightening then."

I shuddered, gathering my courage. For I had never been scared of the cellar before. *How bad could dried beets and a bit of darkness truly be?* "It was the place I was kept in my child-hood home. An exact replica of it. I...thought it was real."

He rubbed my back, still holding me close. "And this distresses you? To be home again? I suppose it was intended to be comforting."

"I do not know why I disliked it so." But there it was. My voice came out in a creaking whisper. He was right. Clearly, I was distressed.

"You said you did not have a room."

"It's...not mine. I only stayed inside it."

"I see. What does the room look like?"

"Dirt floors. And many shelves, but all empty save for old dried roots and bits of refuse. Rather dark, for there are no windows, and the door is always locked."

"Locked?"

"From the outside." And I began to shake even more, despite his careful questioning. My breath hardly remained in my chest, and it felt like my throat might close and block it from leaving altogether. "But if I am quiet and if I remain useful, then...then I may come out. Then...."

It was then that Willen took me over to his desk and lifted me onto it so that I had someplace to sit. And then he wiped the tears I did not know I had been crying. "Aia, who kept you in this place? For how long?"

I sniffled, wishing that I could regain some semblance of composure. "My brother. Whenever he entertained his guests. I was to hide in the cellar so I could not be found out."

"And your parents?"

"They are dead."

"Oh." For a while I thought he would leave it at that. Then he continued. "But...what sorts of guests did your brother host, Aia?"

I shook my head. "I never saw them. Important ones, he always said."

"And how were you treated when you were not locked away? When there were no guests?"

I blinked at him. "What...do you mean?"

"Did your brother treat you with kindness when you were free to walk about?"

I let my palms rest on his forearms as his hands settled on my waist, though I still held the flower, albeit more loosely. "I am not sure I understand your question," I confessed.

"Then I shall try to rephrase it. Did you feel as though your brother enjoyed having you around?"

"Well, I made myself as useful as I could. I cleaned and mended his clothes. Things like that."

"Did he ever thank you? Did he smile at you often? Or play little games with you just to hear you laugh? Things like that."

"Oh. I suppose not. I seemed to be a great burden to Aman. And if I made mistakes, he then had to punish me, which neither of us enjoyed very much."

"Punish?"

I nodded, my fingers gripping his arm once again. "He...there were often beatings. They were to teach me—"

But Willen could no longer remain where he had been standing, with his hands on my waist and his beautiful face very near mine. Instead, he paced about the room with his fists balled up. When he turned the corner of his furious walking, he caught sight of me and stopped, running his hands through his hair.

"Forgive me for my reaction. I did not mean to alarm you."

"I am not alarmed by you, Second Prince."

Willen's voice sounded as tight as mine felt. "I should not have raised my voice at you earlier, Aia. Concerning the flower. I see that now. I mean, of course, I knew I was being brash and I can be...emotional...when I should be logical. But now I know I have wronged you more than I thought I could."

"I did not leave the flower in your room. I promise you I am telling the truth."

He nodded. "I believe you. I always believed you, truly."

I thought about that. "Then, why did you insist it was my doing?"

"Because I was afraid, of course." He ended his pacing and pulled himself up next to me so we sat side by side on the wooden desk. "Aia...you are new to the Palace. And you must understand there are certain rules that must be kept. You and I? We are already breaking some of those rules."

"Oh, I understand the concept of rules very well, Second Prince, though I am not so familiar with the specifics of this particular set. Still, I am sure that the rules, when broken, bear consequences?"

"Precisely. I worry about those consequences. And when I thought perhaps you had broken one of our strictest rules and had gone to my personal chambers, I feared even more that you would be punished for it. There is nothing I would like less than to see you hurt for something as simple and innocent as leaving me a flower."

I thought about this for some time. "Second Prince? Did you break one of your rules by writing me that note?"

He made sure not to turn and look at me, but color tinted his cheeks. "I did, yes."

"Then why did you do it? And if it is against the rules for me to visit you here, in your study, why do you not send me away?"

He blushed even deeper and cleared his throat. "I have been asking myself the same questions and I have not found an answer. Only that...even when I imagine myself telling you that you cannot stay and even when I practice the words that would order you to leave...I see you standing before me and I cannot imagine what those words could possibly be. When you are with me, I cannot fathom possessing the willpower to make you go."

"But...you do *wish* I would leave...."

"I wish the rules were different. Just as I wish you had been treated with kindness all your life and not locked in some dreadful place, alone."

I placed my hand on his and swallowed my gasp at the unanticipated wave of enjoyment I felt. "I wish too that your circumstances could allow you more happiness, Second Prince."

"You must call me by name." The words spilled out of him so quickly it seemed like an accident.

"Is that not one of the rules I should not break? You mentioned this at the ball, did you not? Calling a High Royal by anything besides a title?"

"It is one of the rules. But perhaps one we may forsake when we are alone."

"And there again...is not being alone a broken rule?"

"It is. Very much so."

"Yet, we will break that one."

Willen bit his lip. "I...we should not."

"So I should go?"

But he did not answer me. After some time, I chose to speak at the same instant he did.

"Perhaps I could practice my reading here from time to time—"

"You were beautiful tonight—"

It was my turn for heat to spread across my cheeks. "Oh. I hardly knew what I was doing. Willen, did you happen to see? Did I manage to glow?"

He burst into laughter. Enough to shake the whole desk and to bring a smile to my nervous disposition. "Are you laughing at me, Willen?"

"Of course I am laughing at you!" He slapped his knee. "'Did I happen to see? Did you manage to glow?'" He swiped at tears that squeezed to life along the corners of his eyes. "Are you truly serious?"

"I am indeed serious. I closed my eyes at the very moment I put forth effort. I do not know how it went."

He shook his head in disbelief. "Aia, you glowed, yes, but not at all like the others who put forth harsh, blinding displays of flashing light. You...you were...." He leaned back and closed his eyes as though he was trying to remember it exactly as it happened. "You were the first break of morning light. When there is every possibility for good anew. And the memory of the darkness just starts to melt, so you can still remember how frightening it was to be lost in it. And so you can savor how relieved you are to see the morning come. You know the light; it could blind you with its brilliance, but it shines just enough for you to bear looking into it. So you may feel it. So you may know it." He looked at me as if I were glowing right then. "There is not a soul who could deny wanting such a moment. So yes, I 'happened to see' you glow."

I only realized I still had my hand on his when he lifted it to his lips and blessed it with a breeze of a kiss, leaving the flower behind us at last. "You must not doubt your ability, Aia. Or your inherent beauty. Dare say you could have simply stood there with your arms hanging, and the Palace would have fallen in love with you."

It was my turn to laugh. "Surely I am not so different looking than anyone else." And then I shrugged. "But I suppose I have no idea."

He rubbed his thumb across my knuckles as he spoke. "What do you mean by that?"

"I have no idea how my looks might compare to another's. How could one know such a thing? Although perhaps you could describe it to me."

Willen stood to his feet. "You are telling me, Little Tree, that you have never seen your own reflection?"

"I...no, I have not. I think I did once or twice when I was very little. I peered into a puddle—"

But Willen was no longer listening. "This cannot do. I must remedy this. Immediately."

"Willen, it is alright. I have gone this long without knowing—"

"You cannot go another night, not another moment, without knowing what I must behold whenever you speak to me. It is an injustice that you are blind to it, Aia. Wait here."

He hurried out of the study, leaving me to trace the spines of his books, trying to pronounce the complicated words carved into the leather. When he returned, he dragged something larger than both of us, with a white curtain draped over it.

"Alright," he said, a bit out of breath from heaving it into place. He offered me his hand and led me over to the object, then turned me to face him. Carefully, he examined me, tucking a few loose hairs behind my ears. He seemed to get lost in his task, for he ran his thumb over my brow and then down my temple, his stormy eyes studying me with dreamlike intensity. When he realized he had drifted from his purpose, he cleared his own throat and blushed scarlet. "Forgive me. I—" He did not finish his statement, only shut his eyes as if he needed to go to sleep and wake up to a new turn and fresh start. "Stand here," he said.

He angled me to face the object and stepped behind it. Then, he pulled the drapery from it in one dramatic go.

It took a moment for me to realize that the revealing of the object was not the point of the whole event, but rather that I was meant to look at the contents of the device. On glass much smoother than water, I saw an image of someone who I assumed was...me.

At first, I did not know what to do. I had no thoughts except, *How could this be?* And then I took in the full sight of myself. My height and shape, so much like the other Trees, yet...there was something different. I was neither too tall nor too short, slender, with hips that curved and breasts that stood out from my chest. I knew this already, for I had many opportunities to look down at myself and ponder those aspects of my appearance.

What I had never truly observed was my face. I approached the object and studied the tilt of my chin, the curve of my jaw. The hollow at the base of my throat and the contrast of my collar bone to my shoulders. My lips, they were pink as a ripened fruit one moment and then the silvery blue of pale moonlight the next. In fact, all of my skin followed along in this mesmerizing dance of light and color. The more I looked, the more detail I witnessed. Sparks of gold like lightning crackles and hints of iridescent green and purple. My hair, fair as I had always known, seemed to move as if it were enchanted by a sweet breeze, though no draft could possibly enter the study. At times, the blonde strands glowed golden, and then they moved near to translucence.

My eyes. They were a steady, piercing golden-brown.

"Do I...always look like...this?"

"Well...to some degree, yes. But you are changing now that you can see yourself. I have not witnessed this look before."

I swallowed, my mouth suddenly dry and my head light, as if it were floating away from my body. "What do I appear like to you? When you are the only one looking?"

He circled behind me so he could demonstrate while I watched. "The mirror does not seem to capture it." He reached his arm around me and traced my neck. "More gold." And my skin responded to his gaze, almost as if he were calling the colors to life. "And your hair, as if it's made of diamonds." He touched the ends of my tresses like he did not realize I would notice him doing so. "The colors all move more slowly, as well. Like clouds across the sky at first light."

No wonder my family locked me away so no one could see me. No wonder Aman feared his guests catching even a glimpse of me. No wonder they kept me in the dark, where only sadness and loneliness could color my skin. For if I was seen—or heaven forbid if I saw myself—I would have given away my secret with utmost certainty. For whatever I was, I was so undeniably. "I...am beautiful."

Willen frowned and kissed my shoulder as he stepped away. "And now you understand."

"Understand?"

"Why you have to go, Aia. And you must not come near me again. Not in this study, not at a ball, not in a Palace corridor. For when I am with you, I forget that there are any rules at all." He turned his darkened eyes away. "You fear your past, Little Tree. But I am the great peril of your future. Above all else, you should fear me."

My Fate Was Changed

Leaving the Prince's study did not send me into the maw of the cellar a second time. Instead, I was met with the corridor and a flurry of Trees as they scrambled after Clorente. To both my confusion and amazement, it was no longer the dead of night. Rather, the bright light of mid morning flooded my eyes. I fell in line at the very last, glad to be behind Shrane.

"Where are we going?" I asked her.

"We do not yet know," she replied. "We were only told that we must hurry. But it seems we are going round and round the corridors in circles."

"In circles? But...why?"

"I have already told you everything I know, Aia. Round and round, and do not fall behind. That's it. Now please stop talking; I hardly have any breath left in me."

Shrane was not joking in the least. After nine times around the same corridors at nearly the pace of a run, one of the remaining girls paused to catch her breath, her hands on her knees. We hurried past her, and I tried not to hear her wild screams as we went on without her accompanying us. I had no idea what became of the girl, for she was gone the next time we came around. In truth, I could hardly remember what she looked like.

We did this—chasing after Clorente—for what seemed to be many hours. When finally we stopped, my lungs ached and my body stiffened. One of the girls retched into a crystal vase. Shrane sat flat on the floor, trembling and pale.

Clorente, however, appeared completely unaffected. Her hair, dark as raven's wings, fell to her waist in twisting braids, her brow devoid of even a droplet of perspiration. "Trees, you are not *listening*. You are not paying attention," she said, her cane smacking the shimmering floor. "One of you must bear the High Prince a seed. If you are that one, you must *become* that one."

"She's going to kill us all," Shrane croaked beneath her breath. "It's only a matter of time."

"Not me," Gretaline hissed back at her. "I am that one. I will become that one."

Shrane's already round eyes widened. "How can you be so confident? We have not eaten in *turns*. And we are being made to run for hours and hours. These feats are impossible. This *whole thing* is impossible."

"It's only impossible without your Wonder, idiot," Gretaline snapped. "Why must I be responsible to teach complete newborns how to simply breathe in and out? Why must I be so endlessly benevolent?"

"Who is chatting while I lecture?" Clorente asked, her tone sharp as her upturned nose.

Both girls clamped their mouths shut.

"Now. Prepare your minds, Trees. I have been informed that the High Prince, in all his splendor, will be joining us for a meal this very morning. You will do your utmost best not to embarrass yourselves. Keep away from the food, lest you be tempted to gorge yourselves and bring shame to Trees every-where. Let us go."

Once we arrived at the dining area, which had changed both location and architectural design since our last visit, we sat in our matching green dresses with our hands in our laps. Waiting.

All at once, the doors to the dining area burst open and Theor reared in, his face screwed and his riding boots stomping. "I am to be called away from my important Royal duties? And for what? Tea and cakes with a bunch of half-wit, underdressed *whores*? Whores whose legs I am not even permitted to part?"

He slammed his hand into a tower of pink assorted pastries, sending them flying across the room. One of them hit Shrane in her rather round, rather large eyes. She shrieked and ducked her head to get the crumbs out.

"High Prince," Clorente said with a deep bow. "Forgive me, but I believe it was you who requested an audience with the Trees this fine morning."

Theor sighed with ferocity and grabbed a gooey orange scone, stuffing half of it into his mouth, his other hand on his hip. "Yes, yes, now that you mention it, perhaps I had a mind to see some beauty this morning, but then I made riding plans and forgot all about it. Now I am missing riding, and for what? For whom?" He spit his mouthful of scone on the floor and tossed the other half over his shoulder. He went in for a tartlet instead, ripping it asunder with perfectly white teeth.

"You know what? Why should I not have all the things I want at once? I am the High Prince. And I am entitled to any of the things which I desire." He flopped the rest of the tartlet on the table so that it bounced about before landing square in an unsipped cup of tea. Then, he licked his sticky fingers before reaching out and grabbing my arm. He yanked me out of my seat, knocking my chair over with his aggressive maneuvering. "This one will come with me, then. I will not take the entire host of dull Trees, or the gloom will block out my sunlight."

With Clorente mumbling out a protest and a few gasps from the girls, Theor dragged me out of the room.

"My Prince, please!" Clorente called, speaking up as she chased after us. "Please it is against the rules for you to be alone with a Tree who is not ready to seed. You will disqualify her!"

"If she is disqualified, then I may do whatever I like with her. And there are many others remaining to choose from, are there not?"

"Your Graciousness, you have only five Trees remaining in total. If you take this one, it will leave you with four, your chances greatly reduced. And this one...it seems she shows great promise. She may be your only chance, High Prince. She may very well be the entire realm's only chance. And of course, I would have to inform your father, the High King—"

Theor swiveled and moved in mere inches from Clorente, his grip on my arm all the tighter as he pulled me with him. "Fine." His glare sought to burn her. "I will bring a chaperone. Petrus will accompany me."

"*Petrus*? He is hardly a responsible chaperone, High Prince."

That is when Theor straightened up and bellowed with all his might. "Willen! Willen, bring your self-righteous arse here at once." Then, to the servants who followed the fair-headed High Prince like a swarm of victimized bees, "Find my sorry excuse for a brother this instant! We all know it is he who Clorente deems responsible. Responsible Willen. Suitable Willen. Dutiful-and-noble-in-all-his ways Willen!" Theor raved so wildly that I thought he might snap my arm in half, but not before he punctured my eardrum.

Quick steps on the staircase, which seemed to shift so that he appeared at the top of it out of nowhere, and the voice of Willen Vedan. "Theor, what in heaven's name are you *doing*?"

"Riding!" he thundered. "With the company of my choosing! Oh and you, most holy chaperone!"

Willen took in the situation with haste before his gaze flicked over to Clorente. They exchanged some silent conversation, and Willen swallowed his comment and nodded. "I am at your service, then, High Prince."

"*Are you*? Of course you are! So helpful. So supportive."

I winced as Theor continued to fling me about, my upper arm still trapped in his mighty grip. Willen noticed, his careful, cloudy eyes tracking my every move.

"I will ready the Tree of your choice and pair her to a horse," Willen offered.

"Nonsense. She rides with me. I've a big enough saddle for the both of us."

A muscle tensed in the Second Prince's jaw. "If you wish. But as you know, a Tree must be blessed by her caretaker before leaving her presence for any prolonged time. Leave her with Clorente for this blessing while we mount, Theor. She will join us in no more than a moment."

Theor glared at his brother with such vehemence, such hatred, as he drew near that I feared for Willen more than I ever had for myself. Then, the High Prince, believing the ruse, released me, shoving me forward and turning to leave with a grunt.

I stumbled, but Willen caught me with ease. "Good heavens, Lady Tree, you are undoubtedly injured," he said. He lifted the sheer sleeve of my sage green dress and examined my arm. "The bruises will be tremendous, Clorente. They are already forming."

"I am alright," I said, trying to convince him. But he was not easily persuaded.

"You cannot possibly be alright. He almost broke your arm clean off."

Clorente stepped forward. "I can tend to her, Second Prince. She is in good hands. It will only take a moment."

"In whose *hands* is she, Clorente, and how *good* are they exactly? For the way I see it, your hands are the very ones from which she was just snatched. Is that not true?"

Clorente blinked, squaring her shoulders. "Yes, Second Prince. And you of all people should know that when the Royal Law has deemed another pair of hands infinitely more powerful than yours or mine, all we can rely on—all we have left—is the fact that our own hands are good."

It should have been a convincing argument. One that exonerated Clorente from Theor's less-than-admirable actions. But Willen narrowed his eyes. "I may not be as loud and bold as my elder brother, Clorente. But I pay attention. And I know that you are desperate. I know that you are *failing*. You are cutting corners with these women. You are cheating the rules. And this Tree will not be one of the corners you cut."

Clorente swallowed. "I—"

"*You* will *protect* these Trees. With your life. No matter who threatens them. You will not use them to spare *yourself* hardship."

With that, Clorente bowed. "I shall be more careful with the Trees, Second Prince."

"You will do what you swore. I do not give a damn about how careful you are. You serve the *Trees*. Now find your courage and do so." Willen took a breath and ran a hand through his ashen hair. Then he offered that remarkably steady hand to me. "Lady Tree, if you are ready?"

I took his hand, and he led me toward the set of doors Theor had stormed out of a short time before.

"Are you alright?" he asked me again, his tone hushed compared to the voice he'd used in confrontation with Clorente.

"Truly, the incident was not so brutal as you made it out to be, Second Prince."

"I do not mean your arm. I am inquiring as to your sensitive nature. I was harsh back there. Clorente is meant to look after you, and I had to say something about her inability to do so."

"She tried to convince the High Prince not to take me, your...generalness."

He snorted down a laugh. "'Prince' is fine when we are in public, Lady." Then, he sobered. "Clorente should not be parading you around like she does. You should be kept in private for your many trials. But she is doing so to prove to the realm and the court that she is capable of producing a seed for us all. To save her own neck, she puts yours at risk."

"We can hardly blame her, then. For she is afraid."

"Someone must be to blame."

"Well...it was the High Prince who waved me around like a flag on a breezy turn. Not Clorente. Perhaps the blame should lie with him."

Willen nodded. "Perhaps you are right. I will speak to him when he and I are alone." And then he twirled me around so I walked on the opposite side of him. "May I tend to your arm? You should not be in pain any longer."

"You? I thought it was Clorente who could heal."

"I rarely use my Wonder. When I do, it tends to cause trouble. But for you, of course, I will not hesitate." He nodded. "Your bruises should be much better now."

I lifted my sleeve, and sure enough, there was nothing there but soft, smooth skin. The colors danced as if they were ripples urged on by a stone in the water. "How did you do that, Prince?"

Willen seemed pleased, his eyes clearing for a moment as he examined his work. "It seems you like my particular Wonder, Little Tree."

"I wish I knew how any of it worked."

He frowned, his hand still holding mine as he escorted me. "And I wish I could teach you. Perhaps some turn...." His words trailed away, as did our conversation, for we both no doubt dwelled on the reality that this could never be. If I became Theor's Tree, my life would be forfeit. And if I was not his Tree, my life would still be forfeit.

We journeyed out the door, and the sight of the truest trees in the distance, just beyond the vast gardens, nearly left me screaming with delight. As Willen readied his horse, he grinned, pausing to study me.

"Lady Tree," he called, trying to pull my attention away.

"Mmm?" I answered, my eyes transfixed on the branches and leaves.

"We are about to ride through them. Perhaps you'll like that."

"Through them?"

"Yes. If ever I could find my brother, we will start."

"He has gone ahead," Beralt called, running up beside us. "High Prince told me to tell you, 'whatever in heaven is keeping them so long, curse them for it. Tell Willen to bring the damn Tree to meet me, for I will not be made to wait a moment longer!'" Beralt bowed to the Second Prince. "Apologies for the language. But that is what Theor said."

Willen's eyes nearly thundered. "How can one be so erratic?" he sighed. "Beralt, perhaps you could join us? We should not ride off alone, just the two of us. A third will be needed."

Beralt bowed deeply. "It would be my honor to accompany you both."

I was hoisted up to the saddle, sitting in front of the Second Prince Of All The Realm, not an inch of separation between us.

"The Lady does not prefer to ride herself?" Beralt asked, saddled on his own steed beside us.

Willen's response resembled a growl. "Theor demands she ride with him. We would have an extra horse with no rider on the way back if she took one from the stables."

"It's not only that. I'm afraid I don't know how. I have not even seen a horse up close before this," I confessed. "The carriage that brought us to the Palace had not even one horse pulling it."

Beralt shivered. "Clorente and her Wonder. Gives me the chills that one. It's unnatural."

"All Wonder is natural, Beralt," Willen said, correcting his friend as we moved toward the trees. "Clorente simply wields hers in unusual ways."

"As do you, Your Grace. I've not seen anyone use such clean Wonder before. It is nearly traceless. As if it were reality all along."

"You flatter me." But it seemed Willen sternly rejected the compliment.

"Well, yes, I flatter you. And you *fatten* me in return. A compliment for a copper!" He guffawed and slapped his knee.

"Don't listen to him," Willen warned me. But I could sense his mood lift at his friend's jest.

"Sir Beralt?" I spoke up, my eyes still trained on the encroaching trees as we rode with no particular haste.

"Yes, My Lady?"

"Has the Second Prince always been so serious?"

Beralt liked that question very much. He roared into laughter, so much so that his horse sidestepped and he nearly slipped from the saddle.

"It's not funny," Willen grumbled.

I shrugged. "I suppose those who tease do not like when it's done to them."

On the side Beralt could not see, Willen reached up and gently poked at my ribs, which made me wiggle.

"He truly is not always *so* serious, Lady," Beralt said. "We have good fun on occasion. I would say the true and hidden nature of the Second Prince would be one of mischief. Much like his father."

I grinned and slapped his hand away as Willen tickled my side once more. "I suppose I must believe you are right, Beralt. Though why he hides this nature I cannot understand."

Beralt nodded, his big beard scraping against his wide chest, his short legs not even reaching the stirrups. "Those who shine brightest become targets, My Lady. Best, at times, not to shine at all."

I played with this in my mind for a while. There must have been some truth to it, for Gretaline chose to take me along with her at the ball simply because she thought I would not outshine her. If I glowed more brightly than she, I would have become her target, not her boost.

"If you speak of the High Prince...why does he dislike his younger brother so? They are not competitors. Is Theor simply antagonistic?"

"Ah. I will let Willen tell that story, Lady Tree."

"Look," Willen said, attempting to distract me. "The trees, Aia."

And oh, how I did look. They loomed up over us, so big and sturdy and ancient. Their strength shook the ground as their roots grew. I could feel those roots calling up to me, whispers and hums as they creaked and stretched. I stared for some time at the magnificence of it all, enraptured by the grandeur. And by their...familiarity.

After a while, though, I realized that I had become so engrossed in my tree gazing that I'd leaned my head far enough back to be resting on the shoulder of the Second Prince, and his chin, for that reason I suppose, nestled against my temple. His body was more relaxed than I expected, as if the two of us might fall asleep atop his horse.

But once we realized the wrong we committed, I sat up and Willen straightened his back and cleared his throat. Beralt looked away as if he hadn't noticed our posture, though most certainly he had.

"He stares because of your color," Willen whispered into my ear. "The trees change you."

In truth, my hands held the faintest green, with hints of gold, silver, and blue. I could only imagine what my face and hair must have looked like.

"Is it very strange?" I asked. "The look of me now?"

But before the Prince could give an answer, and when we had gone rather deep into the lush forest, we heard a loud cry.

"Ignore it," Willen said. "That's the sound Theor makes when he's missed his mark. He makes it after most shots."

Beralt chuckled.

"Ignore it, you say? Like you ignored my question about your brother's animosity?" I asked.

Beralt sucked in air.

"Why don't you ride over a cliff, Beralt?" Willen said.

"Still ignoring," I chimed.

"Oh I *like* her," Beralt said, his beard reshaped by the turn of his lips into a smile.

"The story is simply not to be told," Willen responded. "You must forgive me. I did not mean to ignore you, Lady Tree."

Another cry. But this one was different. It was more of a howl, followed by rather loud panting and shrieking.

The two men sobered when they heard it. As for me, chills raced up my spine and down my legs. I quivered in the arms of the Second Prince.

"I shall ride ahead and see what is wrong," Willen said.

"No, Prince, you are escort to the Lady. I will go and warn you of any present danger. You remain behind."

And Beralt galloped forward, disappearing into the trees. Not moments later, it was he who cried out, loud enough for half the forest to hear. "Wyverns, Willen! Run!"

Just then, two horses without riders barreled past us. Their fleeing was echoed by the wild screams of fallen men in astounding pain.

"My brother. I cannot leave him," Willen called out. "Beralt?!"

"I have him, Willen! Ride! Ride!"

And with that, Willen turned his horse, and we raced in the direction we had come. It was not long, though, before a swooshing sound filled my ears and the foliage was swept from under us. I looked up to see, just above the trees, a gray viper winding its way above the branches, its large wings kicking up the wind as it navigated.

The thing—a Wyvern, as Beralt called it—screeched, nearly splitting my ears and causing my heart to leap into my throat. Our horse reared out of frightful protest, and Willen called out, "Let go of the horse, Aia!"

I did as he said, and we slid off our beast, his arms around me and the both of us rolling across the forest floor as our steed took off, the Wyvern chasing after it.

"Are you alright, Aia?" Willen said, righting himself.

"What *was* that?" I asked, catching my breath as Willen helped me to my feet.

"A Wyvern. A winged snake with a bottomless appetite. They never used to fly so close to the Palace."

"Do you think...Beralt is alright?"

"Beralt? Yes, that old man is just fine. He's taken down many a Wyvern in his time. And if he's with Theor, my brother also will be alright. Our horse might not fare so well, I'm afraid."

I took his outstretched hand so we could begin our walk back. "Thank you, Second Prince."

"Call me Willen, if you wish. We are alone now, though not by our design."

I could not help but smile. "You called me Aia. In front of Beralt."

He stopped walking altogether to think about this, then continued on. "Are you sure?"

"Yes. Quite certain. I would not forget hearing you say my name."

He let time pass before he spoke again. I wondered if he noticed he had not released my hand since helping me off the ground. "Yes. My answer to your last question. I do not wish to ignore you when it is within my power to respond."

"My question?"

"When we were riding. Just before the Wyverns. You asked if your look is strange when you are among the trees. And my answer is yes. It is very different. As if you are a tree in truth. Or rather, as if you are becoming one before my very eyes."

"Oh. I am sorry you have to look at me, then, if it disturbs you."

"You are the only thing I've ever witnessed worth my undivided attention." And then he stopped, as if overwhelmed by something I could not quite understand. "Aia, you must never apologize to me for being who you are. Not for looking the way you do nor for saying the things you say. You are to be wholly treasured for those very things. Do you understand what I mean?"

I could only nod, for my chest tightened greatly, and the words I hoped I could find remained hidden from me. The closer we got to the end of the forest, the more this feeling grew until I too was overwhelmed and required for us to stop walking altogether. The forest did not want me to part with it. And I did not want to part with Willen.

"You are hurt?" he asked, coming close to me and putting his hands to my face, so he could examine me.

"I do not want to go back," I said.

His eyes clouded over. "Aia—"

"If I could choose, I would not ever go back to the Palace. Except if *you* choose to go. Then I would never leave it. I prefer to be beside you. Very much. More than anything I have ever preferred."

"Aia—"

"Why can I not speak to you in public? Why can I not say hello? Why can I not hold your hand *whenever* I feel afraid? Why can I not make you laugh if you are sad or worried? I want to be able to say your name all the time. And I want you to hold me like you did last night. I do not understand *why* it's so wrong. Why can these things not be so?"

"Aia." He shut his eyes for a while. Steadied his breathing.

"Do you not want those things? Is that why?"

When he opened his eyes, it was clear they held a thousand worlds, each with their own burdens. "Aia, it does not matter what I want. I cannot have it. I cannot hold your hand or laugh at your wit or keep you pressed close to me."

"But we *already* do these things, Willen."

"And *already*, Theor and Clorente would have us killed if they knew. Theor already plots for my death daily. It will not help matters if I steal his Tree."

"It is not *stealing* me to hold my hand!"

"But I would not simply hold your hand, now would I?! There would be more. And when that was finished, there would be more. Until there was nothing left between us. And then what?!"

"And then?" Anger pulsed in my veins. I stepped close enough to the Second Prince for me to feel his very breath. I could see his heart racing, the pace of it causing his silk shirt to tremble. "And then, Willen, you will hold my hand all over again."

This was when, to my great astonishment and general disbelief, my fate was changed for all time. For the Second Prince Of All The Realm touched my lips with his.

Curse My Eyes

Curse me. Curse my eyes, which only behold what I should not see. And curse my mind, which leads me down corridors I should not enter. And, above all else, curse my mouth, which finds itself on the lips of a Tree who would never be mine. Never in all my life have I managed to be this stupid.

I pulled away from Aia. Well, in my mind, I pulled away from her. But after a moment, I realized I had done no such thing and still held her in my arms. Her hands had not the pristine and untouched perfection of other noblewomen. I could tell she had worked with them. That she'd struggled for the life she lived. A life that was not awarded, but earned. Defended. The same was true of her back, which I often admired as she walked past me, for, though she was slender, her fine muscles rippled beneath the simple dresses Clorente had all the Trees wear. I ran my fingers along those muscles, and she shivered in response.

This was an even graver mistake on my part. For I could not help myself and kissed her deeper, bringing her toward me, my free hand slipping into her hair and—her hair was not what I expected. Like fairy wings, like gossamer silk laced together. I worried then that perhaps I would hurt her. I had not thought she would be so soft, so delicate. But she did not seem to mind my touch at all, pressing her mouth against mine with matched pressure.

We should not. We should not, we should not, we should not.

But I could taste her. Her supple tongue like the dew of berries in early spring. How could that be, when I was sure she had never tasted such treats herself? How could an anomaly like Aia even exist?

She pulled away from me, but only to gasp for air, and then she returned her lips to mine. She gripped the front of my shirt as if she wanted me closer, but I knew. I knew we could not become any closer than we already were. Not with our clothes on. Not in the middle of the forest and out in the open. *What am I thinking?* Not ever could we do this. Not under any circumstances. *Willen, stop. Stop.* But it was so difficult to listen to myself.

I managed, with great internal struggle, to separate myself from Aia.

"Wait," she murmured, coming to me again. How she slipped her hands beneath the hem of my shirt when I was certain it was tucked into my waistband, I would never know.

I let her. I let her touch my skin with those hands. They were neither cold nor warm—as if she matched the temperature around us with precision. And I did not mean for a groan to escape me, but it left me nonetheless.

"Do you dislike...being this close?" she asked.

I kissed the bridge of her nose in response. I wondered if she knew what the sound of her voice did to me. It was like the rustle of the leaves as a cool breeze stirred over the land. As if the pressure were gone, as if the storms had just passed. When she spoke, I wanted nothing more but to lean into it. I swore I would do anything she asked. Anything.

I kissed the place beneath her eyes, the hollow beneath her jaw, and, though I told my hands to go no further, I pressed them against the softness of her stomach, feeling each of her ribs through her dress as I drew my touch upward to the gentle curve just beneath her breast.

"Second Prince!"

I nearly bit Aia's tongue off, heaven help me. Beralt's voice broke through my heady haze, and I yanked my hands away, stepping backwards and stumbling over a root. Aia reached her hand out to steady me and caught the sleeve of my shirt. This action only caused me to return to her, her gaze lifted up toward me, and to those eyes, golden-brown and unchanging, like the heart of a tree itself. They kept me. There was no other way to explain it. She kept me.

Beralt tugged me by the back of the shirt and stepped between us. "Have you lost your mind, Willen? Have you lost it completely?"

I pressed the heels of my palms to my eyes, as if it might change the sight of her. But when I removed them, Aia was there. Waiting. Waiting for me.

"Miss Tree, stand right there and do not move," Beralt said. Then he shoved and shoved until we were a few lengths away, sloshing our boots in a narrow brook. Beralt kicked the back of my knee so I knelt and flushed my face with the cool water.

"Willen, come out of it, man!"

But I could only think of how much Aia would enjoy the sight of the water and how beautiful she would appear if she took on its properties.

"Willen, for the love of heaven, sharpen your mind, boy. Wake up. Wake up!"

I felt as if I could barely see the old Dwarf, but slowly, my focus sharpened. He wore a gash on his forehead and a look of great distress in his beady eyes. "Beralt? What happened? You're bleeding."

"Willen, not a few moments ago, Wyverns roared over our heads, and I went off to aid the High Prince, heir of the crown and future ruler of all the Realm. The same brother to whom this Tree may, we hope to heaven, be fated to match. The same brother who attempts to take your life with great regularity and who does not need further reason to do so. But it is not just your brother—"

"I know, I know." I wished he would stop. Stop speaking so passionately, stop staring at me with such fear in his gaze.

"No you don't know! The Willen I'm acquainted with...*he* knows! He spends all his time knowing. But now, this turn about the sun, I am not sure you know *at all* what you are doing!"

I exhaled once, twice, three times. And then placed my hands on my friend's shoulders. "Beralt," I said, my voice exuding calm I did not feel, "I know. I know, and I made a mistake. That is all it was. A mistake. The pressure is great, Beralt, and no one can withstand such a thing for too long. A lapse in judgment. Momentary. Momentary, is all."

Beralt harrumphed. "But Willen...out in the open? Suppose I had brought Theor with me? Suppose he had found you first? Or...or anyone else, for that matter? It is not only your-self who would pay a price; it would be the Tree as well."

I tried to keep what little I'd had for breakfast down. At the thought of the danger I had put Aia in, my head reeled.

"You are unwell," Beralt said, his frown so deep that his bushy eyebrows nearly met his bumpy nose.

"No, I'm fine. I just...." I shook my head. "It must be the pressure."

"Perhaps a trip, Prince? Perhaps...space?"

I nodded. "Yes, perhaps space."

"You are saying yes and shaking your head no, Willen."

I sighed. *What is wrong with you?*

"She is...very beautiful," Beralt offered, attempting to sympathize.

"That is not it," I nearly shouted. I caught myself and lowered my tone. "It is more than that. She is...she is more than that."

"I thought you said she was a mistake. A lapse in judgment?"

More breakfast. That's what I need. And some gentle tea.

We returned to Aia and found her not at all where we left her, but already marching back toward the Palace, her palms out so she could touch the bark of the trees as she went.

"No one listens to me," Beralt grumbled, hustling on short legs to match the pace. "I say to wait, she goes. I say to take space, he rushes toward her."

"Aia, wait, slow down. It isn't safe," I called out to her, moving ahead of Beralt and, without meaning to, catching her hand in mine.

She removed herself from my grasp. It was then I realized that she wore tears in her honey eyes.

"Aia, what—"

"I do not want to speak with you, Second Prince. For now I know what it is like to be someone's lapse in judgment. And if I am some grave mistake to you, then I will put more effort into avoiding you, per your desire."

"Aia—"

"I am familiar with cellars. And you wish me to return to mine, so as not to disturb you, so as not to distract you from your guests and your busyness. Your important matters." She scrubbed the tear as it fell down her changing skin. "I will admit, I do not have the slightest clue what I am doing or why I wanted to do it with you. Except that I thought, perhaps, you were wonderful. And now I see that I am, after all, a stupid Tree. I will return to giving my life away for something I do not even understand. So if you'll excuse me...."

It was an awkward walk as we delivered Aia back to the Palace. The guards went on and on about why Wyverns dared to fly so close to humans, but for once, for a hint of a moment, I did not care about the state of the Realm and the citizens and the nature. Beralt tried to follow me, but I quickened my pace.

"Second Prince," he called out.

"Give me time."

"But Second Prince—"

"Beralt, *leave me alone.*"

And I brought my Wonder to the front of my heart so I could change the shape of the halls, calling my chambers closer to me. I slammed the door behind me and sought to throw myself on the bed when a note appeared in my hand, uncoiling like a snake. Clorente's Wonder. It wreaked of manipulation. She always used Wonder too close to the lines of legitimacy. It made my blood hiss in my veins.

Your presence is requested at dinner. The High Prince insists.
–Clorente

And the note vanished.

I could not tell which angered me more. That my presence was requested yet again so that I would be forced to meddle too deeply in my brother's affairs, when all the Realm and then some knew he would not find a matching Tree. Or that Clorente had yet again manipulated time. It should not have been dinner at all, but she pushed and pulled the hours to suit her futile quest to redeem herself.

We would not have been in the mess we were if not for advisors like her. Ones who told the Ancient High Kings that the trees could be used for building ships and fortresses, outposts and carriages and bridges. For warring and conquesting. For exemplifying wealth and intimidating foreign rulers. Until the Ancient Trees themselves turned on us. Left us to starve. With no more Trees as ambassadors to the Royals.

Why would they change their minds now? What have we done to earn it, except for torture the few Trees we could find in the hopes of forcing them to bear Seed too soon. It had never worked that way and it never would. But it was not my place to dissent. As Second Prince, it was my duty to help. To support. To lend my aid to my brother and my father in every way. For most of my rank, in times past, that meant staying out of the way, but my father would not have that. We had already been separated long enough, he always said.

And so I would go to the pointless dinner, for staying at the Palace meant pleasing my father and enraging my brother all at once.

I paused my sulking, for I remembered that I was to meet with visiting dignitaries from Tseslar. This was a role my father gave me, to fill in the gaps of diplomacy where my brother fell short. And heavens, did Theor fall short. One dinner with century-long allies and a hundred circles of friendship would be abandoned in the name of war thanks to Theor's lack of decorum. He was brash and rude and...largely stupid.

I pulled off my shirt in favor of another, but in doing so, I remembered the careful hands of the woman I had just kissed. How the feel of her lingered on my skin. Until it seemed my heart would speed to bursting.

Willen, no. No. It was better that she was cross with me. Better that she could not bear to look at me, that she overheard me lying to Beralt about my feelings for her. That way I would not be the cause of her demise. *That way I can save her.* I nearly slapped myself at this thought, for it was treason, plain and simple. Our Realm needed a True Tree, or the people would starve. We would lose the air and water sustained by the Breaths and Rivers of other realms. Aia was not mine. I could not change her fate. Doing so would doom the entire Realm.

Don't be selfish, Willen. You cannot choose lust over the safety of millions.

But I knew with every certainty that it was not merely lust drawing me to Aia. For one, it was my Wonder. And never had the force reacted without my consent as it did when I was with her. To be fair, my Wonder was not a separate thing from me. It was me. The part of me that remained inexplicable. The mysteriousness of a person that even they could not truly dictate or command. I could only ask my Wonder and, if we were good at working together, it would oblige. Except for when it came to the girl with the sunrise hair. Then my Wonder could not even hear me, it seemed.

I sighed, wishing to force thoughts of Aia from my mind. I went to splash some water on my face, for that had worked when Beralt took me aside to the little brook. But before I sank my hands into the porcelain basin, I noticed a glint of sorts. With a keen eye, I examined the basin and found, submerged beneath the water, the smallest of blades. Since it did not have the size to kill me, I assumed it was laced with poison of some sort. This made me sigh even greater.

Forgoing the washing, I used my Wonder to walk straight into the chambers of my older brother.

"Theor, good evening."

"Ack! You know I hate it when you appear like a phantom. What do you want? I'm dressing."

"First off, if you don't want people walking into your chambers, you should have someone Wonder up a ward for you. Second...why is there a poisoned blade in my wash basin?"

Theor snorted. "Go slice your hand on it and then come back and ask me, why don't you?"

"You cannot so clumsily plot my murder, brother. At least do me the honor of discretion. A bit of complicated strategy, perhaps."

"I don't owe you any honor. Besides, you are too perceptive. Exhausting, you are. Like a little beady-eyed snoop, always looking and checking, always making sure. Always meddling."

"It is not meddling for one to use his own wash basin."

"It is meddling, then, for you to not *die* when and how you are told."

I gave up. My brother did not understand the definition of the word 'meddling', and we would get nowhere if I refuted him. "Why? Why kill me? It does not make sense, Theor. I pose no threat to you—"

"You pose every threat to me, *brother*. Why can you not see that? You and your perfection, your shrewd diplomatic sense, your ability to hoard my father's affection all for yourself." He spat the last words out quite literally, spittle flying from his mouth, his eyes growing red with malice.

"All I ever do is my best to support you."

"If that were true, you would be dead." Theor rolled his shoulders as if refraining from striking me where painful. "That is all I've ever wanted from you. Perhaps one turn, *I* will make a way."

I held my finger up to him. "No. Do not even think of such things, Theor. The Ancient Laws are not to be rewritten. They are forever and they are that way for a reason."

"The Ancients did not know I would have to deal with the likes of *you*. With enough effort and with their blessing, I will have my way. One turn. You'll see."

"Effort? What sort of effort do you think will gain you access to the blessing of the Ancients? Will you use your *Wonder*, Theor?"

At this, he roared like a Wyvern, for he and I both knew he could hardly wield enough Wonder to turn a rock on its side. He lunged for me, his thick and heavy arm swinging with the intention of shattering my nose. But he came within an inch of me and howled in pain, nursing his hand and dropping to his knees.

"You *cannot* harm me. It's impossible. We have been through this so many times."

"One turn. One turn, Willen the Wonderful. You will see the true nature of the High Prince, and I will *win*. The crown. The Tree. And the devotion of the High King. All of it. *Mine*."

I left without another word, for all of those things already belonged to my brother, and none of them would ever be mine.

"Dignitaries?" Beralt groaned, meeting me as I entered the dining room. "How many dignitaries can there possibly be in this world? New ones every few turns! When does it end?"

"It doesn't end, Beralt. That is the nature of the crown. Diplomacy is what keeps war at bay. If we want peace in the Realm, we must host dignitaries."

"I must express...most Second Princes I've ever known simply cavort around with noble women and lie out half-naked in the Caramian sun."

"I am not most Second Princes."

"No. Instead you do the work of the High Prince and more while *he* cavorts with noble women."

"So it seems. But dwelling on my circumstances will not make for an accomplished dinner."

"Must *all* dinners be accomplished?"

I stopped my brisk walking and turned to my friend—the one who had been friends with many Second Princes before me. "What is it, Beralt? Out with it."

"Finally, I thought you would never ask."

"You are whining loud enough for the Ancients to plug their ears. Go on. Speak your piece."

"You need a *break*, Willen."

"Well, I cannot have one."

"If what happened earlier—"

"*Nothing* happened earlier."

"Fine. The nothing that happened earlier...it's—"

"I know. It's not like me."

"Well, I have put thought to it, in the unethically brief interval between the midmorning hunt and dinner, and I believe it is actually very much like you. Like the you who would be permitted to exist if only you were given the opportunity. Which is why you need—"

"I know you mean well, Beralt. But your initial reaction to the nothing that happened was indeed the correct one, and I am grateful for it. Now to put it behind me and get back to the work at hand. I know better. And I will do better."

I entered the dining room and headed toward my seat. The dignitaries, who hailed from Tseslar, were by nature boisterous and desiring frequent entertainment. If I had been given more time to plan without Theor's interruption, the Wyverns, and Clorente's manipulation, I would have hired some musicians or perhaps a comic for our evening. But I had been given no time, and so Wonder would have to do the trick.

A touch here and there enhanced the displays of the food so that the wine cracked and hissed into frothing ice and the grapes juggled themselves before landing on plates. The visiting Duchess giggled when a berry with the wings of a hummingbird kissed her nose.

"A special treat for this evening," Clorente said, appearing all at once near the table. "A rare glimpse at the unique Trees of our Realm."

I had to work hard not to snap my spoon in half. It was not to be done, parading the Trees about. They were not spectacles. They were *important*. They were the only future our Realm could hope to have. Yet there was Clorente, having them walk about the room like they were trophies in some sick harem.

"Oh, how majestic," said the Duchess, clapping her small hands—for she was only thirteen circles of age—and bouncing in her seat. "There are such Wonders in the Realm. I always adore visiting, though my cousin warns me against it. Look how the Ladies shimmer and glow! One would think they are human just like the rest of us."

Clorente smiled—or at least attempted to—her skin pulling tight around her eyes. "Duchess Extraordinary, forgive my correction, but Trees are still human, in part. They are descendants of an ancient Arboreal race, yes, but human nonetheless. And they exist in every land, though very few remain."

"Ah, they are ambassadors, then! Very lovely ones, unlike our Trees back home. I never get to enter the Room to see the ones still in match-making, and I find our True Trees to be quite...boring."

Clorente beamed. "Indeed."

I tried not to stare at Aia, at the way her back moved when she made her way around the room. At the sliver of skin just above her collarbone, which I hardly knew the taste of, for I had not savored her nearly as long as I wished to.

She made a point not to look at me, it seemed, but her colors changed whenever she crossed before me.

Finally, Beralt punched me in the knee and gasped. I had been staring. Far too intently. And, while I paid attention to no one but that particular Tree, Theor had entered the room.

Equipped with his entourage of womanizers, Petrus included, my brother charmed his way around the table. I was sure he pinched a few Trees as he went, for they cried out and blushed as he made his way past them.

"Let's eat!" Theor cried out. "But first, a toast!" He lifted a glass of the red wine of the evening. "To my Tree, whichever of these she may be—probably that one with the perfect breasts—and to the little Countess whose breasts have not yet grown!"

He is drunk.

"Heavendamn it," Beralt growled.

"*Duchess*," the young girl corrected, no hint of a smile remaining on her deep brown features.

"Yes, whatever you say," Theor replied. "Now, let's drink."

My mind galloped through possible methods I could employ to rectify the complete disaster that had left my brother's mouth disguised as words. I sipped the drink without much thought, though its sweetness was a much-needed relief.

The Duchess of Tseslar was not someone we could afford to offend. Her cousin, the King, was not necessarily fond of our Realm, and their land served as a buffer between known enemies and us. If they broke our alliance, one which our grandfather had barely managed to establish, our enemies would march straight through their lands and park at our doors.

We would have to—I touched my lips, for they tingled in quite an odd manner. I shut my eyes, trying to force myself to focus. If the Duchess reported my brother's offenses to her cousin, we would have to—the tingling spread to my throat.

I could not say why I looked not to Beralt or to anyone else present at the enormous table. My eyes, they searched for Aia's. *Curse my eyes.*

Ep 12

The Agony Overtook Me

I put it out of my mind that I had not eaten in many turns.
It did not help that the food presented at the banquet looked
incredible. Apples in cinnamon and candied lemons. Meat
soaked in black wine and buttered potatoes. Something Wonderful caught my eye as a young girl in very fancy gold trimmings
giggled. It was difficult to know where the Wonder that turned
a berry into a bird came from, but it was whimsical, and when
I breathed, the air smelled somehow cleaner.

I hoped I would not mistakenly stare at the Second Prince,
who asked the girl kind questions phrased as jokes and jests
to pull laughter out of her all night long. But I did stare at him
whenever I believed he was not looking, for there was nothing
more miraculous in the room than him and the way he tried
not to smile even when he inspired joy in the heart of another.

"Where is Theor?" Gretaline hissed into my ear, her nose
scrunched as she scoured the room. "What is the point of
these meals if he is not present? We should be testing and
preparing if he is not going to be admiring us."

"I hope we never see him again," Shrane murmured. "At breakfast this morning, he pinched my thigh."

"And he pinched my belly. It is a sign of endearment. Don't complain," Gretaline said, lifting her nose. "You know nothing of high society."

But I thought of riding with Willen and the way he so gently tickled my ribs. He did not need to cause me alarm to show endearment. And he was just as high-society as his brother. Perhaps Gretaline did not know everything there was to know about being a Tree.

And as if she'd called out to him, Theor arrived in his usual fashion, his muscular arms swinging and his strong chin high as his title. He did, in fact, pinch a few of the Trees. I was preoccupied with watching Willen's eyes study Theor's movements.

And, after the High Prince said something absolutely preposterous to the girl who, apparently, was a *Duchess* and not a Countess, he made a toast, which meant we all were to drink something. But no glasses were handed to us Trees. We were simply to stand and to watch. Much like plants.

Everyone present took a sip of wine, and of course, I watched the Second Prince, for the way his mouth moved as he went to drink and the form of his neck as he swallowed made me want to touch him, to kiss that throat and to have him touch me in the way he did in the forest. He drank for the toast and then he held his glass at a distance. At first, I thought it was because he admired the flavor of the bright red wine, but when he bit his bottom lip, there was a shadow of discomfort in his cloudy eyes. And then he touched those lips with his fingers as if some malady had been presented to them.

Another flicker across his eyes, but not so much of discomfort as it was of fear. I knew it with certainty, for this time he did not try to avoid my line of sight, but rather looked straight into my eyes. He cleared his throat. And then again. And again.

I wondered how all the room—no, all the Realm—did not stop what they were doing to pay attention, but they all chattered and chuckled and murmured on as if nothing were the matter. But I knew something was wrong. I knew it. And the truth clutched at my heart.

Willen began to cough, still holding the glass in his hands. And then he scooted back his chair, leaning forward and gripping at his throat as if some blockage prevented his breathing. It must have been so, for he began to wheeze.

Finally, Beralt's attention acclimated to the situation. "My Prince, what is the matter?" When there was no audible reply, only Willen clutching at his throat and no air passing from his mouth or nose, Beralt stood up, tipping his chair backwards in haste. "My Prince, you must breathe. *Breathe*, Willen!"

"Help!" someone else called. I could not tell who, for every breath in my lungs wished to commit itself to Willen Vedan. After all, he needed them. "Help, help!"

There was much scurrying and someone crying out that it was a poisoning and that no one was permitted to leave until everyone was searched and questioned. Doors slammed shut, and the little Duchess screamed in terror at her situation, for it did not look good for a foreign dignitary to be present at the poisoning of the High King's second son.

All this chaos, but Willen still could not take a breath.

My legs moved without me asking them to. With grace I did not know I possessed, I took the cup of wine from Willen's hand and brought it to my own lips.

"No!" cried many a guest, including the Duchess and Beralt and Clorente.

Willen reached out to me, the veins in his face and neck bulging and the whites of his eyes going red.

I passed the glass to Beralt. "Hold this and let no one near it, lest it be tampered with further."

And then I sang a little tune, the remnants of the wine still on my tongue. Once my tune ended, I opened my palm and found, resting whole in my hand, a cluster of raspberries. These too I handed to Beralt.

"Lie down on your back," I told Willen, and he did so without question. "I will try." And I did try. I put my hand on his chest and sang my little tune. And then I pulled. The sensation of a strong force, like pulling at a door that was bolted shut, until finally it gave way. And I held in my hand a good deal of fresh raspberries, removed from the body of the Second Prince.

Willen gasped when it was over, air flooding into him once again. His breath was haggard but it was moving, and I could have cried with relief.

The things that happened next were rather confusing. Clorente attempted to remove us Trees from the situation with a tap of her cane, but Beralt lifted a dinner plate and, still balancing Willen's drink perfectly in his other hand, threw the plate across the room and knocked Clorente's cane from her grip.

She shrieked at this and hurried after her cane, but suddenly, it appeared in Willen's possession. Calmly, still coughing, Willen passed the item to Beralt.

"*No one* leaves," Beralt said, his accent thicker than I'd ever heard it before, his chest puffed and bearded chin lowered. "A Royal poisoning means all possible suspects must be examined. Including you, Clorente, and including me."

"If there is danger for my Trees—"

"You *remain*, and so do they, or it'll be a fight between us, woman. And if I were you, I'd not want to take up against the likes of me."

Since my work with Willen was done, Beralt then pulled me aside—as aside as he could, since we remained in a sealed room with dozens of others. "Lady Tree, what make you of the berries? How did you *know*?"

I shook my head, for I barely understood how I knew, except that the fruit called out to me to tell me of its presence in the wine and in Willen. As if the berries knew they were in a place they should not have been, in a place that would cause detriment to me. "The raspberries—"

"The High King! He comes!"

I couldn't tell who called this out, but it caused the people to scurry and scramble.

"Everyone, back to your normal business," Theor said, clapping his hands. "Unlock the doors."

Beralt opened his mouth to object, but Theor brought his hand down across the Dwarf's face. I had the feeling that Beralt allowed this to happen, for his eyes were glazed with anger, but he did not lift a hand to stop it.

"I am the High Prince," Theor said, smacking his own chest. "And rules be damned, as long as I say they be so. If the High King is coming, we will not make ourselves look as if we cannot even hold a dinner. We will make it look right and proper and orderly. Everyone, go back to your business. *Now.*"

And with that, Clorente crossed the room and took her cane back from the Second Prince. She tapped it twice, and the dinner was over for us Trees.

I had hoped we would have a reprieve of sorts, one during which I could gather my thoughts or let out a few pent up tears. I had gone from arguing with the Second Prince about a flower to weeping in a Wondered cellar to being flung about by Theor at breakfast to kissing Willen to saving his life. And I hadn't had the time to breathe, much less to process any of it. One thing about being locked in a cellar for most of my life was that I always had ample time to think, to dream, to imagine. At the Palace, everything was so quick, as if time slid out from under me whenever I stopped counting it.

I landed hard on what seemed to be frozen ground. Something rammed into my throat and propelled me backwards until my shoulders collided with an icy wall. I could not inhale, for whatever it was kept itself pressed firmly against my windpipe. I struggled but could not release it.

"You foolish Tree, what have you done?"

I could not mistake the voice of Clorente and I realized then that the object cutting off my breathing and threatening to crush my neck was her cane. I wanted to ask her to please, please release me, for I was sure she would kill me.

"A Tree does not intervene. She does not act. She simply observes. She stands. She is admired. She does not save lives, nor does she take them. She is a Tree."

Then, something sharp erupted from the wall behind me. It pierced the skin of my back, and my cry of pain was stifled by the cane. Clorente kept me pressed tightly to the icy wall, and I could not escape the second spike that plunged into my spine. Frantic, I clawed at my own neck, ripping my skin but unable to release myself. A third spike. A fourth and a fifth, until the agony overtook me and my body began to fall limp.

When at last Clorente released her cane, she vanished, and I crumpled to the ground. Once my face hit the floor, I realized it was no floor at all, but a sheet of thick ice, black as the darkness in my old, familiar cellar. I shivered there in the darkness, my blood flowing more freely than my tears ever had.

This is what happens to Trees who are not true. To all those girls who were eliminated. They are killed. Painfully. Abhorrently. It was the fate I so feared when I found out my brother had sold me to Clorente, when I learned I would be dragged to the Palace. Not the fear of being discovered for who I truly was, but that I would die a trembling, futile death of shame despite who I was.

My bones ran cold, and my limbs went numb. But I did not fade to the blackness of death as I thought I would. In fact, I noticed the darkness clearing and, like the sun through window slits, a bit of light entering the place.

I brought myself upright onto my hands and knees and found that it was my hands that made the light. And not only that, but they generated warmth as well. I knew this because pools of water formed beneath my palms as the ice sheet began to melt.

Why should I not? Why should I not make light with my hands? Why should I not bring warmth in times of frigid despair? Make beauty out of heartache? My hands grew warmer and warmer, until I breathed once more. *Why should I not hold his hand?*

With a crash, the ice cracked, and I fell through, landing in a cascade of water in a well-lit room. I lay there, in a heap of soaked clothes and blood, waiting for whatever was to come next.

"I should be very cross with you for soaking my floors, but I will forgive you only because there is no time for being cross."

I struggled to sit up, my arms and legs wobbling with strain.

"Oh heavens, Aia, what...who has done this to you?" Glenne hurried over and lifted me so that I could sit in her fine plush chair. She ran her hands over my bruised throat and examined my bleeding back. "Has someone run you through with...with a knife?"

"Thorns, I think...." My voice scraped out of my throat unwillingly. "A...a trial."

"I don't think trials are supposed to look like this, Aia. I have never heard anything so brutal. You are Tree, for heaven's sake, not a warrior knight!" She clapped her hands and revealed a white bottle. "I will stop the bleeding and mend your throat, hold on."

She ripped what was left of my dress and rubbed a creamy salve on my wounds, which stung with white heat and then cooled, numbing the injuries. Then, she Wondered up an oil and rubbed it on my neck until it felt like I could breathe without pain once more.

"Thank you, Glenne," I said, sighing with relief. "So much has happened."

Glenne put her finger up in the air. "Don't tell me! It's better to keep things to yourself among Palace people, Aia, trust me. Though I think I would never betray your trust...situations change, and when people feel desperate, betrayal is inevitable. Keep your secrets. As many as you can. And for right now, we must prepare you, for the High King has requested your presence. He is not to be kept waiting. Not ever."

She clapped her hands as if cheering herself on. "Move your rear, Glenne, get the girl a dress."

And oh, did she get me a dress. It was a long number, down to the floor, dark blue fading into deep purple, with a faint hem that sparkled when I moved, like I was stepping through stardust when I walked.

"It's beautiful," I whispered. "Glenne, how do you come up with these?"

"You are the inspiration, my dear, and tonight, you sparkle like the primordial heavens themselves. Now, for the hair, we should go back to Realm origins as well." She released my tresses and let it hang down past my shoulders. "Do not bite your cheek or tongue off, Aia. I must warn you, this next part will not be pleasant, but the pain is only temporary." She clapped her hands, and some black powder poofed from between her fingers, raining down on my hair and face and arms.

I coughed as it entered my nostrils and the sensation of a thousand scratching insects overtook me. I shrieked but refrained from tearing my own skin off. And, as Glenne promised, the pain passed in moments."

"So sorry, but it's worth it. Now you are ready." Glenne took my hands in hers. "I must ask before you go, Aia...is it true you saved the life of the Second Prince? I heard talk of it among the other servants."

I stared into Glenne's innocent, cheery face and stopped myself from spilling out everything that had happened. "Forgive me, Glenne. Someone wise told me I am to keep my secrets."

Glenne giggled and kissed my forehead. "Well done. You're learning, Lady Tree. Lucky to have me, aren't you? I'm the best, you know, except I'm actually the best, not just saying so. Remember that." And then she inhaled near me. "Sorry, but your Wonder is delicious. I've never smelled anything like it. I had to take one last little sniff. Now...off you go."

I was already walking before I realized where I was, led by Beralt who apparently was so upset that he growled nonsense words without even meaning to.

"*Grumble, grumble,* Theor, *grumble,* in what world? *Grumble, grumble,* I never!"

"Beralt," I interrupted him. "What is happening? Where are you taking me?"

"To the High King! He is not only here unannounced, which throws the whole of everything into an unmanageable chaos that must appear intricately managed, but he has questions to which no one has answers." He moved his short legs at a pace that normally I could beat, but my spine burned with every step I took as the thorn wounds of my pierced muscles had not completely healed.

"Might...might we slow down?"

"We cannot slow down, Miss Tree, are you mad? What part do you not understand? The High King, who hardly comes to the Palace of the Princes, has arrived and is requesting an audience with you. If I had even a bit of Wonder in me, we would already be there!" He waved his muscular arms about. "Poof! Remove that wall! Paff! No more doors to go through! But no, I have no Wonder and the stumpiest legs possible. We must hurry!"

And so we did until we arrived at a pair of dark wooden doors. Beralt licked his hand and smoothed it over his unruly hair to no avail, for it still stood on end.

I reached out my hand and smoothed it for him, only to watch the frizzy strands pop up again. "There. Now you look perfect," I said. And he did look perfect. Perfectly Beralt.

The Dwarf went red and cleared his throat. "Why thank you, Lady." He sighed. "In we go."

Beralt pushed the doors open, and we entered the room. A few servants hurried about, carrying things to and fro. Theor stood very still, his face unusually pale and his hip no longer cocked to one side. Willen sat on a cushioned stool, his elbows on his knees as a servant rubbed some concoction on his bare back.

And in the center of the room stood a man. With fair hair like Theor's and the same chin, broad shoulders and a wide chest. A scarlet cape around his shoulders and the finest of shirts and breeches beneath. The thinnest gold wire knitted itself across his forehead, disappearing into his blond locks. A crown, I realized, though it was less dramatic than any I could have imagined.

The High King turned to me and stared. I meant to remain by the door, inconspicuous at best, but when I looked about, I had already crossed the room.

Ep 13

Heat Beneath My Skin

The red glass of wine I'd handed to Beralt during dinner, right before I pulled raspberries from the blood of the Second Prince, sat alone on a table in the fine room. I felt much like the wine in that moment, standing alone and not meaning to have gone where I went or to have done what I did. But I went and I did, and now I had to answer for intervening with Monarchal matters, when I was simply a Tree.

The High King studied me for quite some time in deep silence. He had so much the look of his eldest son, Theor, that I was certain he would comment about my breasts or attempt to pinch me as he walked by. But when the King spoke, his tone did not resemble Theor's in the least. In fact, his low, gravelly voice reminded me so much of Willen that if I closed my eyes, I would not have been able to tell the two apart.

"So you are the Tree who saved my son?"

My eyes found Willen once again, and, sitting just behind his father, he lowered his head and then mouthed the word 'bow' to me.

Of course. Why have I not thought to do that? I lowered myself, quite aware that I was not performing the gesture properly.

"You may rise," said the High King. "Now, tell me. How is it you knew what ailed the Second Prince?"

I swallowed, biting my lip to force myself to speak, for all I wanted was to hide someplace very far away, in the dark, where no one could see me. But I had to answer for what I had done, an act that Clorente had shown me was both prohibited and rather punishable in nature.

"I...did not do it alone. It was the berries. They did not wish to hurt the Prince. I *also* did not wish for the Prince to be hurt and so we...helped each other."

"And what method did you employ? To remove the berries?"

"I sang to them, High King."

"You *sang* to the fruit? And you expect me to believe that they listened to you and complied?"

"I suppose...I sang, and they danced? I am not sure how to explain it."

The King's expression did not change, though the air in the room was different just from his presence. There was a gravity to him, an importance that did not just come with his title. *Is it Wonder? Is it greatness? Or am I simply afraid?*

"Where have you received your training, Honorable Tree?"

I shook my head. "I have had no training, High King."

"No? And where are you from?"

"Neighboring Lands."

"I see. How are the trees there, in the Neighboring Lands? Perhaps you learned simply from observing."

"I don't remember having seen any trees, but I did not see much of anything for most of my circles. I was kept inside."

"Hidden, I assume. With a look like yours and with the reputation of the Monarchs among those from the Neighboring Lands, I can see why your family thought it best for you to remain unseen. It is different in the Pride Places, where Trees are revered and set apart to be trained with the hopes they will be brought to the Palace. Your lack of training, I understand. But I ask you this, Honorable Tree. Did you *intend* to poison my son, Willen Vedan?"

My stomach clenched itself into the smallest of knots. I could not help but look to Willen once more, for I feared this was a sentiment shared by the Prince as well. I was not gentle with him in the forest earlier, when he'd told Beralt that being close with me was a mistake. *What if he thinks I despise him? Enough to harm him?* But I did not despise Willen Vedan. Not in the slightest.

Willen's eyes had never looked stormier. He held my gaze, trying to communicate something I could not decipher. I prayed it was not contempt.

"I would never harm the Second Prince. Never."

"And why should I believe you? You seemed to know exactly what was in the wine that made him ill. And you seemed to know exactly how to remove it. How can I be sure you did not decipher what would bring about his demise and place it in the wine, then remove it to appear virtuous? To shine a light upon yourself in these trials?"

"Well, Your Greatness, forgive my saying so, but I have not received any shining light as a result of my decision to act on behalf of your son. I have only received retribution. Of the most terrible sort. And questioning. Of the most terrifying nature. If I wanted to be favored, I would have stood closer to the High Prince so he could fondle me at his leisure. I would not have even noticed the Second Prince's condition for concentrating on the one for whom I might be a match."

Aia! Have you lost your mind in every way? For the High Prince was not but a few lengths away, and I had insulted his integrity in front of his brother and father.

Theor both blushed and scowled, but the High King's expression did not change.

"You claim, then, to be at a *disadvantage* due to your intervention?"

"I do."

"Well, it is evident by the way you have insulted the character of my eldest that you do not merely wish to seek favor among the Monarchs. I will alter my line of questioning as a result. Did anyone put you up to this?"

"I do not understand, King. Did anyone put me up to... removing the berries?"

"Lady Tree, I will tell you a story. My second son has been deathly intolerant to only one food his entire life. Raspberries. We discovered his aversion when he was a very young boy, hardly able to remember himself, during a secret visit to his mother, my not-yet Queen. When I brought Willen to the Palace— some circles later—I ensured that *my* dislike for raspberries was well known and that they would never enter the Palace kitchens. But I never explained *why*. Never linked them to Willen or his aversion, for his own safety. In fact, I am not even sure *he* knew he could not touch the fruits. His mother, my Second Queen, is obviously rather dead, as is true of every Queen who blesses the Realm with a son. She and I alone knew this truth. So...how did the raspberries end up in the wine of Willen Vedan?"

"Were they not in *all* the glasses?" Theor spoke up. "My wine was the same, was it not? And the Countess—"

"*Duchess*," I spoke out and afterward clamped my mouth shut.

The High King gave his eldest a quiet look so stern that Theor took to pacing the room. Then, the incredibly tall man returned his attention to me. "What say you to this, Lady Tree?"

"Perhaps it was a mistake. A cook who did not know about your dislike for raspberries and thought it would aid the evening to present something new."

"Perhaps. Is this what you think happened? You think it was an accident?"

I wished I could choose my words more carefully, but it was as if they were being chosen for me. "No, King. It is possible that an accident caused all this, but I do not think so. I think it was done with intention. But I do not know by whom and I cannot say why, for this knowledge is lost to me."

"A final question then," the King said. "What is your name?"

I hesitated. I could not say why I did so. When I finally spoke, I had to force myself. "Aia."

"Aia," he repeated. Strange that even though his voice matched Willen's perfectly, he said my name with a different air. When Willen said it, I felt even my bones shift within me. The King's utterance had little effect. "Aia means 'miracle'. Did you know that?"

Do not look at Willen. Do not. Do not do it. I tried to forget Willen tracing the letters of my name that night in his study. But I could forget nothing about the man no matter how hard I tried. I bowed. "I did know the meaning, Your...Kingliness."

A moment of pause. "Before you go, Honorable Aia, will you see to it that every bit of the toxic berries have been removed from my son. He still seems unwell to my eye, and I cannot have him ill. He is much needed."

"You believe me?"

"I have my ways of knowing when people are telling the truth and when they mean to deceive me. Truth, by nature, enjoys being found."

I was too afraid to make my feet move me over to the Second Prince. Not because I was afraid of him, but because I feared what I might betray if I came too close to him, if I had to touch my hands to his body. How would I be able to hide how I felt? How I longed for him to notice me, to desire me? They would discover it. They would all discover it, and I would be removed. Killed. Taken away from this life and from Willen.

But the King had asked, and so I made my way to the Prince, holding my breath and wishing, like Beralt had, that I knew *anything* about using Wonder to help me.

As soon as I stood close to him and he sat up straight, I could tell that Willen also held his breath. His eyes locked with mine, and I wanted to warn him, *No, Willen, look away. I cannot handle your gaze and touch you at the same time.* But he could not hear my thoughts and so he did not avert that intense gaze of his.

I parted my lips, but no sound emitted from them on my initial attempt. I swallowed and tried once more, my voice little more than a whisper. "How are you feeling, Second Prince?"

"Not too poorly," Willen answered, his voice rough, as though he'd swallowed shards of glass. "I owe you my thanks."

I put my hand on his bare chest and begged for it to stop shaking. It was then I realized that silver and gold twisted together, emanating from my skin. I hummed the tune that came to mind, and Willen groaned in response, wiggling in his seat.

"Does it hurt you?" the King asked.

Willen shook his head. "No, it is not terrible." But, his hands on his knees, he clenched the fabric of his trousers, and I knew that he'd lied to his father and that it was terrible indeed.

"I could stop," I offered.

"No, please. Continue, Lady Tree."

And so I hummed once more until every minute fragment of the berries was pulled from the Prince and rested in my palm. Crossing the room, I set them on the table next to the wine glass, but when I reached to place them down, I over-extended my arm and pulled one of the still raw muscles in my back. This made me jerk my arm away and cry out, ever so slightly.

The Second Prince stood to his feet, and the High King stepped forward. "Are you injured? Is it the berries, Lady Tree?" the King asked, his brow creased.

I shook my head, closing my eyes to keep the tears from showing. "No, I am only tired, High King. That is all."

What a pair of liars we are, Willen and I.

"Then you must rest," the King said with a nod, and I was gone before I could take another breath.

Oh, but my room was not one designed for proper resting. The dirt floor was unforgiving as I lay upon it, and the darkness only made fear creep up my arms and legs until I thought the shadows would eat me whole. I swore, at times when I almost managed to drift to sleep, that I could hear my brother's footsteps outside the cellar door. *But that cannot be. I am not at home. I am in the Palace.* And so I closed my eyes until the sounds went away.

I dreamed of lying atop a large mound of dirt, vast as a mountain. Clorente leaped over me and drove her cane deep into my chest, pinning me deep down into the dirt.

I awoke to the sound of myself screaming. Struggling to bring myself to my feet, I threw open the door and arrived in a place I had never been before. A hallway with no entries or exits, save one. The tall, stately door was carved of gray-white wood. I thought perhaps I should not open it. But there was nowhere else to go.

When all else proved futile, I knocked on the door and waited.

"*What*? I am fine. The incessant physicians with their pointless visits will not aid in a recovery that has already been established." And the door was flung open to reveal Willen, still wearing no shirt at all, face to face with me. His eyes widened as he filled the frame of the door. "*Aia*?" he whispered. "Have you gone truly mad? You cannot *be here*. You can never *be here*."

I nodded my head, for I had not meant to do what should not be done. "Second Prince, I did not mean to come here, I swear to you. I do not even know where I am or how to leave. There is only one...one door in this hallway. If you could show me how to...*where* to go...."

Willen softened, though he ran his hand through his hair, a sign of his frustration. "You simply appeared here?"

"Yes. And I cannot seem to leave."

"Then this is my doing."

"*Your* doing?"

"Well...my Wonder's doing. I...I must have been moving things around without realizing it. I apologize for blaming you. I can send you back to your room, if you wish."

I bit my lip, for I wanted to shout out, 'No! I want to stay!' But if this was Willen's room, he'd made it very clear that I could never visit him here.

But Willen did not send me away. He simply stood in the doorway with his eyes closed.

"What's wrong?" I asked.

"I...am working on it."

"Is your Wonder not strong enough? Perhaps you are tired from the poisoning?"

"No, my strength is not the problem. It's...my Wonder...it will not listen to me."

"Does it not do as you ask? Your Wonder?"

He sighed. "It does what it wants. Or really...what *I* want. But what I want in my soul, not always in my mind."

"Then"—I had to swallow to force myself to continue speaking—"it seems all you must do is *want* me to leave."

He met my eyes, and I pretended that I was not drowning in his.

"As I explained before, I am *trying*," he said.

"You could say out loud that you want me to go. Perhaps that will help."

His hand through his hair once more. He opened his mouth, but no words came out. And then, he seemed to be in great distress, his veins throbbing in his neck, while attempting to force the phrase, but still. No words.

"So you must...wish me to stay?"

"Yes," he responded before I could finish sounding out my question.

"But the rules—"

"I know the rules. I know them better than most. That doesn't mean I want to follow them. I simply *must* follow them."

"So...I must go."

"No. Yes. You must...You should...."

"Then I will stay. With you."

He seemed to be about to mumble something more about rules but he interrupted himself by leaning forward and kissing me.

I thought he would pull away to scold himself, but he only brought me closer, tugging at my lip with his teeth and pressing me to his chest. I could not say when in fact I crossed the threshold to his room. I hardly realized we were inside until I pulled the door closed behind me and my back met the wood. I flinched, inhaling at the rush of pain, and Willen paused.

"You are injured, Aia?"

"No, no distractions this time," I replied, tasting his neck as I so wished to while I watched him at dinner. It was better than I thought it would be. *He* was better.

"Let me," he said, allowing me to kiss his throat, his shoulders as he put his hands to my back. The Wonder flowed freely, and the burning, twinging pain relented, though the heat beneath my skin did not.

"Will you forgive me?" he asked.

"Forgiven."

He laughed breathless against my neck. "I did not specify what exactly I wish you to forgive."

"All the stupid things you've done and said. Forgiven."

More of a laugh at this, and then he plucked my lips with his, though his hands reached beneath the hem of my dress he'd hoisted up to my thigh. "If I am forgiven, then I must next show my gratitude."

"No need."

But traced his fingers along the skin on my inner thigh until I shivered in response.

"You are gracious to me, Little Tree."

"And you are hesitant, Second Prince." *Hesitant, Aia? What do I know of such things?* Who was I to speak to him this way?

"Only because...I am not sure what you want, Aia. How... much you want. When to stop."

At this, and with a confidence I still had not grown used to possessing, I held Willen's face in my hands so he saw my eyes once more. "I want all of it. And I will *tell you* when you must stop."

The fabric of my dress he ripped from my shoulder, biting the curve of me, his breath increasing in speed the closer he came to my breasts until the beautiful number Glenne had invented hung around my waist and then fell to the floor. I suppose the loss of the rest of his clothes could have been attributed to Wonder, but I did not care where they went, only that they were no longer between him and me.

He took me backwards into a bed the likes of which I never knew could exist. It was wide and soft and somehow smelled like Willen. But my attention was stolen by the man who brought his lips down to the space beneath my breasts, just where they met my ribs. I did not mean to shift beneath him but it could not be helped. And further down he went until the sound that left me I wished I had not uttered and that he had not heard. He laughed at this, though, a genuine, true laugh. And when he finished there, he brought himself down and entered, somehow, every part of me at once so that I could not be silent or still.

He did not stop, this Second Prince, nor did I want him to.

When I awoke I could remember no terrifying dream, no Wonder-drenched cane being plunged into me, or any such nightmare. I opened my eyes to the sounds of morning. Little chirps and buzzes from beyond the closed window and light streaming in from behind the edges of the heavy curtains.

I did not open my eyes, for I was frightened that I had imagined my night with the Prince or that somehow Clorente had invented the reality only to strip it away—the ultimate trial of torture and humiliation. Finally, I heard a chuckle and received a sweet kiss on my nose.

"Are you pretending to be asleep, Little Tree?"

I smiled at that and peeked one eye open. "No."

Willen proceeded to leave kisses on my forehead, my cheeks, my chin, and then finally my mouth, drawing from me sweetly until I wiggled closer, another moan leaving me.

Willen pulled away, leaning his forehead against mine. "You cannot do that."

"Do what?"

"Any of that."

"Any of what?"

"Just...anything. Don't do anything at all. I am very late for a vast array of important Princely business, and you are keeping me here."

"So I must simply lie still?"

"No," he sighed. "That will not be enough, for you are naked and far too beautiful. You will have to do even less than that."

I held very still, pretending to be made of stone—or perhaps a tree—but Willen tickled my ribs until I burst into laughter. "Your actions go against your own advice, Your Foolishness!" I said in jest.

But Willen sobered at this. And I had not realized how clear his eyes appeared—a lofty blue-gray—until they clouded over once more. He took my hand and kissed each of my fingers. "Truly, I must go. And you must as well. I am to investigate who tried to kill me, though I know it was Theor. Still an official investigation must commence and conclude, with no one as the culprit and the mystery ongoing. And you, Little Tree, have to stay alive another turn."

"So I can produce a Seed for your soon-to-be murderer?"

"Now you're getting it." He got up and pulled his trousers on. "I must hurry."

"How will I find my way out of the corridor?" I asked, pulling his luxurious sheets around me while I searched for my now mangled dress.

"My Wonder is far more compliant this morning. And I assure you"—he cleared his throat and ran that hand through his hair, as if in his mind he argued with himself—"nothing like this will happen again. I...fear I owe you a great apology, Lady Tree. One I cannot begin to...I don't know how I thought...."

I wished I hadn't hung my head, but I did. "Another mistake, then?"

"Aia. You simply must understand the dangers of what we are doing. We cannot—"

And for the first time, I did not need the Wonder of another to appear someplace other than where I'd been.

Love and Pain Are One

"Where have you been?" Gretaline asked me, latching on to my arm like a winged Wyvern securing her pathetic prey. "It's been half a turn already! Did you get lost?"

I pried her fingers off one by one. For the first time in my life, I was in no mood to simply be dragged about. "I would not trust the time in this Palace if I were you, Gretaline. Three turns could be one moment, for all we know. One of these turns, perhaps, we'll have all our meals at once and just get it over with. Besides, it's not as though we're likely to taste food ever again."

"We are not starving, though. Isn't that strange? One of us should have collapsed by now, but I do not feel unwell. I am not satisfied, but I am not in pain."

I realized that I could not remember the last time Aman had fed me. Actually provided me with a meal. Perhaps it had been circles since I had eaten more than scraps I'd found left over after his guests departed.

"I am quite accustomed to it," I confessed. "I suppose I should not complain. Now...what did I miss? Did Clorente notice me missing?"

Gretaline shook her beautiful head. "She gathered us for breakfast but did not seem to notice you were gone. So strange. It was like she'd forgotten to look for you. I assumed you'd been killed. And Shrane. I mean, I knew she'd be eliminated eventually, but you? It was a surprise to me. I thought for sure it would be you against me at the very end. Naturally, I will be the last Tree. And from the way they speak, it may very well be that I'm the last Tree in all the realm. A prestigious place, to be certain."

"Shrane? Was she not at breakfast either?" I worried for my friend with the round eyes. "The others?"

"Two more were present. The one with the vines in her nose and another I can hardly remember. They are wandering around somewhere. No matter though, for Clorente told us to wait here until she came again with further instructions. It has been some time, and I am quite bored."

I looked sideways at Gretaline. She was the reason the girl had endured the agony of vines growing out of her cranium. She dismissed it like the event was as ordinary as the color of her eyes or the twisting of her hair.

"Tell me, how did you know what to do to save the Second Prince? Also, too bad for you it wasn't the High Prince needing saving, or I might as well have resigned my efforts to gain him for myself."

I ignored her question. I had not the appetite for explaining yet again what I'd already told the High King.

"And I heard you met my Theor's father, the High King. Please, do not withhold, Sister Tree! What was he like?"

But I remembered Glenne's words. That I should learn to keep secrets. And so I did. "He was as kingly as one would think, I suppose. And he wore a crown."

Gretaline squealed. "How majestic! A crown! I suppose Theor will wear his own one turn." She grew solemn suddenly. "Though I will most likely not be present to see him do so."

"No? I thought you were certain you're his True Tree?"

"Well, don't be stupid, Aia. If I become his Tree, I will not be traipsing around the Palace in a dress like a mere mortal. I would be a Tree." She held her arms up and out to resemble branches. "With bark and leaves. Surely you've had the opportunity to see them up close by now. They do not have eyes, so how would I be able to see the crown upon Theor's head?"

"Wait. That is what happens when a Tree matches a Prince? She becomes an actual real tree?"

"Why...yes. How could you not know this?"

I shook my head in disbelief. "*Forever*?"

"Well, of course it's forever. And what an honor it will be. Some even visit True Trees and put wreaths around their branches. Bring the sick to be healed beneath their boughs. Better than all the other Trees who have failed. They are just ordinary old trees. No one will visit them except perhaps future candidates looking for cautionary tales."

"But...those Trees died. I saw them die. Most of them, at least."

Gretaline shook her head. "You saw them die, but you did not see what happened to them once they were dead. You don't look around much, I must admit. I don't know how you've made it this far without ever paying attention. I swear."

"But...I don't *want* to be an actual tree."

Gretaline scoffed. "Of course you do. What else would you rather be doing? Slinking around the Neighboring Lands married to some cobbler who doesn't bathe? At least being a tree is noble. What more could you want?"

I hardly had to close my eyes to remember the Second Prince stretching his hand over the smooth skin of my stomach to answer that. More. I wanted more than a sedentary life apart from him.

But alas, he did not desire what I craved. No, he was too noble for such things. Too concerned with his sense of right and wrong, of appropriate and inappropriate, of should and should not. The only thing worse than being apart from Willen Vedan was being with him and knowing he regretted every moment.

"What is wrong with you? It looks as if you are wilting." Gretaline seemed more annoyed by this than anything.

"Me?" I shook my head. "I was only thinking."

"Thinking? About becoming a True Tree? Goodness, if it depresses you so greatly, put it out of your mind. It's my destiny, after all. You're worried over nothing."

Shrane scrambled into the room, her short hair a mess and a strange look on her small face. She hurried over to us and took my hand. "May I borrow you?" she asked in a croaked whisper.

"Well, I certainly don't need her," Gretaline said with a roll of her eyes. "I have more important things to focus on."

Shrane pulled me over to a corner and squeezed my hand. "Aia, *something happened*."

"Are you alright? You seem...out of sorts."

In fact, Shrane was filthy, her dress torn at the sleeves and dirt smudged on her cheeks, chin, and nose. There were even bruises on her neck and along her collarbone. "Shrane, what is it? Tell me."

She shook her head. "I can't tell you here. It's not...." She looked around as if someone might overhear us. "It's not something I can mention. Not out loud. I swore I wouldn't."

"But if you are in *danger*—"

"No, no, nothing like that. Well"—and then she shook her head even harder. "Aia, I think I am in love. And love can be dangerous, can't it?"

I startled as if she'd slapped me. "Love? What—how? Who?"

"I can't say. It has to be a secret. A very well-kept secret."

"Then Shrane, you should not have told me anything at all. If it puts you at risk, say nothing more. Please."

"But I *must* tell you, I must. You are my closest friend. And if I keep it all quiet, I will burst!"

"Shrane—"

"He is strong. Commanding. And handsome. Quick-witted, though...we did not do much speaking."

A headache was born between my ears. "You...you—"

"Yes. He is very knowledgeable about those things. I am very fortunate, of course. But we cannot tell. We cannot even speak a word."

I nodded, though guilt seemed to explain the source of my headache, for though Shrane spilled her innocent heart to me, I could not take the same risk. I would not tell of my night with the Second Prince, for I meant what I said to the High King. I would never harm Willen. Never. And though I would be relieved to confide in someone—my woes, my fears, my desires—I would not give myself that release.

"Shrane, you must not speak like this to anyone else. I will not tell, but you cannot be sure that others will have your interest in mind. In fact, they may use your love against you."

"But love...it is not a weakness, Aia. It can only enrapture; it cannot betray. This I believe with all my being."

Since she spoke of all her being, I studied the quite obvious bruises on her body. "Shrane...forgive me, but...how did those markings on your body come about? Did you stumble?"

"No, no. He is most vigorous," she explained. "A passionate love-maker."

I bit my lip but spoke nonetheless. "That might be a bit *too* passionate, don't you think? It looks painful."

"Love and pain are one. And fear is simply the pathway to love."

"Did...he tell you that? That it is normal to be afraid when you are with him?"

"Isn't he poetic?"

"I do not think that is poetry, Shrane. I think it's deceit. At the very least, it's nonsense."

She scowled at that. "How dare you? Don't speak of my love like that. He is not deceitful, nor is he nonsensical. I've never felt this way about anyone. And I am a woman now," she said, lifting her chin. "What would you know? What love have you had?" And her round eyes flashed. "You know what you are? Jealous. And I should never have trusted you."

And with that, my only friend at the Palace crossed the room and proceeded to glare at me.

I could not help but wonder who her 'lover' might be. My thoughts went to Theor, but I could not imagine that the High Prince would feel the need to use clever phrases to convince a girl to stay in his arms. He would simply take her if he had the mind to.

Clorente entered the room and, instead of tapping her cane on the ground, spun it in her hands and struck the shimmering marble floor. I felt, all at once, my skin ripping from my bones and my hair tearing from my scalp until I struck the ground just as her cane had. The force took the air from my lungs, but once I regained the ability to inhale and exhale normally, I sat up. This time, I was not alone, but side by side with the rest of my fellow Trees. Shrane coughed and hacked, and Gretaline sat silent with her head in her hands. The Giggler, who still bore one of Gretaline's seeds somewhere in her body, wheezed on all fours, and the other girl—one who had short blonde bangs, long hair, smooth pale skin, and almond eyes— lost the contents of her stomach.

Clorente appeared in a commoner's dress, the plain brown linen shrouding her new appearance. She seemed to be a younger woman with plump arms and large breasts, her gray-brown hair in a messy braid down her back. She'd had too much sun, and her knuckles were caked in dried blood and calluses. I had the distinct sense that the appearance was not fabricated by Wonder, but that Clorente had somehow...borrowed the body.

She clutched her cane in her well-worn fingers. "Welcome to the Pride Places," Clorente said in a voice that was not hers. "This is the origin of our Realm. The home of our ancestors. Where the Ancient Monarchs first chose to create our government. We became a people here."

Gretaline's chest swelled with admiration as she looked out over her home region. It was, in fact, lovely. The streets were paved with white stones and the houses carved out of the same. The grass was green and luscious, the trees placed outside each home dancing in the gentle breeze. The people walking about nodded when they noticed us. Some carried babies and small children; others rode horses and called out greetings. But most were pleasant and happy to be alive.

"It seems beautiful, yes. But you only think it is good because you don't know better, Trees. When your eyes are opened, you see the truth. You see why you are who you are and what you must do." She sighed. "These Places were once the gems of our Realm. The streets burst with green life, and children never hungered, for they could walk the streets and open their palms so that fruit fell from the branches into their blessed hands. But our joy decreases as the blessing of the Arboreal Ancients wanes. We fall into decay when the trees are few."

With that, Clorente struck the ground again, and we were wrenched to a new place. When finally we stood, we were in the presence of true greatness. The vegetation was so immense that it pulled the breath right from our lips. The trees were taller than mountains and the mountains taller than the clouds. Water tumbled down cliff sides, and birds of every color cried out for joy. The few people who lived in this place stayed in small houses made of dirt and mud and stones, but they walked with their arms around each other and their foreheads leaning close as if it were their great joy to tell each other secrets.

"Here are the Stolen Worlds. Conquered lands sought out as tribute after the many wars the Ancient Kings fought on behalf of the Realm. They are of our Realm, but not from it. And so their connection to the Ancient Trees is stronger. More viable. Feel the difference on your skin and in your lungs. Feel the clarity in your mind and the connection to all things around you. The blessing of the Trees. And what our High King greatly longs for."

Once more, she took us away. And when we arrived, I knew the scent of the air by heart. A sour smell and a great deal of dust, nearly enough to choke us as we inhaled. The heat burned the skin of my arms and face, and the sounds were that of metal scraping on metal and shovels against dirt. People either spoke not at all or quarreled loudly.

"What heaven-forsaken place is this?" Gretaline asked, her pretty brown eyes wide. "Where *are* we?"

"Neighboring Lands," Shrane and I answered at once.

"Yes. These are the Neighboring Lands. The places without purpose that the Ancient Kings took into the Realm with grace to give the people hope for a future. Once, they resembled the present-turn Pride Places. Adequate and thriving but not yet overflowing with life. The Monarchs hoped they could lend their aid and, along with the Ancient Trees, bring the Neighboring Lands to glory."

"But they failed," Shrane said, her voice flat. She pointed across the street from where we stood. "I lived just there."

It was a small, squashed structure—hardly a building at all—with open gaping squares for windows and a slumped, thin woman sitting on a stool outside.

"Is that your mother?" the Giggler girl asked. "Perhaps you could say hello."

Shrane's eyes glazed over more and more the longer she looked. "No," she said, her voice flat. "It would be worse if I did. She does not wish to see me."

Clorente's lips tightened. "And so it is among those who live where there is no life. And so it will be in the Pride Places. And then, one turn, in the Stolen Worlds. And on and on until nothing is left but desolation and the dust of what we could have accomplished."

"How do we stop it?" the Tree whose name I did not know asked Clorente.

"Haven't you been paying any attention?" Gretaline spoke up. "We must—one of us—match the High Prince. Bear him a Seed. Earn the blessing of the Ancient Trees once more. Or we will all be ruined."

"Yes," Clorente said, her sharp eyes surveying the scene around her. "And we are nearly out of time. If there is no match for Theor, we would have to wait another generation. For him to become King and have a son, for a new crop of Trees to be born, to grow up, and to be discovered. And then, perhaps, *maybe*, for them to match in the future."

"There will be nothing left by then," I said. Then I turned to Clorente. "Do the other kingdoms and realms have True Trees matched to their Monarchs?"

She nodded. "Some do."

"So this...is worse than what we see here. It means we are weak. It means...we are vulnerable."

Clorente seemed surprised by my insight. "You think deeply, Tree. Yes, we are vulnerable in many ways without a Seed."

"What of your home, Aia?" Giggles asked. "Can you see it from here?"

I could hardly remember. I did not even know the names of the streets and I could not see the old Bakery from where we stood.

"We will not be visiting Aia's home," Clorente said sternly. "But you may not return to the Palace until you bring a flower to life in the Neighboring Lands. Once you do so, a clean dress and fresh water will await you. For some of you...your end draws near. And I do not envy you the task of being a tree in this barren land." With that, Clorente tapped her cane and left us.

"Make...a flower?" Shrane squeezed the sides of her face. "How can someone make a flower? Oh, I am going to die here, aren't I? How fitting. How fitting! My mother always said I would die just like everyone else."

Gretaline took a deep breath. "I am not going to die. Not here. Not yet. When I become a True Tree, I will be gracefully planted in the Royal Garden, among the True Trees gone before me. With wreaths around my trunk and gems dangling from my branches. I am not going to take root in this place. What I am going to do...is make a flower."

But that was not what I planned to do. I left the other Trees and set out to find the Bakery, and then to find the house with the old cellar.

Swear Not to Torture

I could not be sure if it was indeed my childhood home. The dilapidated, squat building leaned against the house beside it as if it could not support its own weight. Much smaller than I ever imagined it to be, but everything seems larger when one is a child. I remembered the last time I walked through the front door. How impossible to know when something as ordinary as entering through a threshold might change a life forever. But once I smelled the thick and creamy scent of fragrant Caram sauce, I knew Aman was cooking. I knew it was my old home.

I did not knock on the door. Instead, I cracked it open and slipped inside. I expected the floors to be filthy since I was no longer living with Aman to do the cleaning. But things were rather tidy, and the objects were dusted and kept in their places. *Has my brother taken up an unexpected interest in housework?* No, I could not imagine his muscular frame on hands and knees scrubbing under the wooden table. It was quite literally beneath him.

I tiptoed through, with no sign of Aman's presence besides the bubbling sound of the potatoes in that heavenly sauce.

But when I approached the small kitchen area, I found not my brother, but a young girl. Perhaps six or seven circles in age. Beautiful olive skin and long, straight dark hair. She wore a tattered tan dress I knew without a doubt used to be mine.

When the girl saw me, her almond eyes went wide, and the ladle she had been using to stir the potatoes clattered to the floor at her bare feet.

The girl fled, arms pumping and hair flying, to the door that led to the cellar, closing it swiftly behind her.

I did not know what possessed me to follow her, but forward I went, my feet taking the same steps it had over and over again. The door to the cellar, with its strong iron bolt, was so familiar in my hand it made my heart ache. I pulled the handle open and walked into the darkness that had been my life for eighteen long circles.

I knew where the girl would be. In the little crawl space I'd made by angling the shelves in the very back of the cellar. From there, she would be able to see out of the slitted window, mostly catching glimpses of the sky and sometimes a view of the feet of shuffling passersby. But they would never see her. And if they did, they would not care. For, I was beginning to understand, no one in the Neighboring Lands could hold much of anything in their broken hearts. Compassion slipped right through their worn fingers.

I knelt on the ground, able to see the girl's toes poking out of the shelving hovel. "Hello there," I said as softly as I could. I was surprised to hear how my voice floated out of me, like the soft petals of the flower I'd clutched in my hand the first night Willen and I embraced. "I see you found my favorite hiding place."

The girl scrunched her toes, no doubt wishing she could disappear altogether.

"I won't tell him that you were near the food. I promise."

She sniffled at this. "He will punish me...if he finds out."

"Well, he will never find out. Don't worry." I sat back against one of the shelves. "But it always smells so divine, doesn't it?"

"Sometimes...I feel I'll die if I don't eat some. Just a bite."

"Yes. He chooses fragrant food on purpose, I think."

"He...does?"

"I believe so."

"But *why*?"

"To make you want it. To see if you can resist. To *teach* you to resist."

"But why can I not have some? Why must I resist?" And the girl began to cry. "I want to go home. I always ate food at home. Every turn! And there was milk sometimes too."

"Who is the man to you? The one who punishes?"

"He is my brother. My parents told me so. That he would take care of me. That I should be very thankful. And make myself useful to him."

"And where are your parents? Why do you not live with them, where you can still drink milk and eat food?"

She choked back a sob. "They grew ill. They...they died. But I have my brother now. I am very fortunate. And I will be very helpful. I will be...I will be useful."

"You know...he's my brother as well."

"Really?"

"Really."

"Does that make us...sisters?"

"I think it does. Would you like a sister?"

The girl scrambled out from her hiding place, her cheeks still wet from her weeping. She wiped her face, smearing dirt from the floor across her nose. "I have always wanted a sister." She gasped when she truly got a look at me. "Oh, you look...scary!"

I grinned. "I suppose I do. I never knew how I looked until very recently. Have you seen yourself since you lived here?"

"No, no," she said, shaking her head. "If I even look into the water of the basins, I am punished very much." She pointed to the door. "He ties me out there in the kitchen to punish me if I am not obedient and useful. It is very dreadful, but if I am good, I won't be punished as often. He promised."

I nodded. "I was punished there as well."

"Oh. Is that why you look so strange?"

I shook my head. "No." But then I thought about it. "Perhaps. Now I am not sure whether I was punished because I look strange or to make me look even stranger."

The girl came even closer to me so that our knees bumped each other. "I'm Dolsie."

"And my name is Aia." She was near enough for me to touch her hair. Led by some instinct in me, some understanding of what it felt like to be uncared for, I rested my hands gently on the girl's cheeks. Human touch was not something that could be replaced with even the grandest of imaginations. "You know...you are very beautiful and kind, Dolsie."

"I am?"

"Yes. No one will tell you that for some time. But you can always remember that I said it."

She gave a watery smile. "Will you be staying here with me, Aia? Since we are sisters?"

"No, I cannot, sweet little one. I have to go. But I will come back for you."

"You will? Truly?"

"Yes. Once I've made a way to get you out safely. And I will take you somewhere good. Where no one will punish you, useful or not."

"Can there be such a place, Aia?"

"I will make sure there is. For you."

And then I heard something that made my blood freeze over. Same rhythm as always. Footsteps descending on the stairs to the cellar. Two quick steps, preceded by one slow. *One...two three. One...two three.*

"It's Sair. He's coming," Dolsie whispered.

A new name for a new girl. My brother went by many names. But I alone knew his true one. I leaned close to the girl and whispered in her ear. "If ever he frightens you too greatly, call him by the name Owul. He will no longer be able to harm you after that. But you must be very careful not to let him know you've heard this name. Do you understand?"

The girl nodded, her eyes so wide she might have swallowed me in her gaze.

I kissed her forehead and placed her little palm in mine. As quietly as I could, I hummed a tune. And when she lifted her hand, a white flower—one identical to the flower Willen found in his room that one night—was left. I tucked it in the narrow space between the shelf and the dirt floor right before Clorente's Wonder took me out of the Neighboring Lands.

"Well done." Clorente's voice greeted me. She had returned to her ordinary form, her high cheekbones glowing in the evening light. "You are one of four Trees who remain—"

"Who is she?"

Clorente eyed me with a warning in her dark eyes. "I beg your pardon?"

Giggles, Gretaline, and Shrane gawked at my boldness, each holding a flower of a different shape and color in their delicate hands. The Nameless Tree, perhaps, could not manifest a flower in time.

"Who is the girl in my cellar? Who is she?" My fists clenched at my sides, and I had trouble breathing at an easy pace, my chest heaving beyond my control.

"I told you not to visit—"

"Well, I *visited*. And I saw her. Who is she? What is she doing there?"

"Tree—"

"He *punishes* her!" I was beyond shouting. *Where has the quiet Aia gone?* She was replaced by a shaking monster. "He beats her and starves her, and you allow this! He locks her away, turn after turn, and you commend this! You plan to keep her there, don't you? For circles. Until she no longer knows any better. Until she no longer yearns for things that humans should want. You replaced me with her. To torture the humanity out of her!"

"You must calm yourself," Clorente warned. "You are making a scene, Tree."

"I have a name! And I have a life! I have desires and hopes, and you cannot, no matter how long you lock a person away, take those parts from them!" I pointed a finger to the woman. "Confess! You arranged for my brother to begin again with another Tree. An innocent little child."

"Was your life truly so *terrible*? That you would confront me like this? That you would risk the future for your vindication?"

I knew tears streamed from my eyes, but there was no holding back my voice. When I stomped my foot on the ground, the earth shook and roots sprang from beneath where I stood, racing toward Clorente.

"My life was dreadful. And you will not force another child to repeat it. *I* won't allow it."

To my awe, Clorente put her hands up, clutching her cane beneath her arms. "I will remove her."

I stopped. "You...will?"

She nodded. "Yes. I will restore her with a loving family. But only if you swear not to speak of this to another soul."

When I looked around, I saw that the other Trees had somehow vanished and that only Clorente and I spoke outside in the Palace courtyards.

"Why should I believe you?"

"Because if you tell of what I've done, I will be removed. And if I am removed, there will be no True Tree found. You must understand my predicament, Aia. If I do not succeed with one of you, we have little hope. I must keep trying. I must try harder than anyone ever has before. The rules, I must break. My methods, they must be unconventional. It would have taken generations for me to breed a Tree as powerful and beautiful as you, but I did not have generations to produce you, Aia. I needed you now. And Shrane...I had to try another method with her. And with the others. And Gretaline—she's a different story altogether. Some I found, but some I planted. Some I pruned. Some I forged, do you see? Without the Seed, the Realm will go beyond suffering. Sacrifices must be made."

The roots that moved beneath my feet fell back to the earth.
"I understand your desperation."

"Do you?"

"If anyone understands desperation, it is me, Clorente. I will
hold your secret, but you must swear not to torture another
girl for the sake of your progress. Each deserves a decent life. Use
the methods employed for Gretaline. For those who lived well.
Who were treated with some measure of kindness. If sacrifices
must be made, make them elsewhere. If this is not done, I will
tell. I will tell *everyone*. What have I to lose? Nothing. I am little
more than the walking dead anyway. Do *you* understand?"

Clorente nodded. "We have a deal." And she tapped her
cane, bringing the other girls back.

"What just—"

"Rest, my Trees," Clorente said, her composure instantly
regained. "Tonight, a ball awaits. And the Trees must make an
appearance. You will create flowers for the High Prince and all
his guests. Study your book and practice as you wish until you
are designed for the night's events."

The book, *Tree Of Light*, appeared in my hand as I walked
toward the entrance to the Palace of the Princes. But when I
opened the door to my room, it was not a cellar as it had been
every other time I stepped past the threshold. It was an ordinary
living space, with clean white walls, average lighting from a
square window, and a comfortable bed with linen blankets.

I sat on this bed and flipped through the book, unable to
make sense of the words, until at last I blinked and sat in the
center of Glenne's fabric studio.

"My muse has arrived!" she said, bouncing on the balls of her
feet, already clutching lengths and lengths of fabric in her hands.

"And it seems she does not come to me bleeding this time around!" She spun me with her Wonder until I stood before her, the seat I had previously been perched on vanishing. Glenne studied me, her head tilted. "Oh my, oh my. It seems you are emboldened this evening. Perfect, for these balls are so stuffy. And women hardly show what they feel. It's all tucked into wigs and corsets. But for you...." Glenne narrowed her eyes and held up her thumbs, measuring me at a distance with her tongue between her teeth. The fabrics she had been holding floated without her. "For you...transparency." She sighed like she was in love. "Heavens, you are so beautiful." Then she clapped her hands, startling herself. "Now, to work we go."

"I am to grow flowers for those in attendance at tonight's ball," I explained.

"And you are not happy about this?"

I sighed. "I am...simply not happy."

"Well...what is the matter? If someone was once happy and then no longer is so, it means their happiness has not disappeared, it has merely gone somewhere else. Where has your happiness gone, Aia? Find its location and perhaps you can get it back in time for you to make some flowers tonight."

My mind went to Dolsie, the beautiful little Tree in my brother's cellar and the life she might have lived if my feet had not taken me back home. I thought of Clorente, who orchestrated these lives for us in the hope of saving a dying Realm. I thought of Theor, who preferred to kill his brother than to extend his kindness to his own blood.

But no. None of them had truly taken my happiness. I had given it away. To one person. And he did not seem to have made any plans to return it.

I could not pay attention to the choices Glenne made for me. I knew vaguely that she dipped me, head to toe, in some sticky solution that burned my skin. I knew she threw some odd-smelling liquid in my hair that made it go stiff for a moment or two. And that she rubbed something cold in my eyes. Once I was ready, she marveled at her work and wished me all the best.

And I arrived at the ball. The very instant I made my appearance, those in the room stopped what they were doing. Glasses fell from bejeweled hands, and fruit flopped from gasping mouths. Even the musician screeched to a stop, his fingers frozen at his strings.

I parted the crowd as I walked, looking for one person.

Shrane found me first, her round eyes bulging as she took my arm. "Aia, my heavens, what was your designer thinking?" She wore a white number, tied up with gold at the sleeves. It sloped downward in the back, showing off her fine spine and freckled skin. A wig made of grapes and branches adorned her head, and gold earrings shaped like bird eggs dangled from her lobes.

"Do you like mine?" she asked, twirling for me and then taking my arm again. "I think I am starting to grow accustomed to these sorts of things. The music, the dancing, the sights and sounds. It was all so overwhelming the first time." She sighed, almost reaching for a fruit on a tray but then stopping herself before she could pluck it. "Or perhaps I am simply in love. I wonder if he has arrived yet."

So she had forgiven me for insulting whoever had tossed her around and called it passion. Maybe if I found him, I could tremble some roots beneath his feet as I had done with Clorente.

179

Once we reached the main ballroom floor, all eyes turned to me. Including those of Willen Vedan, who stopped his conversation and stared my way.

"It looks as if she wears nothing at all!" one woman cried out. "Heavens!"

"Yet, I cannot see any parts of her. A Wonder indeed," another answered. "Who is her designer? I have never seen anything like it."

I glanced down at my dress to find that they were right. It was as if I wore only gossamer threads over my legs and stomach.

"Her eyes are like the night sky," someone else muttered. "Could not you gaze into them for an eternity?"

I wanted more than anything to ask Willen for a moment of his time. A chance to speak to him in private. But I realized suddenly that I had no place to do such a bold thing. He was Willen when he was inside me, yes, but among the dignitaries and nobles of the Palace, he was the Second Prince and not at all mine.

It was then, with the heralding of brass trumpets and many gasps from the guests at the ball, that the High King of the Realm was announced. Theor descended the staircase before him, eliciting nods and bows from many onlookers. And then he waited at the bottom of the stairs until the great man stepped forward. He wore scarlet and gold, and on his arm was a lovely woman with dark skin and long, thin braids that swayed down past her waist, clipped with beads of gold and white pearls. Her lips had been painted scarlet, and her belly burgeoned beneath her rippling gold gown.

The High King and Fourth Queen of the Realm. And not at all smiling. Their happiness, it seemed, placed elsewhere.

Ep 16

All Will Be Lost

Oh, how the crowd gasped and applauded at the sight of the Queen. Women touched their own bellies as if they felt the swell of an unborn child within them. Men elbowed each other and lifted glasses of amber liquid in the air. A few of Theor's friends, the slippery Petrus included, slapped his shoulders like he was the one who was about to be a father.

I noticed Beralt bow to the Second Prince. "Congratulations," the bearded Dwarf grumbled. "Another jewel in the Realm's crown."

Willen did not respond with any show of elation. In fact, he did not appear pleased in the slightest. I wondered if he was, like Theor, jealous of the younger child to be born of his father. Would he plot his demise just as his brother aimed for his death?

"They say it will be a girl," Theor muttered as he pushed through the crowd and past me without so much as turning his eye in my direction. "Nothing to worry about. What could a girl do? Useful for nothing."

181

With hardly a moment in between the High Prince's passing me and his arriving at the drink station, Gretaline was upon him, donned in a crinkled green fabric and looking much like a fresh spring leaf. Vines weaved through her curly hair, and on her earlobes were soft green buds, dew drops on each of her lashes. She was beautiful, but Theor minded his drinks more than her.

"Our King certainly loves the attention," he complained to Petrus, who scoffed in solidarity.

"That's always been his way, though hasn't it? At your coronation, he'll rise from the dead to steal the show. He might even steal the crown right off your head, claiming it would look better on his."

"Tonight is meant to be about *me*. About *my* Trees. Their displays of beauty on *my* behalf. Not him and his fat failure of a wife. A Fourth Queen and she still bears him a daughter after so many attempts. The Third Queen squatted out a girl as well. Who knows what she does with her time? And we all know the Second hardly counts. We pretend her son is legitimate, but he is nothing like me. I was born right. I was born true. I should be the only son and the only heir." And he was angry enough to slam his glass on the table, spilling its contents all over his hand. Disgusted, he wiped his mess on Gretaline's dress and shoved away from the table without so much as glancing at her.

The Brown Beauty's cheeks tinted pink, and she turned, looking for some escape. But I approached her and took her hand in mine.

"Don't fret," I told her. "His unkindness will be returned to him some turn."

"I...am not about to fret. At least he was near me for a moment. Perhaps he will come around and apologize later on, and we may have a discussion. One of wit and virtue."

"Maybe so." I found a napkin and dabbed at the stain on her dress. "You look beautiful," I offered.

"I know how I look," she spat out. "I was made to stare at myself in front of the mirror for turns as a child. I have every fraction of myself memorized."

"I was never permitted to see myself."

"That's stupid, isn't it? How would you know what chance you have against the rest of us?"

"I did not know anything about anything."

"Then...how have you made it this far?"

I shook my head and shrugged. "A miracle."

Gretaline nodded toward the crowd. "Look, it's the Second Prince. The one you saved. What a strange fellow, don't you think? Always brooding and shrouded in gloom. He seems so...stern and unflinching. So different from Theor. It's a wonder they get along."

I did not respond to this, for Willen walked over as the music struck back up. "Lady Trees," he said. "I hope this turn goes well for you?"

"Oh," Gretaline said. "Thank you, yes. It goes well."

"I'm glad to hear that," he replied. Then, he looked at me. "And you, how does your turn go?"

"It is well enough."

His eyes flashed and then clouded, like lightning showing itself in the midst of a storm. "Perhaps it would be better if men were not complete idiots and overall raging cowards."

"Good heavens, they cannot all be that bad," Gretaline said, blinking at his choice of words.

"No, they are often worse," I countered. "And so confusing that even they do not know what it is they want."

Willen nodded. "Because, Lady Tree, they want things they cannot have."

"Seems to me they want things they've already had, Second Prince."

Willen's gaze did not waver. "I hope you receive all the apologies you deserve."

"I don't. Apologies mean nothing. I have things I want, and apologies are not to be found among them."

Willen blushed at this, but we were saved from the most unpleasant of half-conversations.

The High King made his way over to us. "Honorable Trees," he said in that voice that sounded so much like Willen's. "I know it is unorthodox but I require your assistance this turn. Would you lend me your attention and, if possible, your aid?"

Gretaline's mouth clamped shut. I bowed, though clumsily, and waited.

"You may rise," the King said.

"We would be more than happy to do whatever we can for the King," I replied. *When did I become so composed? So confident?*

Collected by servants of the King, the four of us and Clorente were led to a private room and met with the both Princes and the High Monarchs. The lovely Queen sat in a plush chair, her shoulders much more slumped than they had been when she made her grand entrance at the ball. Beneath her eyes were sunken circles.

Theor appeared equal measures bothered and bored to be present, playing with the edges of the curtain as he stood in the corner.

Willen was concerned, his brow knit together and his arms crossed as he leaned back on a desk. His gaze fell on me and held for a moment too long. I wanted to admonish him for staring until I realized I also was guilty of the crime.

"Oh my, it's truly the King," Shrane whispered. "I never thought I would see him. I used to dream of this when I was a little girl."

Gretaline shushed her as the King began to speak.

"At this ball, you ought to be making flowers, I hear. But I have a less fashionable request. It requires your discretion and your talents. For you see, my beloved wife is with child. A girl, it would seem. And while we are thrilled to have a fourth child...her health is not what it should be. We fear for her life and the child's. And we hope...we hope you might possess the skills to heal her."

"Heal her?" Shrane asked. "I can't imagine how."

Gretaline inhaled sharply. "I have healed before. Minor cuts and the likes. But only by mixing tinctures together using various plants. Perhaps there is an herb garden or an apothecary at the Palace? I could try to whip something together."

The King nodded. "Your efforts are appreciated. My servant will show you to whatever you may need."

As Gretaline left, Clorente's lips pursed, her eyes following until she disappeared behind the door.

"I must say this is unorthodox, Great King," Clorente said with a hard sigh.

"I know it is, Clorente. I know. But we are desperate. The last thing this Realm needs is news of a dead child. And it would be our fifth loss. We must try."

"Why can the Realm not bear news of a dead child? Are they all so fragile?" Theor asked with far too much enthusiasm.

"Times are delicate," Willen said, as if his brother should understand.

"Why are times so delicate, then? What's wrong with the times? All seems well to me."

Willen quite literally bit his lip and clenched his jaw to keep from responding.

"My son," the High King said, his voice strained. "Have you not been given the correspondences I sent regarding Tseslar? Regarding Morn?" Then the King looked at Willen. "I thought I asked you to divulge this pertinent information. To make sure he understands."

Willen ran a hand through his ashen hair. "My King, believe me, we have discussed the foreign matters. In great detail. Many times. Over many types of presentations, including having him read the letters out loud in my presence."

"Untrue!" Theor cried. "I have no idea what he's talking about, King!"

Willen stood up straight. "You have no idea what I'm talking about because you don't listen to a word I say."

"I don't listen to a word you say because everything that comes out of your mouth is boring beyond measure and severely inconsequential."

"I cannot help what you find interesting, Theor, but political matters of the Realm are not inconsequential. You will be High King Of All The Realm. These matters are the only thing of consequence for you. The Realm is what should matter, nothing else."

"Alright, enough." The High King put his hand up. "You are distressing my Queen. We are here for her healing, not to discuss the tribulations of our Realm." He sighed. "Do any of these remaining Trees possess skills useful to us in this moment?"

And at this, Giggles quite literally fell over backwards, her eyes rolled up in her head and her knees soft as pudding.

"She has simply fainted," Clorente said quickly. "No need for alarm. Our Trees were not prepared to see the High King tonight."

Clorente tapped her cane, and Giggles vanished, hopefully to her bed.

Then, the King looked to me. "Lady Tree, to whom we owe the salvation of my Second born, would you possess this skill?"

I realized I was clenching the fabric of my dress in my hands and that I was not breathing as I should have been, more than likely preparing to faint as Giggles had.

"She can, High King." Clorente spoke with reluctance. "This Tree...possesses more skill than she lets on."

"Does she now?"

I swiveled to face Clorente. "I do not know such things, Clorente, I promise you. I am not hiding some secret repertoire of Tree-like abilities."

Clorente sighed, closing her eyes. "The guests your brother hosted, they were not there for his fine cooking or to exchange goods. They were there to benefit from services he offered. From services you provided. For you healed them, Lady Tree. From many ailments. Simply being close to you, or...I cannot say I understand your methods. But this is how your brother earned his income. They came, and you healed."

I thought of this, and it made me even more dizzy than I already had been. All those turns spent hidden beneath floorboards or wedged beneath baths or tucked in the cellar. It was not only to develop some Tree-like tendencies in me but also so that I could gain the proximity needed to heal guests without them looking upon me. Without them knowing I existed at all. Aman. He used me in every way.

And Clorente knew.

Did the King know? *Do all of them know and simply pretend they are innocent?* I remembered Willen holding me the night I first found my room, the night of the flower. Was it a lie? Did he know what had been done to me? *Is it part of my formation? To make me into a True Tree?*

"Will you aid us, Honorable Tree?" the King asked.

"I am not sure how I can," I responded, "but I will try." After all, the only one purely innocent in the room was the unborn child in the belly of a mother she would never come to know, for the moment she bore the child, she would be killed. A great privilege, they would say.

I approached the Queen and took her dark, soft hands in mine, kneeling before her. I could feel, within an instant, the struggle of the life within her belly. The child had no room. And its cord wrapped around it, crushing its flow of blood. Except not one instance of this, but two.

"More than one," I whispered to her, still holding her hands. "You are not ill, Fourth Queen. Simply tired from growing them both."

The woman smiled at me, and tears filled her eyes. "I thought I felt two rumbling around in there, but the physicians told me I was mad."

I nodded. "You are not mad. I feel two at once. Quite certainly."

"But...what is wrong with them?" she asked. Her voice sounded like petals falling. "I am tired, yes, but there is something that is not going as it should go. The babies. They are unwell, I know it. What is wrong?"

"There is no more room for them," I explained. "They are tangled—"

"Take them out," she said, sitting straighter in her chair. "Take them out now if there is no room."

"My love," the High King began. "You—"

"I am the *Queen*," she said, taking her hands from me and balling them into fists. "And there is one thing I can contribute to this Realm. Children. These children. And then, when I have done so, my life. Take them in reverse order. Or I will, in the end, have contributed nothing at all."

The King pressed his hand to her shoulder. "I—"

"Not *you*," she said, pounding her fist on the arm of the chair. "Not you this time. *Me*. This time, me." She set her eyes on something I could not see. Some future in the distance she'd imagined just for her. "Call the physicians. Prepare what must be prepared. I'll give birth this very turn and be done with it."

A knock on the door, and a messenger entered. He bowed and handed the King a letter. As the King read, Willen held his breath, studying his father's back when he turned the letter over, folded it in half, and handed it behind him to his Second son.

Theor Vedan noticed this transaction with a scowl of utter darkness on his otherwise fair features.

The High King ran a hand through his hair, much as Willen would have, and then spoke with finality. "We shall give the Queen what she wants. And with great haste." Then, he turned to Theor. "My son, prepare yourself for departure."

"Departure?" He perked up. "Oh good! Where am I going?"

"To Tseslar."

He screwed up his face. "Tseslar? Why in the heavens would I do that? It's dreary in Tseslar. Something is always going on, but nothing worth paying attention to."

"You will go to Tseslar because Morn has declared war on this Realm and Tseslar lies between them and us. We need to ensure the Tseslarian alliance with us holds strong."

"I will go with him," Willen offered. "I can speak with the Tseslarian King."

"You will stay here," the High King said.

"Stay here? Will you be going with Theor, then, High King?" Willen asked.

"No. I will remain with my Queen as she gives birth and is buried. Theor will go to Tseslar. And he will go alone."

"*Alone?*" both sons cried out at once.

"Alone. It is time the High Prince prepared himself for the very real duties of Kingship. If he does not, we will all be ruined. It will only be a matter of time before more wars are declared, more resources stripped. Theor must show that he is capable."

"Wait, Tseslar?" Theor asked. "Is that the one with the little Countess?"

Willen smacked his hands together. "Duchess! She is a Duchess, Theor. Good heavens, man, take it seriously. If Tseslar does not agree to keep Morn from our borders, we will be embroiled in a war we do not have the natural resources to sustain. Do you understand—for even one moment—what will happen to the Realm you are meant to govern if this occurs?"

"Do not talk to me like I am a fool," Theor thundered.

"Stop this, both of you," the King said. "Theor, prepare to leave for Tseslar to strengthen our alliance. I will tend to my Queen and pray to heaven that there is indeed more than one child in her womb and that at least one of them is male. We need all the heirs we can get with a war incumbent. And Willen, you will join your efforts with Clorente and see to it that a True Tree is found by the time Theor returns to us." The High King, if I was not mistaken, looked directly at me then. "We need a True Tree. A Seed. We need resources and we need them now. Or all will be lost."

Clorente ushered us from the room before I could protest the hastened death of the Queen. Perhaps there was another way. Perhaps she could keep her life and still hold thriving children in her arms. But no one cared for my take on the matters of High Monarchy.

"We must expedite our efforts," Clorente said as she led Shrane and me away from the room.

Willen rushed past us and grabbed the older woman by the elbow. "You will do no such thing, Clorente. Are you truly this mad or are you just wicked?"

She yanked her arm away from the Prince's grasp. "You heard the High King, did you not?"

"You cannot *expedite* your efforts. That is insanity. You are down to four Trees in a matter of turns. One of them has fainted before our very eyes, and do not lie to my face and tell me it was because of the sight of the King. She fainted because she was exhausted. Exhausted and starved and deprived of sleep because *you* are manipulating time against all Ancient Laws of Wonder. You will only succeed in turning our Trees to kindling at this rate. Release your pressure, woman. Let sense return to you and life to your Trees."

"We need the—"

"Then we will not *torture* them to *death*. The King said I am to aid you, and so I will. This is how. By providing a voice of reason."

Clorente rolled her shoulders, eye to eye with Willen. "Very well, Good Prince. A moment of rest. And then we must commence."

I blinked and was no longer at the ball in my hint of a dress, but pressed tight into my bed, the blanket pulled over me so my arms and legs and body were bound still. I could not move. I could hardly breathe. And then the blanket crept up and over my mouth, nose, and eyes until all was darkness.

Clorente's idea of rest.

Ep 17

A Scream that Broke My Heart

It took ages for me to break free of the 'rest' Clorente had designed for me, and when finally I emerged from the restricting leaves, my skin felt so raw that my eyes pricked with tears each time I moved even in the slightest. It was then that Glenne finally arrived to my room, carrying a large ceramic jar in her petite arms, her face wearing the tightest of frowns.

"Good. You are awake," she said, keeping her voice small and calm, much unlike her usual boisterous self tended to do. "I did earnestly hope you would wake up Aia. Just as I hoped you would not yet have to endure the peeling of your skin. But alas, my hopes don't make Trees. Why I bother to hope at all, I don't know."

She set the jar down just as a tub appeared in the corner of the room. "We must get you into it, I'm afraid," she told me, wincing at her own words, for she could see that any movement was torture for me. "I know it seems impossible, but we have to try. The leaves you were all wrapped up in secreted quite the concoction. The milk is what will soothe the burning and cause your skin to regrow anew. I would pour it onto you where you sit, but you must soak in it for the properties to take effect."

I wanted to tell Glenne that, with her help, I could manage to get into the tub. Perhaps with her help, I could manage to do just about anything. But I could not move my lips without searing pain shooting throughout my face. Glenne took my hand, and it was worse than if she had not. I made a gurgling sound in my throat, and she understood the mistake, releasing me at once.

Then, I rose from the bed and made my own steps, one at a time until I reached the tub, hoisted my legs over the edge, and sat down. My clothes had long since dissolved—apparently just as my skin had—and so there was nothing left for me to do but to wait for Glenne to administer her mercy.

She poured the milk over my hair and body, and the cooling element was instant, literal steam cascading to the ceiling as it relieved my scorched body. Once I could speak again, I looked to my friend.

"Glenne?"

"Yes, my dear Tree?"

"You are right."

"I *am*? Well...of course I am. I always am. But exactly which perfectly right thing are you referring to? Just so I am basking appropriately."

"You are the best designer there ever was. I am sure of it."

Glenne grinned. "You feel beautiful in my dresses, Aia?"

"When I wear your dresses, I feel...like myself. It is the greatest gift, and you are the finest talent in all the Realm."

Glenne's eyes flooded with unshed tears. "Thank you. I...I must confess to you, Aia. I did not receive very high marks in

training. In fact, I barely qualified to become a designer at all.
My instructors called me a 'hopeless romantic'. Extra emphasis
on the 'hopeless' bit. They said my ideas were both too subtle
and too complex. Simple and extravagant were more what they
desired. But I could not seem to produce what they desired.
And so...I worried when I was paired with you. Especially
when"—she sniffled—"I realized how much I like you.
I thought...I might be too hopeless or too romantic and then
I would get you killed. How dreadful it would have been."

"But your creativity did not result in my demise. Very much
the opposite."

"Yes. Indeed. You have gotten quite far! Though I wish it did
not involve you enduring such feats of pain and terror."

"Those are not your design, Glenne."

As I spoke to her, I felt my eyes flutter closed, my lids growing
heavy. And finally, my eyes closed altogether. Glenne kissed
my forehead, and the door clicked closed behind her, leaving
me to sleep in that healing milk.

Until...something stirred the creamy milk of my bath.
Perhaps, I thought, *it's the wind.* But I was well indoors, and
no wind could stir any part of my room. *Some new terror of
Clorente's?* But there was a chilling jolt down my spine that had
not accompanied the use of Clorente's Wonder in the past.

This is when a sharp, urgent sensation struck me, beginning
at my left thigh and coursing up my leg, spreading throughout
my body. An alarming pain, strange to me, like nothing I'd
felt before.

I plunged my hand deeper into the water, grabbing hold of
my thigh only to find some wriggling...thing...attached to me.

With an emergent flood of energy, I leaped to my feet to find a long, slithering creature attached to me by its gaping mouth.

I was unsure of what to do, for no matter how I pulled, the creature would not come loose. It was only when I thought to squeeze its neck that it unhinged its strong jaws and released its razor fangs, its black beady eyes unflinching while its body writhed and flailed to be free. I did not know what to do with the thing, so I flung it against the wall. It hissed and slithered away, disappearing beneath my bed.

I left the bath and found only one thing to drape over my body. A silken robe of the faintest pink. I tugged it on, not even bothering to dry myself, and reached for the door. Once I threw it open, I was in the familiar study I had come to adore. The fire was not yet ablaze or, perhaps, it had already gone out.

Willen was in the process of pacing, with Beralt sitting behind his desk, spinning a blade on his fingertip and lost to the wiles of boredom.

"I do not see how war can be avoided and I do not see how it can be won, Beralt," said the Second Prince, his pacing leading him away from the place where I stood. "And with Theor gone to ensure the strength of our treaty with Tseslar, we will have two enemies very shortly rather than just the one."

"Why not send you?" Beralt asked in his gruff way. "You have relations with the Tseslarians that could prove beneficial. I am... I am confused."

"I also am confused, Beralt. I should go. My uncle, the King, has never been unkind in his letters. He is no fan of my father, but to me, he shows at least some favor. Why choose now to test the diplomatic skills of Theor, who my uncle will no doubt despise? Am I so incompetent? Am I so...fragile that I must stay here where my father can monitor me?"

"You are not fragile, Willen. It is not that. It is only...confusing."

"Willen?" The word at last left my mouth.

The Second Prince turned and began moving toward me the second he got a look at me. I was in his arms before it made sense that I could be, then set down upon a chair.

"Aia, what is the matter? Are you hurt? Are you ill?"

"Something...in the water...."

He touched his hands to my face, my head, my shoulders, working his way down with vigilant attention as he aimed to locate the source of my malady. I must not have looked very wonderful for him to worry so immediately. Luckily, my skin had healed, and his touch did not bring about excruciation as it would have before my milk bath. I only had the bite on my leg to survive.

"What was in the water? Did you drink something?"

Beralt came over and gave a rough sigh. "It could be poison, could it not?"

I clutched Willen's hand and brought it to my leg. "Something...."

He brushed aside my robe, his eyes widening when he saw the marks in my skin. "A snake?" He turned to his friend. "Beralt, send for a physician."

But Beralt did not obey the command. Only stood staring, his lips pursed.

Willen did not realize Beralt hadn't left his spot. Instead, he held my cheeks, rubbing my temples and getting me to look in his eyes. "My love, what color was the snake? What markings did it bear?"

When I did not answer, he tried once more. "Please, can you tell me what color the snake was?"

I inhaled, trying to bring the memory to my mind. Then trying to move the words to my lips. "It...was a...white—"

"White? A *white* snake?" Willen licked his lips, his irises flickering as he tried to think. "Not a natural snake then. A creation. Someone's creation. So the antidote will not be in the infirmary or the apothecary. The poison was derived from Wonder. And therein will lie the antidote."

Beralt nodded. "I figured as much, Second Prince. And so I did not summon a physician. It would have put you both at risk, and to no avail."

"Help me lay her down," Willen said. And he and Beralt set me on the ground, my head on the cushion of the chair. "Stay with her. I will return with help in a moment."

"Willen, you cannot interrupt!"

"I will do so in a clever manner, Beralt. I must. I cannot do this alone, and there is no one else I trust. Guard Aia well," he told his Dwarf friend before vanishing.

"All will be well, Miss Tree," Beralt mumbled, patting my hand and scowling, as was his way. "Willen will not see harm come to you, for you have made him into the most pitiful of fools. You have him by the heart, my dear. Worry not."

I was not worried about my leg or the color of the snake. I worried that Willen was off telling the world that I was in his study, underdressed, in the middle of the night. That harm would come to him as a result of my irrational behavior.

But I could no longer form words, my body growing stiff and cold as my leg continued to throb.

Willen returned and touched my forehead, then the fire roared to life at the prodding of his Wonder. "She is too cold," he said. "Please, waste no time."

Above me floated the elegant face of the Fourth Queen. Her braids slipped from behind her shoulders and gently touched my cheek. "A white snake, you say, Willen?"

"So she told me, Mida."

The woman, her dark brown skin gleaming in the firelight, touched my lips with her gentle hands. "She is dying." And then she looked in my eyes. "But she will fight, and so must we." She looked to Willen. "You will sit and gather Wonder for me. I will need it. And you, Beralt, I will need your knife."

The Queen caught the blade as it was tossed to her and, squatting beside me with her pregnant belly nearly dragging on the floor, she pricked my thigh and dragged the knife across my skin.

I felt the pain but could not react to it. Darkness crept in around the edges of my vision. I could almost hear the hissing of the snake filling my ears, filling the very room.

"I will pull the venom, and you will put your Wonder in its place, Will. We must not hesitate in between the pull and the push. Ready?"

And the Queen slapped her palm on my thigh and yanked her hand away, pulling smooth black liquid from my leg. Then Willen placed his hand over hers, flooding my veins with the cleanest, strongest Wonder I had yet felt in my limited experience.

I sighed at the relief of it, the ease with which it entered my body.

"Keep watch over her," the Fourth Queen said. And then she groaned, rocking back on her heels so that Willen had to use his free hand to steady her. "I am fine, I am fine," she said in reply to his gesture. "It is almost time for me to deliver them. The childbirth Wonder does not wish to wait."

"Mida," Willen said. "This is madness. It is ridiculous that you must forfeit your life—"

"Willen, stop," she said, shaking her head. "It is too late to bring this up. Too late to rehearse this conversation yet another time."

"But none of us want you to die. My father does not; I do not."

"This is the way it is done."

"It is a stupid way, and there is still time. We can choose another path."

"There is no other—"

"We can create one. But now, you are planning to deliver these children and face your death at the hands of people who love you? Do not ask me to remain quiet, for I cannot."

"Willen. I know you love me. And your father's—"

"And mine," Beralt chimed in. "Your kindness is undeniable, my Queen."

She smiled at Beralt. "Thank you. Thank you, but I will not defy the Ancient Law, will not break Royal Law. I will do as I am meant to do. What I knew would be my fate when I agreed to be your father's wife, I now face with courage."

"I don't want you to face it with courage. I want you to stay here. Alive."

I realized then that the Queen and the Prince were nearly the same age. She was, after all, his father's fourth wife.

"Mida, you are not just a Queen. Or the wife of the King. You are my friend. Besides, what will I do the next time I need you? If a white snake bites another? Or...."

"Or we must drink too much in the Royal pools, and Beralt needs to be reduced lest he drown?" She groaned again, adjusting her weight as she clutched her bulging belly.

"I can hide you, Mida, until we find a way."

But the Fourth Queen touched my lips once more. "Your rebellious heart is meant to protect another, Willen. I have my mate. And he awaits for me to give birth to his children." She kissed Willen's cheek. Then, she looked to Beralt. "Take care of him, faithful one. He will need you."

And then she was gone.

"Willen, I will find clothes for our Tree." And he left like a normal person, through the door, with hastened steps.

The Second Prince kept his hand pressed to my leg. After a moment, he traced the long scar that ran along the outside of my other thigh. "I see you once had another rather serious encounter. You must tell me the story sometime."

It came about on a very ordinary turn, when an old man came to visit and buried a seed in my leg until it sprouted. The turn that changed everything for me. I would bear many scars, but perhaps Willen would hear the stories of them all.

He pressed his hand to his head and closed his eyes for a moment, still thrumming Wonder into me. "I cannot believe she will die for nothing," he said. "Just as my mother did." He squeezed the bridge of his nose. "At least her children will be too young to remember the turn. Too young to memorize the look on their father's face when he witnesses his wife standing before the people."

I wanted to hold him, to stop his suffering, but it was he who stopped mine.

"My father loved us, you know. He loved us. And it will be my great downfall."

I could not know exactly what he meant. But I knew that life returned to my body. "Willen—"

And when I said his name, he scooped me up in his arms and held on. "Thank heaven," he said. "Your colors are returning. And your voice has found its way once again." He kissed my mouth, my nose, my heart. Then he looked at me with resolve. "Aia, someone tried to kill you this turn. We must discover who would attempt this. It could not have been my brother, for he is en route to Tseslar, no doubt to doom us all."

"I am alright. And whoever sent the snake did not succeed. What have we to fear?"

"They will try again."

"And they will fail again." I sat up of my own strength. "Forgive me, for coming to you like this. I hardly knew what to do."

"Always, you come to me when you are in danger, Aia. Always."

"Danger changes your rules," I noted.

"They are not *my* rules—"

"They are yours, indeed. You rely on them. Yet, you were willing to abandon them for the Fourth Queen when she was in danger. And for me. But not for your own happiness."

"My happiness means nothing."

I touched his face then. "And that is why you keep misplacing it. You give it no value, Willen. And if you cannot value your own happiness, how will you ever value mine?"

I kissed him—the need for recovery be damned—tasting the fullness of his lips and, for the first time, detecting the flavor of exquisite sadness. When he slipped his hand over the round form of my breast, his touch betrayed his deep confusion. His breath as he exhaled against my neck revealed the chaos within him. I pulled away from the Prince, to whom I owed my life though I had just the same saved his, and I let my Wonder— that feeling within me that did what it wanted when I could not find my courage—take me away from him once more.

It took me not back to my room, however, but to an outdoor garden, with lush greenery and trimmed hedges, flowers blooming on trellises, and smooth walkways carved of fine white stone. The moon showed its proud face above, and over the rustle of leaves as they swayed in the sweet breeze came the piercing cry of someone in very great danger. A scream I had heard enough times to place with a face in my memory. A scream that broke my heart.

Shrane.

Ep 18

Nothing but Bark and Boughs

Thunder cracked overhead, causing me to halt my steps.
My bare feet cooled on the smooth stone of the Royal garden
as the rains came in. The droplets blessed the petals of the
flowers, bouncing from the delicate curves and onto the thirsty
soil beneath. I was thankful for the rain and the thunder, for I
slowed myself long enough to restore some rational thought
to my mind.

Instead of racing toward the source of the nightmarish scream,
I hid myself among the shrubs, moving with greater care in the
direction from whence came the sound moments before. The
prickled stems did pluck at my newly healed skin, but they were
nothing compared to the enormous thorns that Clorente had
thrust into my back after I saved the Second Prince.

I endured the tinges of pain until I could see ahead of me
a tree. And beneath the tree, a girl in a sage green dress. It was
indeed Shrane, her knees pulled into her chest and her sweet
face buried in her hands, though at such a distance away, I could
not have made out her features.

And a figure loomed before her, tall and imposing and dressed as one of the noblemen of the Palace. He reached out and grabbed her by the arm, wrenching her to the side and pushing her to the ground. He swung his leg over her, pinning her arms down, though the Tree did not scream another time or seem to put up much of an effective struggle. I could only hear, above the plodding gentle rain, Shrane's whimper as she submitted.

What to do? What to do? I would have to do something. To rush out and assault the attacker. To stop him from going any further, for clearly he was hurting my friend, not to mention endangering her chances at becoming the True Tree. Even if Shrane had been a stranger—even if she was my *enemy*—I would have no choice but to intervene.

I began to move forward, but a hand on my shoulder stopped me as surely as the thunder had arrested my progress moments before.

"Stay hidden," he told me. "I will put an end to this."

And the Second Prince stepped out of my hiding place, rain bouncing off his broad shoulders, and approached Shrane and her aggressor. He did not have time to attack or ask questions before the cloaked man hurtled into the darkness.

"Show your face," Willen commanded, running toward the perpetrator.

But the assailant sped away, vanishing before Willen could get close enough. He stopped at Shrane, who lay on the ground weeping, and lifted her into his arms, bringing her back to my place among the flowers.

"She is injured," he said, setting her down atop the dampened soil. "And if Clorente were to know she was out here with this man, she would be removed from the Palace."

I shook my head, caressing the battered face of my round-eyed friend. A bruise swelled beneath her eye, and her nose bled down her lovely lips. "I would never tell Clorente. But did you see who it was, Willen? The man who did this?"

Willen shook his head. "A noble of some sort, I think, from the smell of his expensive fragrance and the look of his clothes. But I did not see his face. Perhaps if he had used his Wonder on me, I would have recognized it from experience."

"You can tell the difference between Wonder from experience?"

"Yes. If one learns to pay attention. Each person is unique, and so is their Wonder. Not only how they use it, but the sensation of it. And since I have trained with many of the nobles—those in fighting condition at least—I have a good feel for most of their Wonder. I might have identified it if I could have come in contact with it. Safe to say, whoever the man was, he now knows it was I who intercepted his attack."

He put his hand to my cheek, regarding me with so much affection in his cloud-cast eyes that my heart nearly moved to meet his palm. "How did you find yourself out here, Little Tree? You just nearly died in my arms this very turn. I thought you would be resting. And besides that, someone is very likely trying to destroy you. Thus, you should not be walking the grounds alone at night."

When I did not answer him, he frowned. "Are you still very unwell? Aia—"

"I'm...fine, Willen. Fine. Really. Your Wonder and the Queen's as well...I can never thank you enough for saving me."

"Aia, you should never *thank* me. I owe you my life, and that will always be so."

I nodded. "Debt repaid, then."

"No. That is not how it works. Not for me." He studied Shrane, who had faded to sleep among the flowers. "I know this is not what you are hoping to hear at such a moment, but...I came this way looking for Clorente. That is, before I heard this Tree screaming for help."

"For what purpose do you seek Clorente?"

"She is needed by Mida. Well, I should not say Mida is the one who needs her. Something...has complicated this entire thing even further, I'm afraid. We need Clorente for identification. And the servants cannot seem to locate her. So I am helping."

I blinked in the rain. *He needs Clorente to help with identification?* That could only mean one thing, for I had fallen victim to Clorente's identification before, and nothing was ever the same after that. "Has the Queen given birth to...a Tree?"

"It seems so, from the whispers I've heard. Perhaps it explains why the second child was undetected. But a Tree has never before been born within the Realm's Royal line. It's unheard of. In the Realm, Clorente would be the highest living authority on the matter and so must be summoned at once."

"Is the Fourth Queen *from* the Realm, Willen? Perhaps her lineage can be traced to some unique source?"

He shook his head. "We grew up together in the Palace of the Princes. Her family has always been close to ours. There is no hint of the arboreal race in their bloodline as far as we know. There will then be talk of the Queen's infidelity. So many... issues...are raised now."

What issues could be raised? I thought the Realm so desired Trees that they would go to any lengths to find them. And here one was born within the Palace. Should it not be a good thing?

A happy, fortuitous occasion? Unless.... "They think, if she has given birth to a Tree, that she was unfaithful to the King."

"Precisely. And the penalty would be death. Not only for her, but for the infants as well."

"They would even kill the baby Tree?" My eyes widened. "The children are innocent!"

"I...do not know, in truth, what will happen. But I know the Royal Law. And that is what it dictates."

"But what do you think of the accusation? Could it be true? Could the Queen have been unfaithful?"

He sighed. "Aia, it is not possible. Mida...she loves our family. She loves my father. And she loves this Realm. More than any-one I've ever met. Perhaps even more than I. She would never do such a thing, never jeopardize the Realm, no matter what lust or love might have whispered in her ear. She could not have done it. It's simply not who she is. For heaven's sake, she came to your aid and mine in the throes of childbirth! I cannot believe she would do anything like this. I refuse to believe it."

"So...what will you do, Willen?" I clutched his arm, for a gradual fear was overtaking me. That he would perform some reckless feat in an attempt to save his childhood friend.

"I will...try to buy us time. Perhaps if I pursue the course my brother has always threatened he would take...perhaps if I seek out the Ancients, the ones who made the Laws, I could have them amended. Perhaps these deaths, needless and cruel, need not continue."

"And every land would be free of the Laws?"

"No, Aia, no. There is Ancient Law and Royal Law. Royal Law is made by each land in an attempt to better uphold

Ancient Law, for breaking the rules of Ancients...it is detrimental...I'll just say that."

"So if you can change the Ancient Laws, the Realm may be willing to change Royal Law?"

"Exactly. The Council may see reason. The absurdity of the Royal Laws may be discarded at last."

"Willen...this is not only about the Queen, is it?"

His hand left my cheek, trailing down to my neck, his fingertips tangling in my hair as he held me. "I cannot simply let you go. I cannot. No matter what good it would do for the Realm. There has to be another way. A way to help without harming."

"Will your father permit you to embark on this search? To find Ancients? I thought...a war may be near. Does that not impede travel and such things? Can it be safe for you to leave?"

Willen kissed my forehead and then pressed his lips to mine and kissed me again. "Take this Tree and find her rest. Perhaps you have enough use of Wonder to heal her wounds, to hide them from Clorente. Apply your hands. That will help you focus."

I gasped. "Willen, you cannot show me how to use Wonder! The rules—"

"Rules be damned." And then, the rain still blessing us as it did the petals and the leaves and the soil, he grinned at me, his eyes leaving mine and devouring the shape of me as we knelt. "You look beautiful, by the way, all soaking wet like this." And then he brought me in, as if to kiss me once more, but tugged my lip with his teeth instead. "And if you dare to wear something like that to a ball again, or to walk about as you do now with nothing between us but the thinnest of fabrics, even you will wish we had rules to keep me in line, Little Tree."

And the Second Prince Of All The Realm left in a swirl of Wonder to find the woman who would either condemn or redeem his friend.

And I watched him go, wishing we had more time in the garden. For whether my happiness was well placed or not, it all rested with Willen vedan.

'Take her back to rest,' he said. How will I accomplish such a feat? I did not have the brute strength of a man nor the command of Wonder that Clorente or Glenne displayed. I could manage to move myself about with Wonder from time to time, but I hardly knew *how* I managed to do so.

Use your hands. But how would I use my hands to transport another person? And then I realized...I could use my hands to heal Shrane, perhaps, and then we would walk back to our rooms like ordinary pedestrians.

And so I placed my palms on her face and waited. To no avail, for nothing proceeded and no shimmers of enchantment left my being and made their way to Shrane's. I sat all the way down on the ground and closed my eyes. The rain dripped down my arms and slid to the dirt beneath me. I felt the smallest kisses and opened my eyes again to witness baby clovers. They'd sprouted where my fingers aimed and were so glad to be alive and drinking heaven's water.

"Hello," I said. "Welcome to the Realm."

And it was as if they giggled, stretching their tender stems and spreading their tiny leaves. "Would you know what to do, little green ones? I am lost. In fact, in this world, I am perpetually lost, it seems. But you look like you know your way about being alive."

And the kisses the clovers gave me turned to tingles. After some moments, the very look of my hands changed, and a light flowed from my pores, as if the sun had been sleeping in my palms and could no longer keep from peeking its eyes open.

Remembering Willen's advice, I put my hands on my friend and waited. The light flowed out warm and thick, like how I imagined honey would feel if I soaked in it. And then, Shrane's gorgeous eyelashes fluttered, and she sat up, wiping away the rain and remnants of blood.

"Aia? What...what happened?" she asked. And then she gasped. "You are almost naked! What are we doing in the flower bushes?"

"Shrane, someone attacked you. I heard you screaming and came to your aid, but I did not see who the man was. It is important that you try to remember. Did you get a look at his face?"

Shrane laughed—a strained sound, to be sure. "No, no...you," she sniffled, "you misunderstand, Aia. No. That man was no attacker. That...he is my *lover*. You see—"

"You cannot be serious, Shrane. You think...that man is your *lover*? That he cares for you? You were bleeding!"

"I would never expect you to understand."

"But I *do* understand!"

"No. You don't. I am beginning to think you do not understand anything at all. Sometimes you act as if you were just born. Or...or as if you simply stayed in a bed all your life and merely walked into the world for the first time this turn. He and I...we are *passionate* with one another."

"That is not passion, Shrane. You were lying here in the dirt, unconscious and unmoving. Where is there love in that? If I had not chased him away"—I made sure to make no mention of *my* lover, lest Shrane learn secrets that needed to remain hidden from the world.

"You chased him away? No!" And Shrane wobbled to her feet. "I must find him. You may have *wounded* him, you stupid idiot! Or...or he may no longer desire to see me. I may be too much trouble for him now. He may already be in the arms of another, Aia. Why would you do this to me?" I could not tell if the tears or the rain left trails on her newly healed cheeks. "I thought you were my friend!"

Then Shrane gasped and pointed a quivering finger at me. "Unless...unless you came here to meet him! Why of course! Dressed in nothing but a night robe, with the skin of a freshly strewn moon beam. You came to meet him and found me already enwrapped in his affections. And you chased him away and now you seek to convince me that I should abandon our love."

"What? Shrane, no. There is no way I could ever express enough how deeply and utterly uninterested I am in your lover. I am...*disgusted* by him, not attracted to him. His nature is averse to mine, Shrane, please. You have to listen to reason. You have to believe me. If Clorente found out you were out here with him in the middle of the dark—"

"Just as *you* are out here, isn't it so? And if you tell Clorente, she will know you were doing forbidden things as well. And we will both be made into nothing but bark and boughs. So you will keep your mouth *shut*. Or...or I will put a seed in your nose. I will have Gretaline teach me, and when you sleep, I will explode it into a forest."

"You do not mean that, Shrane."

"Stay away from me. And stay away from my lover. Do not intervene again. Ever. Or I will find a way to destroy your happiness, as you are so obviously plotting a way to steal mine."

And she ran off, slipping on the slick stone and fighting for her footing as the thunder broke through the clouds once more.

I suppose I ought to put myself in clothes that qualify as such. I was no Glenne, and I could not stitch with unbreakable Wonder like Clorente, but certainly I could form some simple, woven thread. I put my hands to my chest and spread the Wonder everywhere I hoped to cover with fabric until I was satisfied that I was less revealed.

And then, quite exhausted, I attempted to walk, one foot after the other, to my room for what I wished could be a normal bout of restless sleep, even if it only lasted a short while.

I entered the Palace to find Beralt running, his stumpy legs flying as quickly as possible. He spotted me as he rushed past and waved his arm at me. "Go to your room at once, Lady Tree, and do not come out. You will be no help here. Go!"

But I did not listen and instead followed swiftly behind the Dwarf, my energy replenished by the sight of his drawn expression. Truth be told, it was not very difficult to keep up with the fellow.

Once we arrived to the next hall, I saw why Beralt begged me to return to my room. There was so much to see. The draperies flew about like Wyverns, and the crystal glass of the windows shattered, raining down in much a less the gentle manner than the droplets in the garden. The columns cracked like thunder had shaken them, and the marble floor trembled beneath my feet.

But, in earnest, there was only one thing worth beholding amidst the chaos within the Palace walls. A slough of men wielding both Wonder and weapons gave every effort they possessed, it seemed, to wrangle one man into submission.

"Oh, heaven help us," Beralt whispered when he finally arrived beside me, our halting position overlooking the turmoil. "They have made a decision on the Fourth Queen it seems," Beralt continued. "He will rip them all to pieces, I'm afraid."

Oh, Beralt. I too am afraid.

Ep 19

And Those Who Suffer

I wish I'd taken more wine at the ball, but Beralt, along with half the nobles in attendance, watched every swallow I made as if it could be my last. As a result of their unswerving vigilance—and general inability to mind their business—I entered the second half of the night depressingly sober and exponentially annoyed.

"Must every single pair of eyes linger on me with such devotion? Do none of you waiver in your attentions? Does not one of you feel the need to blink, at least on occasion?"

Beralt stroked his wide beard. "We worry, is all, and can you blame us? The poisoning of a Prince should have that effect on the people of the Realm."

I rolled my eyes at the Dwarf. "*You* worry, perhaps, but these people do not care what happens to me. They are probably happy *something* has finally happened, in fact. My life is as boring as the stack of taxation papers I have yet to sort through back in my study." I dodged the gaze of an older Lady who held pity out from the tip of her long nose. "Besides, I was

hardly *poisoned*. It was an allergic reaction. Is that not the
story they were all told? Raspberries gone astray?"

"That was the story circulated about, yes. But the nobles
know when a scandal is afoot, Willen. And afoot it is."

I scoffed. "There is no scandal. Only my brother and his
failed efforts. And me and my wasted ones."

"Your efforts on behalf of the Realm are never wasted, Prince.
You serve the King well in every way he has required." Beralt
frowned and sloshed back a bubbly pink drink with a shiver.
He was more a man of hard spirits or warm ale. Not frilly Palace
concoctions. "You are far too hard on yourself, you know. You
do much good for the Realm and for your father. Heaven knows
I could never juggle the tedious work you do."

"Beralt, if I did much good for the Realm, we would not be
on the cusp of war with Morn. Not only Morn, but the Wyverns
and the Stolen Worlds we took from them. And we would
have the resources needed to defend ourselves. We would have
trees. Water. Food for soldiers."

"The shortage of trees is not your doing. And the hostilities
between the Realm and Morn are not your fault either. How
could they be? Did you go back generations and steal their
Breaths, using them as objects for barter and manipulation
against their Monarchs?"

"Well, to have done any of that, I would have to be permitted
to leave this Realm, and I've never made it past the Forest of the
Deep without my father reeling me back in." I sighed, but it did
not rid me of my frustration. "I know I could not have prevented our hatred of one another, but I could keep animosity
between Morn and the Realm from growing. For example, it is
a misconception that my predecessors stole the Mornish

Breaths. They were offered to us for diplomatic reasons from the realm of Impera, who could no longer harbor them."

Beralt raised a bushy eyebrow. "And the land?"

I took his pink drink from his hand and finished it. "Well, we did take that."

"And we'll not give it back?"

"Our Laws have become quite complicated."

Beralt grunted. "All laws should be the same. That's how the Dwarves do it. Simple. Straightforward. Easy to follow and clear when you've broken them."

"We once had all Law as one, Beralt. Technically we still do. The Ancient Law governs above everything else. Rules over Dwarves, Aelves, and every Human domain. We are all are subject to them. But we humans have made further layers of insulation. Royal Laws and the likes. More restrictions to keep us from coming close to breaking Ancient Laws."

"But this only leads to confusion and war."

"At first, it did keep people from accidentally breaking Ancient Law and simply being swallowed by the earth with no warning or catching flame while walking through the market. But now, I do wonder whether this can be worth it. For one, we kill pre-emptively. Queens are made to die after giving birth to one child. To protect the Ancient Law: a Queen must be held in highest esteem."

"Heavens, why not just *esteem* the woman? No need to take her head off in the process."

"People became unsure of what 'highest esteem' could mean. Higher than the King? Higher than heaven? Higher than the Law itself? And so...people who did not esteem her would—"

"Be swallowed by the earth or catch flame in the market?"

"Yes. So the easiest way to make sure she was esteemed most highly—and to ensure that a nobleman who did not bow deeply enough did not simply fall over dead—was to give her the most honorable of endings."

"And what is honorable about executions?"

"I believe they are meant to be more...ceremonious."

"Then just have a ceremony, man! A bit of cake. A bit of wine. Some dancing. Put her in a nice dress!"

"I see your point, Beralt. But what can be done? I am neither a Lawmaker nor an enforcer."

"You know, Willen, we Dwarves observe these Laws as well. And we mostly get along by giving the Queen Of Dwarves the biggest axe and letting her lead the charge."

"Perhaps your definition of esteem is different."

"Perhaps yours is *wrong*."

"I cannot argue there, Beralt." I felt the eyes of some Duke boring into my shoulders as I reached for a glass of wine. "When will the stares end?"

And then, to my great surprise, the stares did end. For every eye was taken by the Tree who walked into the grand hall. Aia was...everything.

And I could see...everything.

Her long hair hung loose, covering only some of her breasts, the ends of those fair tresses fading into translucence. Her skin shimmered nearly fluorescent beneath the sheerest of fabrics, the dress taut on her frame so that when she turned, only a hint of its existence materialized. It was as if she was completely, devastatingly naked. Every curve, every line, I could see...but then I could not see. Not truly.

"Heaven help us," Beralt gasped. "I...I don't know what to do. I don't know where to look."

But he looked at *her*, as did I. There was no one in the room who could avoid it.

She noticed me, it seemed, and I could tell she was quite angry with me. Her eyes a swimming, fluid gray and green—I never knew what they would be when I looked. They used to hold a steady brown, but not anymore. They shifted and stirred, as did her skin, her hair, her presence. She glared at me from across the room, but I feared her fury did not have the effect on me she hoped it would.

I wanted her.

I wanted her all the way. In every fashion, but especially the one in which we were alone and I could have her close to me. So I could hear whatever words of correction she had stored up for me. So I could beg for forgiveness. So I could earn it with every stroke, every kiss, every bite.

"Second Prince, I dare say you will crack that glass if you clutch it any firmer," Beralt said, interrupting my thoughts. "I can hear it straining in your grasp."

I cleared my throat, though I had nothing to say, and I turned, though I had nowhere to go.

"I was thinking...perhaps we could practice making it more obvious." Beralt elbowed me and handed me another of his leftover drinks. I used my Wonder to transform the pink liquid to something a bit sturdier. "You could walk up and simply pull your pants down."

I was already redder in the face than I wanted to be. "Shut your mouth. It's not that obvious."

Beralt guffawed. "Tell yourself that. Just make sure you don't take her to your bed, Willen, or we'll have all sorts of problems."

Too late for that. I had not only taken Aia to my bed, I'd taste every bit of her. There was no mistaking what we had done. I made an effort not to press my hand to my head to alleviate the ache. Stressed was not close to enough of a descriptor for my mental state.

And then, the attention of the room shifted yet again. For in walked the High King and Fourth Queen, both regal and unexpected.

"The High Monarchs are in attendance?" Beralt asked. "This is not even a High ball. Why would they come out to the Palace of the Princes? And with the Queen in such a vulnerable state, no less?"

The only reason my father would come out to a lesser ball was because he needed an audience with someone in attendance and thought it would cause more of a fuss to summon them away from the festivities. No doubt, my father would confer, but I did not know if it would be with me. And I did not know why Mida would need to be involved. She should have been resting.

The King put a hand on my shoulder as he approached. "Good Prince, I hope all is well?"

"It is, yes. I'm honored you asked."

"Mm." His mind was far away. When I was a child, he always felt far away right before he had to leave my mother and me to return to the Palace. "I would like to personally request your presence if you can spare the time."

If I can spare the time? For the High King Of All The Realm and the only man who has ever been my father?
"Of course, anything."

He nodded. "I will join you shortly. Look after the Queen until I arrive."

The Queen. She nodded and tried to smile as the attendees cooed over her large belly and bowed in overdone extravagance as she walked past them.

I got close enough to offer her my arm. "Fourth Queen, your most *swollen* Excellence."

"I should push you down the stairs," she said, narrowing her eyes at me and looping her arm in mine. "But it wouldn't be worth the effort."

"Mind telling that to my brother? He is exhausted from scoping out staircases I could be pushed down."

She flashed a smile. Good. It had been too long since she had given a genuine one. "He's already spent all his energy scowling in the corner. He won't listen to me."

I patted her hand as we made our way to the private meeting room. "I think all the Vedans wear matching sets of frowns these turns. You included, Mida."

"Well, *I* have the best excuse."

The hair on the back of my neck stood up. Mida did not like discussing it but she was always the one to bring it up first. Over the turns, we'd learned it was best not to talk at all. We would only erupt into arguments.

"It's not an excuse, Mida. It's ridiculous."

"Honestly? We cannot begin to argue now, Willen. I have only just arrived, and we have not seen each other in so long. Can we not enjoy each other's friendship for a few moments?"

I paused, falling silent as I counted to ten in my mind. "There, now it's been long enough. I will begin the debate."

Mida laughed, her white teeth flashing in contrast to her dark skin. "That was a moment?"

"That was ten moments, to be precise. I am a generous Prince."

"No, what you are is a stubborn Prince."

"And you, a stubborn Queen. Too stubborn to listen to your oldest, truest friend."

Mida sighed, leaning her weight against me as we took to the stairs. "Will...I am already with child. What would you have me do?"

"I don't know, Mida. Something. Make a fuss. Stomp your feet. Throw something. Threaten someone. Or, if you are too tired to do these things, I will perform them and more on your behalf."

She glanced at me. "I thought you were well behaved these turns. You now love and follow our Realm's beloved rules, Will."

"I love that they are stable when everything around me is chaos. I love that they can be steadfast and unbiased. But I do not love them more than you."

Once we were in the private meeting room awaiting the others, Mida let me help her down into a plush chair. It was unlike her to accept such a gesture from me, but she rubbed her belly, wincing in discomfort. The gestational period had not been kind to her. Her body could not hold up as it should. "Willen, do you remember when we were children and Theor pushed me over the garden wall?"

"Of course I remember." Anger coursed through me as if he had just done it again. *What sort of fool hurts someone simply because he can?* "He broke your arm."

"And you...?"

"Broke my hand."

"Mmhmm...how exactly did you manage that, Second Prince?"

"I...tried to punch Theor in the face."

"And the Ancient Law turned the bones of your hand into tatters, did it not?" She grabbed my hand and held on to it. I never told her that it still ached from time to time, especially when I thought ill of Theor. "You knew very well that the Law would not allow you to hurt your brother, yet you swung at him with all your might."

"He deserved it."

"He deserved it, but *you* paid the price."

"Mida—"

"You will not pay the price for breaking this Law. I do not want you in tatters, Willen Vedan. I want you whole and living a fine life. One of privilege and...and gallivanting with lovely Ladies. Public indecency—"

She was trying to make me laugh. And ordinarily, it would have worked. "Mida, this isn't a broken arm you are anticipating. They are going to put you to *death* once you give birth." I knelt before her, squeezing her hand in mine. "I couldn't stand to see you hurt then and I surely can't watch you die a pointless death now."

"It's not *pointless*."

"It is pointless. I can tell you for a fact, Mida. I have watched, with my own eyes, my mother suffer the same fate you prepare to embrace—"

She shook her head. "*That* should not have happened. You should not have had to see that, Willen. You should have been an infant, too young to remember."

"But that *is* what happened. And I was not an infant. I remember all of it. I will always remember. How she stood there with dignity and how my father said nothing and let her go. Let them—"

"Willen."

"He let them *kill* her. My mother. And I can tell you, with all certainty and after many circles of trying to see it as honor, that the whole thing was utterly pointless. Nothing is better with her gone. Nothing. And nothing will be better with you gone."

"Except that I will be esteemed. Except that I will uphold Royal Law. The Laws that protect the people."

"It is pointless, Mida! You cannot uphold anything if you're dead."

She took her hand from me and placed her palm back on her belly. "If the roles were reversed, you would hear none of this. You would face your role and your responsibilities with no hesitation. You would be honored to uphold the Law, to be esteemed this way."

"And if the roles were reversed, you would bring the council to its knees and force them to see reason. You would not let me die without a fight."

Mida bit her lip. "Willen."

"There has to be a way for Queens and Trees and those who suffer beneath the Royal Laws to be free of their bondage, Mida. All I ask is that you give me a chance to find it. Talk to my father. Force him to see reason, to let me leave the Palace grounds and to search for the Ancients. Let me solve this problem before it is too late."

"He will never let you leave, and you will never find them, Will."

"Why? Why will he never let me leave?" I could go nowhere, do nothing but receive diplomats and send out paperwork. "Has he told you, Mida? What have I done wrong? Does he fear my inability to travel? Is it...is it the raspberries?"

Mida sighed a smile my way. "Yes, Second Prince. It is not the fact that you are all he has left of his greatest love. Or that you are the only one of his children he was able to see beloved in the arms of his mother. It is not because he adores you and fears losing you above all else. It is, of course, because of the raspberries."

I could hear the footsteps of whomever my father had summoned to the meeting. I took the few remaining moments to reach out, to kiss the hand of the girl who'd once left me stranded in a tipping tree because she couldn't see why she had managed to climb down with a broken arm while I couldn't with two rather useful ones.

"Please, Willen. Brother of my heart. Let me do what I married Harrod to do. Enough of this talk of crying out for justice and seeking the Ancients to rewrite the Laws that have held together our world for circles upon circles. Enough of this. And let us savor the time we have left. Let us remember our friendship and celebrate the life I will bring into this Realm. Please, cannot you do this? For me?"

"Very well, my Queen," I told her. But truly, fully in every way, I lied. It was not very well. And loving things, like mothers and rules and Queens and Trees, was not supposed to turn Princes to tatters. I could only be ripped to so many pieces before there was nothing left of me to tear.

Ep 20

I Would Have Begged

"What is going on?" Beralt grabbed on to a servant who was determined to run for his life, refusing to let the man go until he answered him. Others rushed past us, screaming and ducking from the debris that flew through the Wonderful air. "This sudden display of rage? What happened that has the Second Prince so out of control? It is not like him. There must be a reason."

The servant panicked, trying to scramble free, until Beralt slapped his knuckles against the poor man's cheek. "What is happening? Tell me now, or I will make you pay for your hesitation," the Dwarf repeated with even more growl than the first time he made the inquiry.

"The Prince...I was told to notify him."

"Notify him of what? Out with it man! You are wasting our time with your shite storytelling. What message did you carry to the Prince?"

I put my hand on Beralt's shoulder, hoping to calm the situation. "It must be the Fourth Queen," I interjected, my voice as calm as I could keep it. "Please, gentlefellow, is that what this is about? Is it about Queen Mida and her delivery of the babies?"

The servant nodded, a bruise already forming on his lean face where Beralt's hand had dealt its blow. "I was told to notify the Prince that a decision had been made in his absence, though his absence itself was brief. Regarding the Fourth Queen, Her Royal Excellence Mida Vedan."

Beralt sucked air in through his teeth. "Heaven help us. What is the decision that has been made? Go *on*."

"The Tree Woman. I forget her official name or title. Please forgive me for this."

"Forgiven, forgiven. Now, proceed."

"She came and said that indeed of the two children born to the Queen this very turn, one of them is a *Tree*," the servant sputtered. "Can you believe that? A *Tree* in the Royal line. It's...why, it's impossible. Not in all the circles—maybe more—have the Realm's Monarchs been known to breed their own—"

"Get to the point, man. Focus your mind." Then, Beralt paused and leaned forward, sniffing the man's face. He straightened back up, a look of disgust causing his beard to twist. "Are you...are you drunk?"

The servant's eyes grew larger than the rims of the glasses into which he had undoubtedly poured his drinks earlier that turn. "I had...a bit of mead. And a dab of honey in it, for the sweetness. I thought my duties for the turn were over, and my wife, she is not the friendliest sort to come home to—"

It was my turn to interrupt the babbling man. "Clorente? She made it back to the Queen before the Second Prince even found her?" How could that have been so? *Unless...unless it* was orchestrated that the declaration regarding Mida and the children would be made as soon as he was sent out to find Clorente. I should have found it odd that a Prince was sent to do the work of a servant, to locate a woman in the dead of night. But I had been busy with Shrane and had not paid it much mind at the time.

"Yes, yes," the servant continued. "As I said, the Tree Woman declared that the little one is a Tree. And everyone in the Palace made a big fuss over it and decided the only way to make things right is to put the Queen—bless her in all her esteem—and the bastard children to death."

Beralt spoke a string of words with such violent astringency that I knew it was a Dwarven curse. "They will take not only the life of the Queen, but her children as well? Even the little babes will not be spared the cruelty of the Laws?"

The servant nodded. "The King cannot be soft on this matter, I am sure. Infidelity, Sir Dwarf. It must be addressed." And the servant smacked his hands together to make his point. "Royal Law is not faint in its meting of justice. That's also what they told me to tell the Prince. And I did tell him. And he did not take it well." The servant flinched at the sound of something smashing against the marble floor not a length behind us. "He said he would go to the Queen at once and speak to his father, who is the High King, as you know—"

"We know how the Monarchy works, heaven curse you, just tell us the rest! Skip only to the parts that matter."

"Well, the King has made his choice. He put up his own personal Wonder on the doors and windows to the Fourth Queen's chambers, and no one—not even the Second Prince—can break through it. And so, the Prince, not liking this at all, put up a fuss, as he is doing now."

A 'fuss', the servant said. Most of the entrance hall had been completely wrecked. It was a bit more than a fuss. *I can get to him. I can help him to calm down.* Of course, then everyone present would see me do it. They would be witnesses to my affection for him. They would at least see that I preferred him. For it could not be a coincidence that I had saved him from the raspberry wine and that I had the ability to steady his storm and bring him back to the shore.

"We must find the King," Beralt said, his sharp brown eyes darting around in search of the Royals. He released the servant, who took back up his present occupation of fleeing the premises. "We must find Harrod at once, Miss Tree."

I did not understand why the first thing we should do would be to locate the father of the one who clearly needed our help the most. *I should help Willen. He needs me.*

I stepped toward the Second Prince, whose back was still to me and a great distance away, but Beralt clutched my arm and held firm. "If the Second Prince makes a mistake—even a slight misdirection—and all that Wonder he has brewing right now moves in the direction of King Harrod, the Ancient Laws will turn it back on him, and it will be a dead Prince you are so persuaded to help." Beralt pointed. "I will go right, and you go to the left, Aia. Find the King and bid him not to intervene. Beg him to stay back, if that's what it takes. At all costs—at any cost—we will protect Willen, even if from himself."

And so, I was assigned a role as the savior of the Second Prince yet again. I ducked as a bit of glass clashed with the wall and shattered right where my head ought to have been. I sucked in a bit more air to strengthen my resolve and did what Beralt asked. To the left, I ran in search of the High King, though I secretly hoped the Dwarf would stumble upon him first.

But no, of course, it was I, the misplaced Tree, who found the King up the stairs and to the left. His servants and guards attempted to stand between him and the explosive Wonder on the ground level of the Palace, but clearly the great man had a mind to go down and confront his distressed son. The floor beneath my feet trembled as the waves of Willen's energy shook the columns upholding the balcony.

"High King!" I was forced to call out, for the guards impeding the way to the Royal tossed me aside like I was naught but a wilted flower. But the King did not hear my feeble cry nor turn his attention to me. Instead, he did his best to encroach on the disaster he'd once lovingly named Willen.

Do not let him die, Aia. Do something. Do something. But what could I do against armed guards on highest alert and the most valiant King—though the only one—I had ever met? I could only do, I supposed, what a Tree would do. And so I imagined I was singing to a little weed or humming to berries or whispering to clovers, and the light that came to my palms I assumed was my Wonder. I hoped somehow it could get me through the armed guards and to the King. I closed my eyes...and tried.

And then when I opened my eyes again, the sight before me held a dozen and more surprises. Such a thing I could not have imagined, even if it were read to me from the pages of a storybook.

The guards had slumped over, much as though *they* were the wilted flowers, their arms and torsos limp and their waists bent. Muffled grunts escaped their drooping lips, but they could not right themselves. They could only stare down at their own shoes while I tried to remember how exactly breathing worked.

His eyes wide, the High King turned to me. "How—?"

Oh, but I could not think of what I was commissioned to say to him. I could hardly even remember what Beralt had explained to me at the entryway after he pummeled that servant. All the thoughts left my head in one flush, and all I could think was that I would very much like to crawl into a cellar and never come out again.

"Why have you *dismantled* my guard, Tree?" The King's voice chilled me, and I had the very real sense that I was in very real danger at that particular moment. "What is it you *want*?"

"I...." I found I could neither inhale or exhale. "I do not want you to hurt him."

"Are you telling me how to care for my own son? You are a *child*. You know nothing of parental responsibility nor my Monarchical oversight of the High King over the Second Prince of the Realm. Leave *now*, or I will make certain you do."

Could a misunderstanding be more terribly germinated between us? "No, no. I do not mean disrespect, King. It is only...Beralt—"

"Beralt? Beralt the Dwarf? He is not even human. And hardly fit to be my son's nanny, much less his advisor."

I swallowed, shivering from the glimpse of darkness I discovered in the King's eyes. "If you were to step in the path of Willen's Wonder, it could destroy him."

The King narrowed his gaze, his voice black as ice. "*What did you just call him?*"

If I could have reversed time, perhaps I would have in that moment. For I did not know what else to say or do except to wish that I had not used the name of the Second Prince as if we were familiar. As if we close. As if he were mine.

The King seemed to have forgotten that he sought to engage with his son and stepped toward me. In one instant, I was on a balcony overlooking Willen, and in the next I was in a bare room, alone. Well, alone, except I was joined by the High King Of All The Realm.

All at once, Harrod slammed his Wonder forward, and I was pinned to the wall. A gasp escaped me, followed by the groan of my rib cage against the pressure of his will.

"How do you know my son?" he roared.

I shook my head, for it was all I could manage to do.

The King then stepped forward until he could pin me to the wall himself, with a strong hand around my throat. I knew for certain he would crush me and my breath would be no more, for he squeezed until my eyes nearly burst.

"Tell me the truth," he said, his face close enough for me to feel the wind of his words on my nose. "How dare you call him by such an intimate name? What power do you have over him? What influence?"

None! I had no power or influence over the Second Prince. I had been, in all the events of my life thus far, completely and irrevocably helpless.

"Please," I squeezed out of my mouth. "Please."

But the King slammed my head against the wall once, twice, until I whimpered, much like Shrane beneath the body of her passionate lover.

"Who taught you, Tree? Who taught you this Wonder you command? Confess to me, and I will let you die quickly."

I clawed at his hand, but his strength was undeniable, as if fortified by his own brand of Wonder, one that I could not begin to alter.

"I know...nothing. No one."

"A Tree of your beauty and power simply...ended up this way? An ordinary girl from the Neighboring Lands wielding direct Wonder from the Ancient Arboreals?"

"I am..." and I could feel the light fading from my vision, "...ordinary."

"Ordinary, is it? Just like the woman I married? A simple noblewoman with loyalty to my family and to my crown? Who, in her very ordinary fashion, thought it permissible to open her thighs to another man, to have him put children into her womb? Ordinary children and not at all Royal? One with no Wonder and the other with the faintest traces of Arboreal blood. And good news on that account, or I would have accepted those ordinary lumps of refuse as my own children, as my own body. But now I see my wife is...ordinary." He squeezed even tighter until I felt blood trickle from my nose down my lips, until I felt it forced from the corners of my eyes. "I had one once. A woman who was nothing close to ordinary. A Queen in more ways than one. But she was a curse. A curse to me. For now, every turn I am forced to put myself into these women who reek of putrid mediocrity. Every turn, I am forced to devote my attention to their crusty-eyed, freckle-faced offspring and pretend they are anything worth loving.

"But love is dead. Even when it is yours, it's dead. And all the while you are within its embrace, it is killing you right along with it."

The King released me then, and I fell to my knees and gasped and coughed and let the tears flow from my shut eyes. At the feet of such a man, I knew it was hopeless. I could not convince him that I was no one. He had already made up his mind that I was important enough to taste his wrath.

"You are no ordinary Tree. And you will be kept at a distance from the others and from both my sons until your fate has been decided," the King said. "If it is you who holds the ability to give my eldest a Seed—if it is you who proves to be the True Tree—you will do what you are told. Willingly. Do you understand? For if I believe you do not understand the words I am saying and your role in this Royal story, I will kill you now."

I nodded my head, my hand trying to reshape my neck, which I was sure had been crushed beyond proper usefulness. The King bent only to take a handful of my hair, pulling me to my feet and bringing his lips close to my ear. "There is nothing—nothing—I will not do to ensure Willen is safe. For he is all I have left of her. He is all I have left of anything worth having. Mind my words. If I must choose him over the Realm, I will. Never shall I make the mistake of letting another loved one die before my eyes."

Never? But he would allow his fourth wife, Queen Mida, to die. And he allowed his third wife as well. And his first. Was it only the second—Willen's mother—to whom the King's heart belonged? Did Theor not matter? Or his third daughter? Or the ones issuing from the womb of his wife at that very moment?

My hair still tight in his unrelenting fist, the King took me to the wall and shoved my face against it. He pushed without relief until I felt the bones beneath my eye give way. I cried out, attempting to free myself from his grip, but he did not release me, nor did he seem to mind causing me such pain.

A cold, frightening emptiness came over me. Perhaps it was fear. Perhaps it was despair. For I knew as my skull began to crack and wince that there was no one who would come for me. No Willen to put his hand on my shoulder and tell me to stay hidden while he did the rest. No Queen to pull the venom from my soul and leave me to mend. No Beralt to swing a sword on my behalf and chase away the tormentor descending from above me. Not even Clorente, to tap her cane and take me to a different nightmare altogether. It was only me and the King and the twisting of the truth, so much like the twisting of my bones.

"The next time you see the sun, Tree, you will be planted in the ground as it rises above you."

And all while he spoke these things to me, he embodied the voice of my Willen. When I could not turn to see the King—whose look was so much like his eldest—I was left only with his words. And that voice held no pity, no endearment for me.

I would have begged the High King to stop if I could have moved my jaw at all, but it was impossible for me to speak, even if I could have found the words. The courage I'd enlisted to use my Wonder to move aside the guards left me, as did my own blood. Even the hands of the King stung like ice as he wrung my arm behind my shoulders. And then, as if it were mercy, he pushed me through that wall and into the darkness. For when a girl wishes she could hide in a cellar for all of time, the cellar has a way of finding her once again.

Ep 21

Right Side of Madness

Finally buried. Beneath the glittering floors of the Palace of the Princes, cold was king. I was thankful for the darkness, if only because it kept me from seeing the suffering of those around me. I could hear them, poor souls groaning and wailing in the black cells that held them. My special place was a stone compartment, only wide enough for me to reach my arms out in front of me. I curled myself tightly, squeezing my knees to my chest for warmth and for comfort. My face throbbed, the bones bruised and most certainly broken. Each inhale and exhale exhibited a horrendous rattle, courtesy of my nearly crushed throat.

My incessant shivering threatened to rip my ribs apart, but my body was beyond its ability to remain still. There was nowhere for me to go besides the places my mind decided were safe. I imagined I was in Glenne's soft chair while she twirled about, tossing fabrics over her shoulder and prattling on about how great a designer she was—better than any of the others, in fact.

"Oh my good heavens, would you please excuse me? Pardon me." An exasperated sigh. "Oh, these are just bones I'm stepping on. Dear."

I heard the voice coming from somewhere in the dungeon and thought perhaps I had lost what few wits I'd developed during my time at the Palace, for the voice sounded as if it belonged to the person I had just been dreaming about.

Sure enough, in the dark, a knock came to the stone wall. "Aia? Lady Tree...are you in there?"

"Glenne?" Oh, how even whispering her name produced an explosion of pain in my beaten face.

"Yes, it's me. I've been looking everywhere for you! Did you hear that the Second Prince lost control of his Wonder and wrecked half the Palace? Some say he is in love with the Fourth Queen and sired her children right beneath the nose of his own father! It's difficult to believe, but he and the Queen are about the same age, you know, so one must speculate, I suppose. Anyways, all this was going on, and I was busy trying to make sure my workplace was not catapulted straight out of the Palace—can you imagine losing all those fabrics? And the *shoes*? Oh goodness, I would weep. But then I got to wondering...did they manage to spare the Trees? And did they manage to spare *my* Tree? You are mine, after all. I considered whether you were caught up in all the drama and the chaos and how you were handling it just after the milk bath and realized...I could find you nowhere at all. I searched and searched, and no Aia. Finally, a servant told me to check the holding cells. What *happened*, Aia? Why are you in here?"

"I...." I did not know, truly, what I had done to deserve being put in the holding place. "I upset the High King, I think."

"What? No, impossible. The King has always been fair and steady-handed. He's known for his nobility. He would not punish you for simply *displeasing* him. You must have done... *something*. Something more. Something *terrible*."

The tears burned my cheeks as they spilled out. "These things happen...when I am merely being myself. It seems I must not be a very good self."

"Well, I wish I could make them unhappen. You're a fine self, Aia. A fine one. Besides, who will I dress if you freeze to death in this wretched debris? That will not do.... If you're gone, I'm gone."

I sniffled, then grimaced, then shivered. "Gone?"

"If you are no longer a Lady Tree, I'm no longer your designer. I thought you knew how it worked!"

"You'll be...replaced?"

"Aia, I'll be *dead*."

I sat up, placing my hands on the stone separating Glenne and myself, trying to ignore the throbbing blue-green glow of my skin. No door or bars separated us. Only the thickest of walls. "That is *madness*."

"Ha! The whole thing is madness, from start to finish. You just have to end up on the right side of it."

"There is no right side of madness."

"Maybe so, but it seems if there's a wrong side, you've found it." Glenne hummed as she thought. "I could perhaps talk to Beralt, the Second Prince's Dwarf guardsman. He is secretly a very sensitive soul, you know. Or—I shudder—but I could speak to Clorente. She might not even know you are here. Perhaps she could get you out. You are one of her Trees after all. She will want you taken care of."

I recalled with not even the slightest fondness, Clorente's reaction to my pulling the berries from Willen, how she choked me with her cane and forced thorns into my back and shoulders, leaving me alone in the ice as I bled.

"No. No Clorente."

"Beralt, then. Though...he might be preoccupied with clearing the Second Prince's name. They will no doubt test the Royal children to see if he is the father. And if he is...."

"He is not."

Glenne paused, for my words were bold and sure and she had not expected me to be so confident in my assertion. "Oh? You know more than I do, Aia? So you have been keeping secrets from me!"

"I know nothing. It is just a feeling."

Glenne made a sound in the back of her throat as if she was concentrating on a very complicated puzzle of sorts. "Aia, why do you sound so *strange*? At first I thought your voice was being muffled by the thickness of the wall, but now...are you wearing a gag? Or...are you injured?"

I did not know what to say. *Yes. Yes, I am injured. And frightened. And alone. More than anything, I fear what Willen may do—what secrets he might betray—if he knew what has happened and where I've gone.*

"I'm...alright."

"I don't believe you, Aia. You sound pained. In fact, you sound *very* pained. But I cannot send my Wonder through this wall to help you. It is locked. No doubt with Royal Wonder. But maybe you could heal yourself? Or at least ease your discomfort." Glenne sighed. "It is very difficult, though, to heal oneself. You would have to be a Master Wonderer to do something that tricky." Glenne tapped on the wall once more. "If you can handle it, you glow up some warmth for yourself, and I will see if the Dwarf can lend his ear to my plea. I'll return, Aia. For your sake and for mine."

And though I could not see her, I was quite certain from the pattern of her footsteps that Glenne danced away. She was the only one I knew who could twirl through bones in utter darkness and not be bothered one little bit.

Glenne was right, for I had forgotten how I survived Clorente's assault in that prison of ice. I made my own heat then and I could do it again. I concentrated on my hands and let the warmth flow from the center of my body to my palms, just as Willen had taught me.

"You'll want to do that in reverse, deary."

I gasped. *Someone else is in here? But who?* I could see no other person in my cell, not even with my warming hands providing a bit more light. "Who...who's there?"

"You're a Tree, are you not?" And when I didn't answer, the voice barked, "*Are you not?*"

"Yes," I whispered. "At least, that's what I've been told." For in my heart, I still could not fathom such a ridiculously magical truth and I certainly could not apply that reality to my own.

"Only a Tree would answer that way. Uncertain. Like the world's most powerful fool. Always so confused, you Trees." The voice grumbled a string of complaints I could not decipher and then coughed and hacked before continuing on. "Trees don't make Wonder like Humans do. Humans pull it from their souls and send it out to the world. So whoever taught you that sorry little bit of Wonder must have been a Human.

A man probably, since you approached it with no elegance, no nuance. A woman would have taught you the way of beautiful Wonder, rather than simply the functional sort. No, it was a man. A Royal, in fact. Uppity. Yes, rather uppity. But you don't want to use your Wonder like him. You want to use it like you."

I leaned my tired, quivering back against the wall once more. "How? How do you mean?"

"A Tree pulls Wonder from outside of herself in. She is inspired by the world around her and then she adds her own song to the symphony, if you will. But she's got to hear the symphony first. Inhale and *then* exhale. That's the way for a Tree. Should be as natural as breathing. Did you not see all the world as beautiful when you were a child? Every Tree does. What's wrong with you?"

"I...could not see much of the world at all as a child."

"Mmm...blind were you?"

"No. I was kept inside."

"Sickly, then?"

"No."

The voice quieted. Then, a rattled intake of breath. "Ah. Torturi Arbore. Someone must have been desperate."

"What does that mean...*sir*?" He sounded like a man, but I couldn't be sure. His voice was all gravel and dust.

"It's a very old, very outdated practice. Means Torture The Tree. A cruel strategy, but it accelerates a Tree's growth while keeping her awareness of that growth at a minimum. Hasn't been used in some time. Hundreds of circles. I thought it outlawed, to tell the truth. And if the Arboreals knew...ohhh, there'd be heaven to pay, let's just say that. Also means whoever implemented Torturi Arbore kept you from the beauty around so you wouldn't *fight* them. Keep you stupid. Keep you Wonderless. Helpless. Obedient. They needed a Tree who would comply. Quickly."

"They could have just asked for help. They didn't need to torture me."

"They needed to make sure you'd say yes. Had to be *certain*. Couldn't risk you running off. Not if you're True. Not if there's no time left. If they could hold a blade to your throat and pull that seed out of you, they would have already. But they can't do it that way. You have to be willing." The voice sighed. "So tell me the whole of it. They beat you, girl?"

I swallowed. People did not usually ask so bluntly, with such a direct approach. It made me nervous, but it was also surprisingly refreshing to simply be honest. "Yes."

"They keep food from you?"

"They did. And they still do, yes."

"They keep you from seeing your own beauty?"

"How did you...know that?"

"You might have inspired yourself if you'd know you were beautiful. Can't let that come about. You might have gotten in your head that you're worth something. Might have gotten some Wonder to your heart, deary. Might have told the Ancient Arboreals on them, too."

"How...who are you?"

"What is your name?"

"Aia. Please, I would like to know yours...."

"Miracle. Miracle, miracle. Oh, they do need one of those, don't they? I can count the number of trees left in the Realm. Devastating it will be. Unless they have a miracle, of course."

"How can I hear your voice so clearly, sir?"

"You can't. It's not my voice you hear. It's my Power you feel."

Even amidst the oppression of the cold, my skin prickled. "I...don't understand."

"Confused Trees." He clicked his tongue. "Child, I have been here so long, you could not find me if you searched for the rest of your turns. I am this place. I have become nothing more than the stones against your back. Forgotten, am I."

"Forgotten by whom?"

"The Humans. The Royals. The Realm and all the lands with all their petty rulers. They do not hear me. They are not listening. They left me here. They leave me here still."

And I felt I would cry on his behalf, for his words, though heartbreaking, carried so little emotion. As if he truly were dead and I were the mere witness of his fading ghost. "Who put you here?"

"I cannot remember the name of the King. It has been too long."

"Don't fear and don't worry. I will get you out. I will. Even if it takes many turns, many circles."

The voice laughed, and the stones cracked. "Deary, you can hardly warm yourself with your clumsy Wonder. You think you can bring the dead to life? Bring joy back to fleshless bones?"

"You...you could show me how. And then I could help you."

Suddenly, the voice increased in both volume and intensity, so that I felt very small when I heard it. "Do not promise me things I do not ask for. The more you see, the more you Wonder. Open your eyes and make it your mission to see. See the world. See the people. See your lover and your love. See the trees. See the dying. Open your eyes and make your own Wonder. This is what I wish you to promise."

"Yes." My own voice hardly remained audible. "I will."

"Unless something changes, I will be the last. The last True Stone. And they do not realize what will happen when I am gone. But I will hold. For them. For them. For them. But you...you must take a different path, Tree. Your name is not Death. It is not Sadness. It is not Effort. It is *Miracle*. And that is what you must be. Will you?"

"I will try, Sir Stone. I promise to try." But I did not know what really he meant or how he could speak to me even though he no longer lived.

"Then you are very welcome."

"Welcome?"

"For my healing your broken body as you lean back against mine. And for the gift of the white snake that slithered from within my many cracks."

I brought my hands to my face with a gasp. *He's right!* There was no more pain. No more excruciation. No longer was I even shivering. *But...the snake that nearly took my life?*

"You tried to kill me?"

"Always. Always so confused. No, deary, I did not mean to take your life; only to change its *direction*. For you to meet the Queen once more, to feel the hands of your precious Prince, to hear the screams of a wilting Tree in a moonlit garden. You are welcome."

I swallowed, my mind dizzy, for all that time I thought I'd been alone. "Th-thank you."

A hush fell over the dungeon. The Stone spoke no more, and I hoped it was simply because he was tired and not because he was gone.

I closed my eyes for a moment. Wonder. Not only had the simple joys of life been kept from me, but also this...thing. This Wonder. And the knowledge of how to wield it. They hoped I would die for them without ever understanding what I truly was. A True Tree with no knowledge of herself. With no power of her own.

But not Willen. When I could not read, he taught me how to interpret letters. When I could not glow, he made me brave. When I had no power, he taught me of Wonder. And when I thought I was no one, he kissed me. He held me. He showed me pleasure and passion.

The Fourth Queen, as well, had been taught she should give her life away, just as I had been. And he could not let it be. He could not let her go to her death without knowing why she lived. This nature of his, Willen's father wished to keep hidden. To keep sequestered.

For of all the things Willen Vedan could do, the most important—the most true—was his ability to show people who they were.

And I will not leave him to struggle alone. To write notes to Trees in secret. To charm diplomats out of harrowing conflict in the shadows. I will help him. I will help Willen Vedan, as he helped me.

I was no stranger to the darkness. I was not afraid of deprivation. I could find beauty in the blistering cold and inspiration in the insidious. I got on my knees and put my palms to the rough, slick stone of the wall in front of me. *How lovely that you are a stone. How I adore the many facets of you. And the darkness...how resolute you are. When all else goes—even the light—you remain.*

And so I continued, finding beauty in the few things around me until I felt my swelling heart would burst. *There truly is nothing mundane in the world. Everything is glorious, if only we let it be so.*

My lungs filled with air, and still I pulled more in. I dreamed of the Prince and his strong hands and the way his mouth moved against my body. How lucky I was that I stumbled into *his* study on that very first night and not into the arms of Shrane's lover. How it felt to stare into the mirror for the first time and to see what Willen saw. To know myself.

And then I exhaled until, like the sun rising at the start of every turn, I lifted from my place on the ground and landed on a glittering marble floor in another room entirely. Which meant, of course, I had broken through a Royally Wondered lock. All on my own. Just a little Tree. Hopefully, Glenne would not be too disappointed to find me missing from the confines of my cell.

"Aia?" On a grand bed, seated comfortably on a mountain of silken pillows and tucked into a scarlet velvet blanket, was the Fourth Queen, her full breasts leaking down her nightgown and her cheeks streaked with unaddressed tears. "How...how in heaven did you get in here?"

I stood up and dusted my ruined, half-Wondered dress. "Apparently, Fourth Queen, I'm not as ordinary as I thought. Now...where is your coat?"

Forfeit Your Own Life

Mida scrubbed her cheeks with the delicate sleeves of her silken robe. "I...I cannot leave."

"Noble Queen, you must. I don't know how much has been disclosed to you, but they...whoever *they* are...have decided you cannot be allowed to live. And yes, perhaps you knew this would come about—"

"No, Aia. I cannot leave without *my children*. My babies were taken, and abandoning them...." Mida rose to her feet, struggling to steady herself. "I was always prepared to go. To...to die. To be esteemed above all else. But I knew in my heart that I could face this for the sake of my children. That...they would live long after I was gone. It made me brave. It made me fearless. And now...."

"They threaten the lives of your children as well."

Mida, who up until that moment was composed and collected—demure as she spoke, postured in elegance—let out a sort of wail that both terrified and enraged my heart. "How could they believe I was unfaithful? How could *Harrod* believe it? I would never endanger the life of my children. Never destroy my friendship with Willen. I would never betray him. *How?* How has this happened?"

I stepped forward and took Mida's arm, keeping her stable. Her dark skin was warm to the touch. "Mida, you are unwell."

"Because they will not let me nurse. And...I fear they have not taken a nurse to my babies at all. They have not cared for them as they should." She began to sob, leaning her head against my shoulder. "I know...I know the twins are crying for me and I cannot bear the truth of it. They should have taken my life by now. I cannot endure this."

"Then you will not be made to suffer any longer. We will find your children. And then we will leave this place."

"But"—the Queen sniffled and hiccuped—"you would leave Willen behind? I know he is in love with you. I have never seen him so enraptured."

"He will forgive me when he learns I am doing it to save you and his siblings. And I can come back for him."

"Aia." Mida shook her head, her braids swishing about her shoulders. "This room is sealed with the King's Wonder."

"I do not care whose Wonder it is. We're leaving."

Mida grabbed a gloriously woven coat and pulled it over her shoulders with trembling hands.

I took in the beauty around me. The sorrow of a woman— a mother—who had lost her only true treasures. The softness of the tears on her cheeks and the sweet milk that spilled for those she was not permitted to sustain.

And with all that beauty pulled inside me, I breathed out, Mida's hand in mine. I rushed forward and through the sealed door, praying I would not collide with the wood face-first. But I did not break my nose. Instead, the stone around the frame gave way, twisting out of shape so that the door simply fell over and we slipped through the shimmering Wonder that remained.

Exhilarated, I stopped in a chilly room—no fire raging to warm it and rather sparse light trickling in from the tall but narrow windows. Sure enough, there lay, in a pile of blankets, the Royal twins.

Mida swallowed her outcry and rushed forward, nearly tripping as she scooped the wailing infants into her arms and held them against her body.

"Do we have time?" she asked, sobbing through her words.

"Quickly, Queen."

I took one of the children and warmed my hands, pressing the bundle of arms and legs against my own breasts while Mida latched the other to hers. Kneeling, she kissed the face of the small thing. I worried that the children were too cold, but their lungs seemed strong and their wills unflinching. The one in my arms glowed a faint purple whenever her cry faded into silence. It was marvelous to see her changing skin before my very eyes.

Mida smiled through her tears. "A boy," she said with a laugh, stroking the infant she nursed. "They would not let me even see them. That is custom, of course. I did not think it would hurt so badly to have them taken. When I learned that they also would be killed"—she wept again as the child suckled and she kissed the Fourth Prince Of All The Realm.

Then she passed the boy to me and took the flailing baby from my arms, shushing it and pushing her breast into its gaping mouth.

"A girl," Mida said. "This one they say is a Tree. But how it can be so, I fear I'll never know. My family have always been nobles. We keep careful records. There have never been Arboreals in our line, Aia. I promise."

"You need make no apologies or promises to me, Fourth Queen. I do not care if the child is a Tree or a Stone or a Dwarf or a Wyvern."

Mida grinned at me. "I see why he likes you."

"Well, we can talk all about Willen after we've gotten you very far away from here. Then I will leave you and return to tell him what I've done." I helped Mida to her feet, and we wrapped the children in as many blankets as we could Wonder up. "He fought for you, Queen."

She nodded. "I knew he would. He cannot help himself, that foolish boy."

I looked to the stone walls, the ones that formed the room around us, the ones that had shifted right in time as we ran from the Queen's chambers. "Can you help us get out of the Palace?"

Mida looked about. "Who...are you speaking to?"

"A very old, very new friend," I explained. And then, I felt the slow breaths of the sleeping Prince in my arms and knew I would have all the beauty I needed to break through the King's seal once more. "Let's not hold back, Queen. Are you ready?"

Mida only blinked at me. "Ready? Ready for wh—"

The floor itself gave way, sending us plummeting down through the many levels of the Palace until we landed in the servants' quarters. The rough stone walls crumbled, leaving a rubble-filled path to the bright sunlight.

Servants scrambled to bow before the Queen, but we wasted no time. Instead, we took to running, aiming our sights at the edge of the forest.

"Send the Wonder to your feet," Mida said. "It will make you faster."

I inhaled the beauty of the gold-speckled clouds and bid my feet to fly, keeping pace with the Queen as we met the edge of the forest.

"They will send guardsmen after us, Aia." Sweat poured from Mida's face, but she did not slow her pace. "They will aim to kill us, I am sure."

I ducked beneath the boughs of the trees and skipped over the bumped roots underfoot. "Then we will have to hide."

"It is not too late, Aia," Mida said, gasping for breath as we kept on. "You can turn back. Save yourself. I do believe you have esteemed me highly enough."

"I'll not leave you. I've already decided."

And so, we darted our way through the bold woods, stopping only when Mida could no longer take another step.

"You have gone too far," I told her, taking the baby from her arms.

Her body shuddered, soaked in sweat and, I noticed with a gasp, blood pooled down her bare feet.

"Mida—"

"A rest is all I need. A rest." She lowered herself down at the base of a tree and fed both her children before leaning her head against the gray bark. "They will find us. Unless you can make us...a hiding place." Her words were accompanied by long pauses and heavy breathing, despite her reclined position.

"I will figure something out, Mida," I told her. "And I will take the children so you can rest well. They need you to be at your best."

"Where—where will you take them to? I...do not want them to be far from me."

To ease her worry, I made slings out of the blankets and hung them from the tree branches, nestling the sleeping babies safely within so the gentle breeze might swing and soothe them. She smiled as her eyes fluttered closed.

I had no idea how to keep us from being found out by the guardsmen, so I sat down and wept a bit myself. I cried because the High King had broken my bones and I did not know how I could bear telling Willen the truth of what he'd done to me. And I cried because the King had indeed seen the truth, for I was stronger than I knew and not at all ordinary.

But what would I do with my extraordinary self? Who was I meant to become? I could not know. I only knew that I had taken a High Royal and two Royal infants destined for death and run away with them. I only knew...nothing.

It was then I noticed that the trees themselves were not only swaying in the breeze, but creaking and groaning, their leaves shaking and then their boughs twisting and reaching until we were enclosed among the blessed bark of a grove.

With the trees as our fortress, I took the time to close my eyes. I drifted to sleep dreaming of how I would need to take the Queen very far away so she could not be recognized by those of the Realm. A new place, a new name, a new life. And she would need food and a house. So would the children. But above all, we would need Willen.

I awoke in the dead of night to the shouts of men just outside our grove. The noise stirred the sleeping children, and Mida had already risen to retrieve them from their slings.

"Guards," she whispered. "They are here."

I took the little Tree and rocked her to keep her from fussing. After a few moments, the men moved on, and we sat back down near each other.

"Do you think Willen is alright?" I asked Mida, our elbows pressed together. "He defied his father's wishes. And the King... the people think he is filled with kindness...."

"Harrod is kind, but just. And he simply cannot tolerate threats to those he loves. And above any living thing, he loves Willen."

I was not sure that the King's hand crushing my throat was my idea of justice. But it made no sense to argue with Mida about him. "Their bond...it is so strong because of Willen's mother? His Second Queen?"

Mida sighed. "Fara came first. His Woman of the Woods. A runaway Royal from another land. From Tseslar. He found her and loved her but could not bring himself to marry her. Could not make her his Queen, for by doing so, he would lose her. And, of course, the King is permitted to have his lovers. So he married a Queen, hoping no one would find out about Fara. Hoping the Council would be pleased. Satisfied with an heir. And it could have gone on that way, him with Queens and his secret woman. Until...."

"Until Fara bore him a child...."

"Willen's birth meant that the King *had* to marry her. It's Royal Law. And so he hid Willen for as long as he could. But once they were found out, it was over. Fara became his Second Queen and Willen his Second Prince. And let me tell you...he adores Willen. Divinely. Perhaps more than he should. So trust me, the Prince will be unharmed. Harrod will make sure of it."

"And us?"

"Us? We are trying to escape Law, Aia. It will not go for us as it will for our Willen Vedan. But for the sake of the children, we must try. We must do something to save the purely innocent. If it were not for the Arboreal blood in my baby Tree, all would have gone as planned. I would have died. And the twins would have lived long, happy lives as High Royals. They might not have been doted upon as Willen is, but they would have been safe and happy."

I let Mida lean her head on my shoulder. "You love Willen too, don't you? You have known him such a long time."

"Oh, I do love Willen. Very much, in fact. I cannot deny this. But our love is not as the nobles all seem to suggest. The Second Prince, he is like a brother to me. A dear, unwavering friend but also someone I would like to roll up in a thick carpet and toss down a steep hill. We argue, he and I, about my role and my destiny. But I have only ever lain with Harrod, Aia. No one will believe me, I see, but I swear it. No man has ever entered me save the High King Of All The Realm." She found and squeezed my hand in the dark. "I wish I could repay you for saving the lives of my children. Your actions were beyond noble. Reckless, even, but I am so grateful for your courage. They both would have died in that stony room if you had not intervened."

"I already owe you my life. Don't you remember? For ridding me of the white snake's poison. And even if I did not owe you, I would have done the same." I did not explain to the Queen that the snake meant me no real harm. It was too complicated to unravel, and the whole thing seemed hardly believable.

"And this, my friend, is why he is so in love with you. You have an unfettered spirit. You both would sacrifice everything to help another."

We fell asleep once again, and when I awoke, the Fourth Queen no longer held my hand. She was gone, nothing but a flower left where she once sat. The twins, too, were nowhere to be found.

"Mida?" *Perhaps she left the grove to find some water or berries for food.* "Mida, where have you gone?"

I lifted the scarlet flower and, to my shock, the petals shivered and released a sound. It was the voice of the Queen. "Aia, my brave Tree and noble friend. I owe you my thanks and my love. If you receive this message, it means I have done what is right. My children, I have sent away. I will not tell you where or with whom to keep from you the burden of carrying the secret. They are safe. They will be happy. And as for me...I will do what I was always meant to do. Please, do not save me. Do not try to stop me. I know my role. And when the time comes, I hope you will know yours. In love. Mida. Oh, and tell Willen...I'm sorry."

I begged the trees to part for me. And with all my strength and Wonder, I ran. I knew I would not find her children. They would be lost to me, I was sure. But I could stop Mida. I could still save her. I tore through the brush and the fallen leaves and even past guardsmen who could hardly gurgle responses before I'd left them behind me. I only stopped when I cleared the forest and found Willen on horseback, racing toward me in much the same fashion I raced toward him.

He leaped from the back of his steed and threw his arms around me, his words choking in his throat. "Aia, you mad Tree, I looked everywhere for you."

"I'm sorry," I told him, my body tight against his embrace. "I'm sorry. I feared there was no time to tell you of my plans."

"You took the children and fled? Aia, you could have been killed at any point!"

"Willen, no." I pulled away from him so I could see his eyes. The blue of them had gone dark gray. "I took the Queen as well and planned to return for you. But she's hidden the children. I know not where. And returned for her own death. Willen, I could not stop her."

He turned, his anger forcing its way out until he cried aloud in one burst. "Why is it branded in her mind so? Why?"

"We could stop her. We have time."

"Aia, I will not endanger your life for someone who insists on throwing hers away. It cannot be so. You tried. I tried. She wants to die, and we cannot stop her. Your life is too valuable to risk it again on vain attempts."

"But, Willen—"

"Do not," he said, holding my face with both his hands, begging me with his eyes, "do not say you are destined to die anyways. Your life is not forfeit, Aia. It is precious. It is precious to me."

"But...I will be punished for what I've done. I must be punished. And I fear...the consequences will be too great for me—"

"You've suffered enough. Already, you've paid in your innocence for more than you will pay for your crimes."

"Your father—"

"If my father wants me to continue living, he will not punish you for this."

I struck my fist into his chest. "Do not say that! Never say that!"

"My life is the most treasured thing the King owns. I have nothing else with which to gamble, Aia."

"You will never—never—forfeit your own life, Willen Vedan."

He set his jaw, a solitary vein bulging as it ran along his perfect neck. "If you go, I go." He tucked loose strands of my hair behind my ears so he could see me all the clearer. "If I must barter for your life with my own, I will. For what have I left outside of you?"

"This is madness. You must see...all this is madness."

"Let it be madness, then, my love. You and I? We shall stand on the right side of it."

Willen put his mouth to mine and kissed me with such vehemence that I thought my spine might bend in two. Then, he lifted me onto his horse, and we rode back to the Palace I had tried so hard to escape.

In some corner of my mind, I knew that I could have escaped it all. Could have run through that forest and used the trees as protection. I could have kept going until I knew not where I was, lost to the Royals and with no need to stop for food or water. But I could not separate my living from my very life. The one whose chest I leaned against as we rode back to his home. I knew then that the Realm was doomed. For I would choose Willen Vedan over every tree in every land. Every time.

Ep 23

A Horrific Silence Ensued

Willen dismounted his horse and lifted me from the saddle, the pressure of his hands on my waist as he lowered me to the ground.

"Remind me to tell you later how beautiful you are when you blush," he said in a hurry. And then he took my hand in his. "We should make haste. Perhaps...I could talk sense into my father. Or maybe the Council will listen this time around."

They would not. Willen had tried everything, including bringing the very walls of the Palace hall down around him. The High King had not unlocked the seal on Mida's room then and he would not spare her life now.

But still, we ran up the stairs, my hand tight in his and the steps rolling like a ream of Glenne's fabric beneath our feet.

Beralt met us at the top of the stairs and stood with his legs apart and his hands out. "Second Prince, stop."

"Beralt—"

And Beralt raised his voice, his cheeks flaming with red hot passion. "You love, Willen, but it is a reckless sort of love. You will not free your friend; you will only endanger the few you have left. Because if you go up against your father, I will be at your side. No matter the cost. And this beautiful creature whose hand you hold...she will be with you as well, Willen. We are with you. But you hold the power here. And you must think of us. Think of all you risk. Think."

Willen swallowed, running his free hand through his bedraggled hair. "Beralt...how can I let her die? Without *trying*?"

"You *have* tried. But she has chosen. Respect her wishes. If she is truly your friend, respect her."

"But it's the stupidest thing I have ever heard!" And his words were choked in his throat.

Beralt sighed, lowering his arms. "Focus on problems you can solve. Who put a white snake in our Lady's tub? And how will she evade questioning regarding the whereabouts of the Royal infants?"

"I don't know where the children are," I explained to both Willen and Beralt. "And the snake...it was a friend who placed it there. To help me."

Willen turned to me, narrowing his eyes. "A friend? A friend does not force you to tempt death, Aia. What sort of friend? Who?"

I bit my lip, trying to find the words to express what had happened in the dungeon without letting my love know how I had ended up there in the first place. The last thing he needed was to know his father had tormented me and locked me away.

"A Stone. A True Stone."

Beralt made a noise I'd never heard another living thing make. A gurgle mixed with a harsh gasp, his eyes so wide I feared they might tear out of his head.

"You saw...a True Stone, Miss Tree?" His whisper was barely audible.

I nodded my head, very glad to still be holding Willen's hand. "Heard it, I suppose is more accurate. It helped me save the Queen."

Beralt fell to one knee. "You are a True Tree indeed if a Stone has come to you. They are most precious to my kind. Most precious."

"Beralt...please stand up. What are you thinking?" I asked, hoisting the Dwarf to his feet. "You are bowing to me because I heard dungeon walls speak?"

"Dungeon walls? Why would you have heard *dungeon* walls?" Willen asked. "Aia—"

"Beralt is right. We should focus on what comes next," I said, hopefully not with too much haste.

"They will make the Queen's death as immediate as possible. Willen, we should prepare. If they interrogate our Tree here, they may do so after the ceremony."

"That is when I will face my punishment as well, I suppose. My defiance of his rules will not be ignored."

"Your father—"

Willen interrupted the Dwarf. "My father will punish me for what I did. He will make sure he does. His fondness for me will make him appear weak, and that is the last thing he needs right now. Instead, he needs to be threatening, imposing, dominating. We are at the brink of war, and I'm not a child to be spared."

Beralt grunted. "You will...incur your own punishment? Second Prince...."

"I am not asking your advice on the matter, Beralt. My punishment will come. Without fail. It's the way of Kings."

Suddenly, it seemed Willen realized he had taken my hand in his again and that it was not something we were permitted to do in public—or in private for that matter—and he released me. "I will do everything in my power to make sure you are spared, Honorable Tree. I...I should not have pulled you onto my horse the way I did or kissed you out in the open as I did or...I should not lose my mind as I do whenever you are near." He faced the Palace once more. "Beralt you are right about one thing. I am reckless when it comes to love. I have endangered you all. My friend, please see that the Lady is reunited with the other Trees as I...prepare."

I said nothing as Willen took to the stairs. And once he had disappeared inside the Palace, I slowly climbed beside the Dwarf. "Why does he never make up his mind, Beralt, regarding whether to want me or not?"

"Because, Miss, the Vedan men destroy the things they desire."

"Does this happen...always? And to what end?"

"For as long as I have known the Monarchs. And I have known them and served them loyally for quite some time. For many, many, many circles. Harrod destroyed Fara. And see now how he destroys his relationship with his most beloved son. Theor wants his father to be proud of him—"

"That is not going well for the High Prince."

"No. It is not. And Willen...."

"Wants justice?"

"Willen wants you."

"Then it should be easy. For I am already destroyed, am I not? It's my destiny." I stood atop the final step. "Perhaps the Vedan men desire that which is destined for destruction and not the other way around."

Beralt tilted his head at me. "You are wise as usual, beneath the glowing skin and the quiet tone." He held a finger up to me. "I would not speak of the Holy Stone you met, Miss Tree. Not to anyone and certainly not to that tainted-Wonder wielder, Clorente."

"Thank you, Beralt. I am very glad I met you." I stooped and planted a kiss on his bristly forehead.

He blushed crimson. "You treat me too nicely, Lady. One of your stature need not be kind to Dwarves."

"Why ever not?"

Beralt chuckled. "That's the same thing Willen said to me when I protested his choice to have me at his side." He cleared his throat, and we proceeded to my room in silence. "I would be honored to stand by your side at the Ceremony Of The Queen, Miss Tree. If you'll not mind it."

"If it's possible, I would love that."

And I stepped into my room, closed the door—as well as my eyes—and braced myself for the tap of a cane.

I was sure I heard it reverberate beneath my feet, but when I opened my eyes, I stared into Glenne's beaming face.

"Hello, beautiful. I see I saved you just as I'd hoped. That scary woman has been waiting for you in your room for some time, but I'm quite the clever designer. I set a Wonder trap for you just inside your door. See, usually a Wonderful person like her would smell that a hundred lengths away, but I used designer Wonder so she wouldn't think anything was out of the ordinary. And look! It worked! I caught you before she could sink her claws into you, Aia."

With a snap of her fingers, Glenne Wondered up a chair and pushed me down into it. "You look exhausted. I'll have to admit,

I was rather terrified when I returned to that dungeon with the Dwarf and found you'd gone. But then I heard you'd defied the King, broken his seal, and run off with your lover, the Fourth Queen, and your bastard babies."

I blinked. Either Glenne spoke quicker than usual or I was more tired than I knew. "How would we have...made children...?"

"It's just a story, Aia. It's not supposed to make sense."

"I didn't...we didn't...."

"Don't mind that. Just know that you and I will probably be dead soon." She sighed, frowning as if some imagination of hers had come between her words and her expression of them. She snapped out of it with another sigh. "Yes, as I was saying, we're doomed, the two of us. And so you might as well go to the Ceremony Of The Queen looking like yourself, should you not?"

"You're...going to design me? Now?"

"Of course I am!" She gestured to the dress I'd Wondered the night I tried to save Shrane. "No offense, but you should be offended by this outfit, Aia."

"I...did my best."

"Oh dear. That is sad." Glenne opened her hand, and a pile of fine, gold glitter cascaded into her palm. She wound her arm back and tossed it directly into my face.

I coughed, I gagged, I choked. It entered my eyes, my nose, my mouth. "Are you insane, Glenne?"

The designer giggled. "A bit."

"At least warn me next time!"

"Then you wouldn't have inhaled nearly enough of it. Trust my methods, Aia. I am a genius, you know. The best designer.

The others will say they are the best, but I am actually—
literally—the very best."

I fought back a gush of tears. "Thank you for everything
you've done for me, Glenne—"

"No, no. No death's sweet goodbyes for us yet. First, you have
to glide into that Ceremony like you know you're the one who
broke the King's seal. Think you can manage that?"

"I did not do it with the intention of being rebellious. Nor
did I do it so people would admire me."

"No, perhaps not. But you *were* rebellious. And people *do*
admire you. So you will look the part. That is my contribution,
my friend." Glenne paused, her hand to her chin, and then her
eyes clouded with tears. "I truly could not have designed a
kinder Tree myself—"

"No. No 'death's sweet goodbyes', Glenne." I sat up in my
chair. "You must do something with my hair. I slept in twigs
and leaves last night, and the forest orphan look won't do,
will it?"

"Forest orphan? Ha!" Glenne grinned, hopping up and down
and clapping her hands with a squeal. "It won't do at all! But I
know what will!"

Glenne turned my chair into a bed and had me lie back.
A bath somehow occurred in this process—and one with no
white snakes involved, thank heaven—and then she lifted a
rather thin blade.

"Aia, darling, I have an idea. But it will require a level of
endurance from you as it will be the most painful design I've
attempted yet. Are you able?"

"Seems you have indeed been assigned the right Tree, Glenne.
I am quite friendly with pain at this point in my life. Go on."

But I did not expect so much of it. With slow and careful precision, Glenne seemed to be carving the blade into the skin of my hip, my abdomen, my neck, and then up to my face, slicing at the delicate area underneath my right eye. She stopped to dab at the issuing droplets of blood but otherwise kept quiet as she worked. When finally she was finished, she administered heavy doses of more and more fine glitters so that I was quite literally buried in shimmering dust.

While I lay beneath the pile, Glenne wove my hair and dressed my feet. She even addressed the state of my fingernails.

Then, she lifted me up and the dust flitted away like a thousand tiny butterflies.

"Beautiful, if I may say so. And fitting for a Ceremony Of The Queen."

"Glenne...may I see it?"

Glenne slapped her knees. "It's not usually allowed, Aia, but why not? We've quite broken all the rules by now. What difference would it make?"

She waved her hand in front of me so that one of those reflective surfaces, like the one Willen had brought to his study, appeared before her. "You are quite good at pulling objects out of nothing, Glenne."

"Designer Wonder. We are skilled at storing and retrieving the tools we need. I am nothing more than a squirrel with scissors."

I looked at myself. And I could not look away. Glenne had carved into my skin the very patterns of leaves. But not only green. Also fiery red, burnt orange, deep yellow. The intricate networks of veins stretched over my stomach and all the way to my face, curling around my eye. Where she had sliced, in every slender crevice, remained a haze of shifting glitter and dust so that when I moved, I shone like I had emerged from a light rain. The veins flowed seamlessly from my skin into the fabric of the gown, the train cascading out behind me.

"In some seasons, the leaves change color, from green to gold and red. Just so, everything is changing, Aia. Because of you and what you did."

My hair was woven into a golden crown. And the closer I looked at my face, the more I realized that my eyes shimmered just like the dress.

"I look...strong."

"Mmhmm...and?"

"And...good."

Glenne grinned from over my shoulder, winking at me in the mirror. "You look like yourself. They won't know what to do with you, Lady Tree."

And then she wrapped her arms around me. "It's not the last hug," she assured me. "I just...wish you the best at the Ceremony. That's all."

"You don't need to wish me the best, Glenne. You made me the best."

"Now, go on. And don't let that old lady push you around."

I was beneath an enclave, keeping pace beside Shrane and Gretaline. Clorente led the way, but by the time she noticed I had joined them, we were already beneath the public eye. Nobles and commoners and everyone in between seemed to have gathered in the outdoor arena.

Displayed in circles between the stone seats and the magnificent platform in the center of the circle were many of statues of beautiful women, all with their arms outstretched and their heads lifted to the sky.

"Those must be the Queens," Shrane muttered to herself. "All the ones who were esteemed over many circles...."

As soon as the noise and bustle of the crowd was loud enough to distract Clorente, Gretaline fell back and hooked her arm in mine. "Where have you been?" she hissed in my ear. "What did you do?"

"What have you heard?" I asked her. It made little sense to implicate myself, especially if the stories circulating were as wild and irrational as the one Glenne had mentioned earlier.

"I heard you ran away with a guard who was meant to be keeping watch over the Royal Infants, and now they have been kidnapped and you have been tainted."

"Wait...tainted?"

"Yes. A man has ruined you. Tainted. Soiled."

"Why would running away with a man ruin a woman?"

"You truly know nothing, Aia, honestly. A woman must keep her legs closed. She must not let a man or his member near her. Or else she will be tainted."

"Well...what happens then?"

"If you're tainted? Why...then you are tainted."

"But...why? What does it do to you? Do you shrivel and die? Does your body ache? Is that what happens to girls who are sold to men for their pleasure?" I'd thought, back when Clorente had first come for me dressed as an old man, that perhaps that would have been my fate.

"Well, those unfortunate girls are ruined automatically and forever, sorry to say. But not in the way you are thinking. It's a societal posture, not a physical ailment. Although a human woman could bear a child. Then she'd *really* be ruined."

"I thought children were a *good* thing to have. As long as the couple are loyal to one another."

Gretaline sighed. "There are rules. The couple must be married."

I remembered how ferociously Aman had wanted a wife. Did the King have the same enthusiasm for collecting his brides? "But the King wasn't married to Fara—"

"He should have been. But he's the King." She shrugged. "He's allowed his women."

"Why does everyone keep saying that about Kings?"

"Because that's how it is. Now"—Gretaline tugged hard on my arm—"tell me what happened."

Thank heavens. We were interrupted as a herald appeared on the platform and began to dictate the events about to unfold. We all took our places, the Trees standing just in front of the nobles' seating area, commoners in the back behind a sturdy railing. I did not wish to be so close to the platform, but so it had to be. *There are rules.*

"And now, silence be upon you for the entrance of the Royal family."

When the herald beckoned us to complete silence, we could all hear—and quite awkwardly so—the clattering of some objects and the shouting of two men from behind the closed door to which he'd gestured. Finally, the door flew open, colliding with the wall, and the Second Prince marched out and took his place facing the crowd, his fists clenched at his side. He was the most beautiful thing I had ever seen. All torment and caution, rage and reverence. It was not long before his blue and gray eyes found mine and held.

Next came out a younger girl, not yet a woman, who I had never seen before. She was carried out by a servant and placed in a chair that had been prepared for her.

Gretaline leaned in. "She cannot walk, poor thing. No use of her legs."

The girl, all red hair and with a sharp, upturned nose, looked to be just as furious as her older brother.

"And of course, the beautiful High Prince is not here. He is off claiming victory over our allies, or at least so I heard."

I wondered why Gretaline thought it important to keep updating me so, especially when Shrane could not manage to look in my direction without her lips curling in a snarl.

Finally, the High King appeared. He was regal as ever, his long scarlet cape flowing behind him. His crown still a sliver of gold twisted across his brow. The crowd bowed when he stood before them, and so did I.

And then, the herald raised his voice once more. "And now, to be esteemed most highly, as countless Queens before her, the Fourth Queen of our Blessed Realm. Mida Vedan."

The crowd cheered and yelped and whistled as Mida was brought onto the platform. She was not in chains. Indeed, no form of bondage impeded her. She walked with elegant grandeur, as if her steps were made of diamonds. She wore a white gown, the train of which was so endless that it spilled over the long platform and seemed to go on and on, like the clouds in the sky.

The white shone against her dark skin as she took center stage, and without the herald directing them, the entire crowd fell silent.

"My people," Mida spoke out. "It is I, your Fourth Queen. And I give to you my parting words. They will be heeded so I am esteemed in all ways. Listen closely." Mida seemed so much older than she had before. Like a Queen and not like a woman or a girl. If her breasts leaked milk beneath her pillowy bodice, it did not show. "I raise my voice to you in an effort to bring forth the truth. I, your Queen, have not been esteemed highly."

The crowd gasped. I turned to see people rise to their feet. "Who has not esteemed the Queen?" they cried. "Tell us! Tell us!"

The Queen lifted a hand to silence them. "My esteem has been degraded by none other than my beloved husband, the High King Of All The Realm."

At this the people did not cry out. A horrific silence ensued. They did not want to diminish their King, but they had to listen to Mida, lest they also be guilty of breaking both Ancient and Royal Law.

"Despite what the King and the Council believed about me and my children, I was not treated with wholeness and kindness as they deliberated. For even if I were to have failed my King, I should have been esteemed. And I say now, aloud, that I have not failed him. So the lack of my esteem is doubled."

Mida did not move one step as she spoke. It was as if she were already a statue, like the women who came before her, who held her crown and a place in the bed of a High Monarch.

"But the King must not be punished for breaking the Law. And indeed he has not been thus far. Because of one Tree. One Tree who acted not only to spare me from indignity but who acted to spare the King from the consequences of breaking the Law. Her quick and courageous feat meant that my esteem was restored. The Tree who freed me, who buried my dead children in the forest out of kindness, has saved the Vedan family yet again. First the Second Prince, and now the High King. If I am to be esteemed"—and then Mida looked to me—"this Tree is to be honored."

All eyes turned to me for a moment. I was incomparably grateful to Glenne for taking the time and the risk to make sure I looked like I should. For in that moment, with the judgment of the Realm streaming onto me, I needed to feel as strong as I looked.

Mida stepped forward and stretched out her arms, and no one cared about me anymore. All attention was the Queen's. She tilted her face up to the midturn sun, and it bathed her long, thin braids and gleamed off her obsidian skin. She was, in every way, the epitome of beauty and grace.

I saw, out of the corner of my eye, King Harrod reach out and hold tight to Willen's arm. The veins in Willen's neck were near to bursting, but he kept his mouth clamped shut. I wanted to move, to speak out, to fight.

"Keep your feet on the ground and your heart steady," I heard. It was that gravelly voice. The Stone speaking out through the pillars of the arena, though no one else seemed to hear it but me.

Heeding Forgotten, I did nothing. Willen Vedan, also, did nothing. We did nothing as, out of nowhere and seemingly for no reason, an archer sent an arrow flying through the air and into the heart of the Queen. Red blood soaked through her white dress, unfurling like the petals of a rose in fresh snow.

She fell in one swoop, her train providing a soft landing for her weakened body. And after a few moments, with the sun still looking on from above, The Fourth Queen Of All The Realm was esteemed right to death.

Orchestrating My Own Demise

The fallen Queen lay still. Strange, for the wind, it blew, and the sun, it slid down the sky. People still murmured and steps still resounded as the crowd dispersed. But Mida would never move again.

All around me, nobles and commoners alike whispered and pointed and stared. The Queen's words had not met deaf ears, it seemed. I was to be thanked for esteeming her when others would not. Thus, I had not only saved myself but everyone in the Realm from breaking Ancient Law. It made me a heroine of sorts, but not one to be admired. One to be watched with careful eyes. Suspicious and untrusted.

Clorente gripped the end of her cane. "You have made a fool of all Trees," she said loud enough for me to hear her. "The trust of the people has turned from us."

"I didn't mean to—"

"But you did, foolish girl. A selfish move, to procure sanctuary for yourself while turning the eye of suspicion on your sisters."

"The Queen needed help," I argued."You heard what she said. If I had not helped her, suspicion would have been the last of our troubles."

"You think—"

"I think you owe me your thanks, Clorente, not your admonition."

Gretaline groaned. "None of this matters. We are supposed to be finding a match for the High Prince, not embroiling ourselves in Realm politics and the fineties of Ancient Law." She threw up her arms. "*Where is Theor*? When is he returning, and who will he choose to be his True Tree?"

"Very well," Clorente said with a nod. "We must focus on preparing ourselves for the High Prince's return. One of you will have the honor of paying the ultimate price to provide the Realm with the vegetation it needs, and when the time is..."

I could focus on nothing else but the Second Prince. He remained at his father's side, trying very desperately not to look at the platform where his dear childhood friend had just died. After what felt like a hundred moments, he approached, bowing his head ever so slightly to me but looking to Beralt. "I want to leave."

Beralt blustered out a sigh. "I think it would do you some good. But we need to first convince the King—"

He turned fully to his Dwarven companion. "The King has no use for me here. He only pretends to. He only—but now he will set his attention on acquiring a new Queen. The Fifth. And another child. And another death. I need to get *out of here*."

I tried to bury the fact that Willen would not look at me as he spoke. It made my stomach ache within me, but I tried to pretend it was nothing.

Beralt, bless him and curse him, noticed my discomfort and cleared his throat. "Second Prince, perhaps we could discuss this in private...."

"My inability to control my emotions is detrimental to the Monarchy. Everyone knows this, Beralt. There is no reason to whisper in the shadows. Not only is it detrimental, it is ineffective. Which is worse. If I could destroy one thing to save another, at least there would be some point. But no. I destroy everything for nothing. And I refuse to cause further harm to those I care for."

"Prince—"

"I will leave whether my father likes it or not. Or who knows? He could be next in my reckless path of destruction. Or perhaps his punishment for my defiance will be...maybe...."

"Prince Willen, you would only be defying the King *again*—"

"If I do, I will go alone. I only tell you so that you will not follow me, Beralt."

Beralt shot out one loud burst of laughter, his small eyes hardening in his ruddy face. "You think I will leave your side? Never. Of all the Vedan Royals I have ever served, you are the most worthy of my loyalty."

But Willen turned and left with long, quick steps, probably so the poor Dwarf could not keep up. He worked his Wonder, moving through the crowd and disappearing without warning.

I turned the opposite way and stepped into the crowd, using my own Wonder to pull me out of the arena and to match my steps to Willen's. It worked, and I appeared beside him. We were inside the Palace, stepping over the debris Willen had created in his efforts to break into Mida's room when the King had sealed her in.

"I do not want you to follow me. We will be seen," Willen said, his voice all darkness and grit.

"I thought you said 'if I go, you go'. Did you not—?"

"You are safe now. Mida made sure of it. And now that I am relieved of the burden of your wellbeing—"

I grabbed his arm so that he stopped moving. "Did you just call me your *burden*, Willen?"

He snatched his arm back, his eyes flashing. "Do not talk to me like that in public, Tree. We could be seen. You could be overheard. You cannot casually use my *name*."

"No one is listening to me, Willen. Certainly not you."

"I cannot decide whether you are stubborn or stupid, Aia."

I wanted to hit him. I had never wanted to hit another person so intensely, not even Gretaline when she was at her worst. But I kept my hands to myself, though they trembled with unspent anger. "You think this of me? *You* are either so stubborn it has made you stupid or so stupid you cannot detect how stubborn it makes you. Your only constant is in how inconsistently you treat me."

"Because you will not *leave me alone*."

"Which is it, Willen!" I stomped my foot and felt the floor shake beneath me. "Do you want me to go or to stay? Would you die for me *or* do you hope to abandon me here? Am I yours or not?"

"I want you to go but I cannot make myself believe it! Ever since the first night I met you, I have not been able to free myself from you, no matter how hard I try. You absolve me of my clarity of thought!"

"Then...why did you *hold me* like you did?" I shoved his chest, but really I wanted to grab his shoulders and shake him. "Why did you take me into your *bed*?"

"Because I'm *selfish*. I'm selfish and I *love you*."

The words hung like a death sentence between us. When Willen spoke again, he was more careful, more measured. "Perhaps you cannot see it, Aia. But I *know*. I know how careless I am with you. I know how much I am putting my own needs and desires first. I know that by loving you, I am choosing myself. And perhaps you see me as something else—as *someone* else—but I am inconsistent because I am a coward. And because I am grandly selfish. So please...do not be stupid enough to humor me anymore. And since *I* cannot manage to leave you alone, you must ignore me. Or hate me, if you can. If you cannot do it for your own good, for the love of heaven, do it for mine."

And he attempted to walk away from me. But I circled back in front of him and stood my ground. "You listen to *me* now. I am not some object of desire. I am not something for you to regret pursuing. And my life will not be a consequence of your actions. It will be a consequence of my decisions. If you want to be a coward and you simply cannot decide to want me, then you will live with the choices you make, Second Prince. But I am not doomed because of *you*. I am perfectly capable of orchestrating my own demise."

It was I who left him then, though I had to pretend a few servants had not stopped their work on remodeling the hall to stare at us while we argued. I stared back at them, unsure of what to do until I cleared my throat and they all snapped back to their tasks.

It took me about ten more steps to realize that I had just berated a man who had witnessed the pointless loss of his dearest and oldest friend and who was forced to do nothing to save her. Of course Willen did not know what he wanted. Of course it was easier to call himself a coward than to tell me the truth—that he was experiencing sorrow beyond measure and feared that he would feel it a hundredfold if I were to meet a similar fate.

I should have been kinder. I should have been more understanding.

But it made little sense to turn back and attempt to repair things. The Prince wanted nothing more to do with me. And perhaps he was right. Perhaps distance was what he needed, even if it was not at all what I desired.

I had better figure what Tree responsibilities I am to—

A strange creaking filled the bedraggled hall, and I paused my steps. *What could that be?* I had not yet heard anything of that nature in the Palace, and the place was always riddled with surprises. *Has another Royal decided to take out their wrath on the poor windows and walls?* Another creak, that time longer and louder than the last.

And then something more than a creak. A screech that split through the air, the waves of sound blowing the dust of debris over my feet. The sound was followed by a few cries from the most skittish servants. The rest looked upwards in concern. Following their lead, I too tilted my head toward the patched ceiling. Shadows flickered across the bits of sunlight streaming in, but I could not make sense of the shifts of light.

Another creak, followed by the overwhelming groan of the very building itself. As if somehow the ceiling were being tortured. Dust snowed down from above, and bits of rafter fell through the golden molding, smashing into the floor and sending servants screaming and running for cover. I too—little more than a servant in the grand schemes of politics and Royal dealings—should have lifted the hem of my dress and set to fleeing, but I held my ground, my head still facing up.

A swooshing noise, like a great fabric flapping in the wind. And then someone bellowed out a warning. "Wyverns! Run!"

Just then, the ceiling peeled off, and the walls strained to remain upright. Plaster and rafters and stone were caught in the clutches of razored talons as three villainous faces roared through the opening above us.

Their nostrils oozed slime, their tongues dripping saliva, and their slitted pupils bulged as they screeched. The gray scales of the first Wyvern rattled as it swooped down into the Palace hall, releasing its haul of refuse and wood onto those fleeing below and snatching up a helpless servant woman. She screamed, but before anyone could even take a breath aimed at saving her, the Wyvern stretched its legs and ripped her into two haggard pieces.

A voice rent through me then with such violence that I fell to my knees, my arms over my head. "Where is the one who is called the Prince?" The shrieking and roaring translated into some language that shook my very chest, though it did not seem that everyone could hear it. "Where is the Prince Vedan?"

Willen. I tried to stand back up, to use my brain toward being of some sort of help, but the voice of the Wyverns would not stop calling out.

"Aia!" To my shock, Beralt raced toward me, taking the stairs three at a time, though he had to use his hands to do so. "Hold your breath, or it will turn your innards to mush!"

Hold my breath? How would that—

"Hold your breath, Aia! It is speaking through your Wonder." He caught up to me just as I clamped my mouth shut. The reverberating words stopped when my breath did. "Now, tell me, what did the beast say? I have no Wonder, it speaks not to me."

"Willen." I squeezed out the words without taking in air. "It calls for the Prince."

"Which Prince? There are two...no three now, if you count the lost babe!"

"There is only one *here*, Beralt!"

I aimed to follow Beralt, taking little breaths so I did not become overwhelmed by the communication of the Wyverns, but he put a rough hand on my shoulder. "Aia, we are in great danger. All of us. Either the Wyverns have grown too strong for our defenses or the Realm has grown too weak. I need you to find and protect the Trees. I will do what I swore and protect the Prince."

I nodded my consent to the plan. Though it was my instinct to help Willen, the Trees...they needed me. Beralt put his gruff arm out and opened his palm, holding it there until I grasped it. Then, he clenched hard. "With more honor than any man," he said. When he released me, we parted ways.

I took off running and hoped my Wonder would take me to the Trees. It worked, and I appeared where they were huddled in the room we'd first slept in when we arrived. Clorente stood at the door, waving her hands over the wood. *Did I bring me here or did she?*

Gretaline and Shrane both paced in the bare room, Shrane ringing her hands and Gretaline deep in thought.

"*Wyverns* are attacking the Palace. Real ones, like in the stories. They will tear us to shreds. They will eat us alive. We are all going to die. None of us will become Trees." Shrane's pitch grew higher and higher, her words bumbling together faster and faster.

"We are not going to die," Clorente corrected her, still waving her hands over the door. "I would never let that happen. We will be safe in here as long as my Wonder holds. The Wyverns are not looking for us."

"They are looking for the Prince," Shrane said. "They are looking for the Prince, and then my lover will have to come and defend him and he will be shredded like roasted meat!"

Gretaline stomped her foot. "Would you shut up about your *lover*? Good heavens, Shrane, no one cares that you've gone and wasted yourself on some man whose name you're not even sure of! There are Wyverns *eating* the Palace. We have no time for your sordid drama." Gretaline turned to Clorente. "Should we not...run away? Will we not be in danger here? Surely your Wonder alone cannot stave off three starving Wyverns, Clorente."

"They have plenty of Wonder to consume elsewhere; they will not look for ours here."

"But—"

"Running is no option, Tree. If the Wyverns have torn into the Palace, we can assume they have raided the forests as well. We would be running straight into their jaws."

I breathed, realizing that Clorente's Wonder seal made it more difficult to hear the Wyverns, though their call still echoed faintly, like a ringing in my ears. "Why are the Wyverns doing this? What do they want?"

"They are Wonder-eaters," Gretaline said, disgusted as usual by my lack of knowledge. "I swear you've never even read children's stories."

"But the Palace has *always* been packed with Wonderful people. Why now? Why this large of an attack?" *And why the Second Prince?*

"They did not organize themselves," Clorente said with a sigh as she sat on the floor. I had never seen Clorente require any level of rest, so seeing her sit down made me more nervous than the screech of the Wyverns as they drew nearer. "Wyverns are known for their power and strength, not their strategy. If they've come bearing a message, it is because someone has inspired them to do so."

"They called for the Prince," Gretaline said, still pacing furiously. "But which one?"

It is Willen. I could not explain, but I knew it was him they wanted. And not only because it was him I wanted.

"Who would want a Vedan Prince?" I asked. "And why?"

"I do not know," Clorente said from her seat on the floor. "But if they sense the Wonder in you Trees, they will become overrun with lust and the gluttons will seek to devour you. Truth be told, there are many reasons I did not hold your training in the forest among the trees. The Wyvern problem is one of those reasons."

"One attacked on that turn the High Prince forced me to ride with him."

Clorente nodded. "It is a sensitive subject for the Royals. They do not wield the power they once did to hold off the Wyverns from the Pride Places."

"They did not come to the Neighboring Lands looking for my Wonder," I pointed out. "Or Shrane's."

"Another reason you were not taught the ways of Wonder," she said. "You would not have had adequate protection, as Gretaline did."

"So you left us both ignorant and defenseless?"

"I did the best I could for the Realm, child. You may be bitter about that for as long as you wish, but I had to try. Do you not understand? We will all be doomed without the necessary sacrifices."

"A person must choose to make their own sacrifices. You cannot choose on behalf of another, especially not a child." I thought of Mida then, who was willing to be esteemed for her Realm but could not allow her children to die, not even to bring justice to the Royals.

"We can hash out all the wrongs done to us after the Wyverns have been sent away," Gretaline interjected. "I have my own list of misdeeds to air out in my own time, believe me." And she glared at Clorente until the older woman closed her eyes and pretended to rest.

More screams outside our door as the Wyverns came closer to our hiding place. The walls trembled, and the thrashing of stone made me wonder how Forgotten was handling having himself torn apart. I could sense nothing from the True Stone, though. Perhaps he rested soundly while this catastrophe unfolded.

"There will be nothing of the Palace of the Princes left standing," Shrane whispered, her round eyes somehow the widest I had ever seen them. "Nothing and no one."

"This room alone will stand, even if all else crumbles," Clorente said. Her voice was more feeble than usual, her skin more ashen. Whatever she had done to seal us from the Wyverns continued to drain her Wonder.

"What have you done?" Gretaline asked, her hands on her hips as she noticed Clorente's state.

"It's draining her," I said.

"Take it down," Gretaline demanded. "If we lose you, Clorente, we will be lost. We don't know enough about the trials of the Trees without you."

"I will not let Wonderlusting Wyverns conclude our story. I will protect you, even if it means I perish while doing so."

"Now Clorente is dying?!" Shrane cried, a bubble of mucus popping in one of her nostrils as she wept.

"Shut up, Shrane, for the love of heaven! How are you possibly one of the only remaining Trees? Honestly, how?" Gretaline took back up her pacing, and Clorente continued her paling. Shrane wept in a puddle in a corner of the room. And as for me...I stood up.

"Let's go," I told them.

No one listened to me.

"Trees. Let's go. Now."

"What? What do you mean?" Gretaline asked, pacing past me for the fourteenth time.

I caught her arms as she went and yanked her toward me. "Look at you," I said. "Look at how truly stunning you are." The Tree wore a silver number that faded to white at the hem. She looked like she was born of the snow on a stormy turn. "And Shrane, you are more beautiful than a human could even comprehend. Stand up and let me see you!"

Shrane stumbled to her feet, revealing her sky blue number and her long, pale legs.

"We are not going to hide in this room and hope that fate favors us while Clorente dies to protect us. We are going to step out there and do exactly what this Realm has hoped we would do."

"What is that exactly?" Gretaline asked, crossing her arms and scowling.

"We're going to protect it."

Clorente opened her mouth to speak, but Gretaline was faster. She kicked Clorente's cane from her hand and thrust her palm into the side of the woman's neck. Clorente's head lolled to the side, and she slumped where she sat, her back to the wall.

Shrane sputtered. "Wh-where did you learn to do that, Greta?"

Gretaline shrugged. "I'm a Tree of great mystery, I suppose." She put her hands to the door and strained. "Probably going to need this Wonder," she explained. "Better take it with us."

"You can use someone else's Wonder?" I asked as I opened the door.

"No. I won't use it. Might make nice bait if I can keep it concentrated long enough."

I nodded as we left the room, Shrane so close behind us that she stepped on my heels every few moments. "But Aia? What are we going to *do*? Shine? Look beautiful at them?"

"We need to get to the center of the entrance hall and then we will do what Trees do, Shrane."

So we moved counter to those fleeing for their lives until we were back to the place where it all started. Of course, the Wyverns shrieked, and the sound of their wings nearly overcame us as they raced toward all the Wonder we carried. Gretaline set Clorente's Wonder on the ground, and we each sat down facing it, legs crossed.

"Hold your breath," I told the girls. "And we will make use out of ourselves for once."

And then, like the grove of trees that unified to shield Mida, the twins, and me in the forest that night, we called out, and the roots heard us. They raced toward us, those usually slow-moving entities, and trees sprang up inside the Palace walls. Faster and faster, until it was more forest than Palace. The Wyverns were forced out, their talons thrashing at the bark, the trees bearing thorns and twisting vines around their arms and legs.

I exhaled, letting air fill my lungs once again. For the people would be safe within our shelter. And with that inhale came the victorious cry of the Wyverns as they took wing. "The Prince! He is ours!"

I stood to my feet and thanked the trees as I made my way out of the shelter we had just constructed. My sisters would have to forgive me. For there were Wyverns in grave need of correction at the hands of a Tree.

Watered With
My Own Blood

The forest loomed the night the Wyverns took the Second Prince. The winged beasts flew just over the tops of the trees, but I could hear them hissing to one another. "Take the Human's Wonder. So much Wonder!"

They would drain Willen of his Wonder right there in the open? To what end? What purpose would it serve to capture and then kill one Prince?

"No," the other snarled. "Bring him whole. Wonder and all. We must follow orders. We must, we must."

Orders? Orders from whom? Clorente was right. The Wyverns had been commissioned by someone to commit this heinous misdeed. And whoever it was, they wanted the Second Prince delivered to them alive.

But what are you going to do about it, Aia? Something. I knew I had to do something. I spotted Beralt's horse racing across the forest floor, aiming to catch up with the Wyverns, and used my Wonder to carry me toward him until I sat upon his horse. I wrapped my arms around his short but wide waist.

"Miss Tree! What have you gotten into your head?" he shouted over the sound of wind and branches snapping against us. "I thought you were to be protecting the other Trees!"

"The Trees can protect themselves now," I replied. "Those beasts have Willen, Beralt."

"Aye, they do. But not for long." He pointed up to the monsters. "Was his plan, you see. To get them away from the Palace. Didn't know a mighty force would seal us all safe inside, rendering the plan almost useless."

"Your plan was to get Willen *killed*?"

"*His* plan was to get the Wyverns away from civilized society. And now that's on it's way, the plan will only work if we fell the beasts properly."

"You really ought to share your plans with me in advance, Beralt. Then I can tell you how utterly ridiculous they are before you implement them."

Hearty laughter exploded from the Dwarf, and he spurred his horse on as we neared the flying beasts. I contemplated how we could possibly catch up to creatures of the sky, but it would have to be a question for another time.

"It seems your plan was to weigh down my horse and chastise me endlessly. What role do you see yourself playing in this conquest, Miss Tree? I will oblige."

"I thought I might serve as a decent distraction...if you wouldn't mind eliminating them?"

"Think you'll conjure up enough Wonder for that, do you?"

"I have plenty of Wonder left, Beralt." I felt the moisture of the woods in the very air, the steep darkness soaking into the trees as we rode past. "Besides, this is a forest. And I am a Tree."

I gave the Dwarf's belly a little squeeze. "Take care of yourself, please. You're very dear to me."

"I am?" He laughed again. "Good old Beralt, won himself the heart of a Tree. Wait until they hear of this back home!" He patted my arm with his calloused palm. "I'll do as you wish. Now, let's get our boy down from there."

I released Beralt and slid off the back of his horse, the leaves on nearby trees reaching out to catch me, responding with grace to my Wonder. *Dear forest, will you help me be more than I am?* I stood very still and put all my hope in an idea. In a notion. That there was more of myself outside of me than within.

I shone. I did not have to imagine it or wonder whether the light came from my body or not. I was brilliant. A beam of glory up to the heavens. And the more trees who heard my request, the more they lent me Wonder, until the Wyverns had no choice but to surrender to their Wonderlust. I heard them swooping toward me and then the rugged slice of Beralt's sword. Another cry from the brave Dwarf and the thud of a body colliding with the ground.

"Go, Beralt!" I heard Willen shout before the final struggle of man and beast, the gnashing of talons and the cracking of tree trunks, the splintering of wood and shattering of boulders. It must have been well over three Wyverns, for all the chaos that ensued.

At last, cool hands met my face, and I knew they had to be Willen's.

"Aia...." He rubbed my cheeks, my shoulders, and shook me gently. "Aia, enough. Enough. It's over."

Though he held me, he seemed far away. Distant, as if in a memory or a dream. He kissed my forehead, his thumbs rubbing my temples. "Aia, please. Enough."

But I was not sure how I could stop. Most likely because I was not entirely sure how I had begun in the first place. The light kept on, and the Wonder built and built until I thought the entire forest would flow through me.

"I sent Beralt for help," Willen said through the haze. "Aia, breathe. Breathe for me."

I was not dying. At least it did not *feel* like dying to me. There were many other times, with hunger in my belly or my brother's blows on my back or my lungs filled with water or my body wracked with the poison of a white snake, where I felt like I would perish. But this...felt natural. *So why is Willen asking me to breathe as if I am not doing so already?*

It was then I realized no air passed through me. And I could gamble that my heart had no need to beat, either. I was...alive, but there was no need for living.

"Please, please, don't." My love's voice trembled as he spoke to me. "Aia, I need you to stop. I need you to breathe. I *need you.*"

And then, with much effort, I opened my eyes. I could see him. He bled down his neck and his hands. Deep scrapes had been torn into his arms, no doubt due to being carried through the air by the Wyverns. But his blue eyes were clear, his soot-covered cheeks streaked with perspiration.

I was able to bring myself back. Enough to reach up and hold his hand, enough to lean into his kiss.

"What were you thinking?" he asked, embracing me fully, half relieved and half agonized with worry. "So much Wonder from one person, Aia? You did too much. Too much."

But I could not answer him. Not with my words. I wished I could tell him that very few things truly mattered. That rules could help but had never saved a life. That honor was selfish. For only the one who sacrifices gets to keep it. The one honored is left only with regret. I wanted to tell him that I thought he was kind and beautiful, and that should be enough. No business of realms and Trees and wars and Royals. No business at all.

Why could not two bodies meet and that be love? Why could not two lovers kiss and that be life?

"You should rest," Willen whispered. "You have done too much this turn. All these turns. Aia—"

But I kept on kissing him. It was all I could think left for me to do. I prayed he knew this. I prayed he could see that all I had was the kissing of him and the feel of his hands on my skin. I prayed that he would not insist on some moral code that did not exist between us.

I slipped my hand beneath his shirt and begged through my fingers that he would listen. *Listen to me.* We were in the open, yes, but the trees would protect us. They would hide us. And perhaps he was tired from fighting Wyverns and Kings and himself—more tired than me—but if he could find the energy, the strength, then we could find our way once again. One last time.

Willen started at the beginning.

His full lips traced a path along my calves and against my thighs, his hands tugging at the tatters of my dress.

"You...should rest..." he argued with himself, it seemed.

But can I blame him? I could see how I still glowed against him, my shine reflecting in his eyes like the sun breaking through a storm. The trees still weaved and grew around us, vines curling around my ankles, twisting into my hair.

But it was not time for rest. It was not time for hesitation. If Wonder could beg, that's what it did.

He brought himself up to my abdomen, his hand pressing along my skin and his Wonder parting the fabric like a blade. Finally, he looked into my eyes.

"I don't want to hurt you."

And there, underneath it all. Willen's truest fear. For, of all people, he had witnessed what had become of the love his father and mother shared closer than anyone. How loving someone could lead to their pain. How wanting someone could bring about their destruction.

I had to carve the words out of nothing, for speaking at that point was nearly impossible for me. It would cost me time, those words—time of which I had very little remaining. But I knew he needed to hear them, to hear me. I knew he needed my voice imprinted in his mind, so he had something he could remember. So that in the future, whenever he doubted himself or questioned the integrity of what we were, he could replay my words and feel whole once again.

"It only hurts..." I breathed out, my voice little but the rustling of foliage overhead, "when you leave me."

I knew he was frightened. Perhaps at the sight of me, for I was not in appearance as my usual self, though I could not imagine what sort of creature I began to resemble. I hoped he could find it in himself to love me as I was...as I became.

"Alright then," he said. And he looked into my eyes like he saw all at once the birth of a thousand stars. "I promise I will not leave you."

That night, I learned something new. That the True Stone was not entirely correct. For Trees do not only pull Wonder from without to within. We have Wonder to give as well. The more Willen gave to me, the more I returned. Until I could not tell which of us was Human or Tree or earth. Until there was no more weeping and no more laughing. Only the breath of a man and the silence of a Tree.

When finally our bodies lay still next to each other, his hands still tangled in my hair and my bare legs crossed over his, Willen told me a story.

"It's not fair, Aia. That you spent your childhood locked away in the dark. When I spent mine in heaven. I never speak of those turns, you know. Not with anyone. But as a very young child, I spent every turn with my mother in the deepest part of the forest, where no one would ever find us. Except one man who knew the way, of course. But...my happiest times were not when he came to visit. They argued so much, he and my mother. He wanted her to marry him...but she refused." He gave a gloomy chuckle. "She refused to follow his customs. And when he was gone back to his Palace, she would take me out hunting. Foraging. Exploring. We'd sleep under canopies— though nothing as Wonderful as this one. And she would tell me, 'Willen, you must make your own way. I did not come all this way for you to forget yourself in some Palace'."

He sighed. "My father always says he wanted nothing more than for my mother to live. But he's lying, Aia. He did not love her as much as I did. He did not love her as much as she loved herself." He pulled me somehow even closer. "It was hard for me to watch her die. I knew she did not want to. It was not esteem. It was an execution. It was murder. But there was nothing I could do then. And there is nothing I can do now. Except, maybe, if I can stop being so afraid, learn to love you well. Learn to *listen*."

He kissed my cheek, his voice growing slow and heavy with the need for sleep. I knew Beralt would be searching for us, but I would keep him and any guardsmen away for as long as I could.

"It will be the greatest story of my life, Aia," Willen said, drifting off with me in his arms. "Learning to listen to you."

He slept, and I was grateful. For I could not hold back my Wonder any longer. I too had stories in my heart that wanted to burst from my lips, but that could not happen. They would have to stay with me.

Down. I had to go down first, just as when we'd been dropped into the deepest well on our first turn at the Palace. As I lay still on the earth, my arms and legs and back pressed into the soil. From my skin, I felt the roots grow, small and slow at first. Merely the tiniest of tendrils. Until they gained both strength and momentum. They buried down into the warm soil, bypassing rocks and boulders, finding their way in the dark. Oh, how I was used to that dark. It did not scare me to go home once more.

And then came the sprouts from the backs of my hands, my belly, my legs. They trembled as they unfurled, the smallest of green leaves opening to the moonlight that broke through the canopy. But then they gained stability and power. They pushed themselves outward and upward, twisting together to form oneness. Cohesion through vulnerability. Their fragile stems braided into a firm trunk. And this they repeated over and over until my pain could no longer be beared.

The roots below were watered with my own blood, my own tears. And still I grew. For I had little choice left in the matter of destiny. Could one choose how tall they would be? Or what color hair would sprout from their head? The tone of their own voice or the curve of their lashes? I could not decide to stop or to go on. To die or to live was no longer my choice.

I did not cry out for help. And I was glad no one could see me suffering. Except, of course, for the trees. But they did not judge me for weeping. They only loaned me their Wonder, their beauty, their steadfastness. They entwined their strong roots with mine. Sisters of another kind. Through those networks of roots, they sent nourishment and love. They spoke to me in warmth, though I could hardly say which words they chose. I only knew for certain that I was loved. That they would always love me. For trees...they never changed their minds about such things as love and devotion.

Finally, I spread my arms up to the sky. *In an attempt to free myself of this becoming? Or is it a celebration of a sorrowful victory?* Was I little more than Mida Vedan, my head tilted up and my arms open to the trees who had gathered to esteem me? All my branches shook free of their constraints and spread out about me. My leaves forced themselves into existence, bursting forth from their tight buds and tasting the luscious moonlight for themselves, each its own entity, each its own being, but all together...me.

But oh, I was not quite finished with my becoming yet. For at the base of my trunk, nestled among my new and ancient roots, slept a Prince. Merely a man, I could see at last, and not even truly a great one. Not yet, at least. But one who needed me. And I still remembered all the times I had needed him.

Before my memories were transformed into nothing but sap, before my thoughts became light, before my sentiment turned to water and air...I reached into the collective heart of my ancestors.

I require a Seed, I told them. *As a gift.*

I could not see them as one might see a person standing before them. They were an idea still, to me. They were a truth, but I could not reach out and touch one of those Ancient Trees. The Arboreals. My grandmothers from many lifetimes ago.

These people deserve no Seed, they answered me. *They are wicked. Deceitful. Cowards. They raze our trees and leave nothing on which our forests can feed. They break cycles. They deserve for their cycle to be broken in return.*

And I wept at this. I realized, somehow, I had always been weeping for this. For time was not as it had been when I could walk around on two legs.

Please. Perhaps these people do not deserve a Seed. But this one...this man...he does.

We cannot give a Seed to one man. If it belongs to him, it belongs to his people.

I felt myself burning beneath their gaze—they were too Ancient for me to behold, but they certainly could see me.

One more. One more chance. For his sake.

If we grant you this Seed, you must understand. It is the last time. This is the last one. There will be no more patience. No more sacrifice. You will be the last True Tree. And you choose to risk it on the one sleeping at your roots, child?

I bowed my boughs, my body creaking as I straightened again, my leaves shivering while I stretched. *It is no risk,* I answered. *It is Willen.*

And so, unbeknownst to him, on a dark turn in a Wondered forest enclave, with no Human in all the world to bear witness to the event, the Second Prince Of All The Realm received the gift of the very last Seed. From the very last True Tree. At the very last possible moment.

He wiggled and coughed as the drop of light entered his chest but otherwise did not stir.

And though I knew it would break Willen's heart, I closed my eyes to my humanity. For good.

Ep 26

You Reek of the Forest

I could not understand, not for the life of me, what persuaded this Tree to let me do such things to her body. It was as if Aia had no idea what power she had over me, over my will and my mind. Somewhere, my thoughts told me no. *No, Willen, let her rest. Do not go this far again. Not now. Not like this.*

After all, I could hardly understand why she'd set her ambitions to follow after me when the Wyverns took me to the sky. *But here she is. Here she is. And when I slid my hand up her thigh, she exhaled and parted her legs for me.*

I knew, when I entered her, that the whole of it was changing. The Realm, the earth, the two of us. My cowardice fled with each thrust, and my courage grew with each sigh, until I was sure of it. That all the world had been orchestrated for me to be with that Tree in that forest at that time. Whenever my mind struggled, thinking she could not possibly want more of me— *she must be tired now, she must be through*—she tangled her fingers in my hair and urged me forward with the arching of her back.

It was absurd of course, to go from fighting monsters to finding pleasure within Aia, but since the moment I'd met her, nothing made sense. I used to think, perhaps, she'd taken my life's compass when she crept into my study looking for a physician for an ailing Tree, but no. She'd not taken my compass; she'd given me one I could not read. The lines and measurements spun and switched, and there was no longer such a thing as true north. There was only to be with Aia or not to be with Aia. She was not the distraction. Everything else was.

When I could go no further, when there was nothing left for me to give, I collapsed beside her and pulled her onto my chest, for we had no blanket beneath us and I was quite out of Wonder. We would have to use each other for both warmth and comfort, and that I did not mind.

For the first time, with Aia's slender body half stretched over mine and her skin glowing pink and green and gold as I stroked her arm, down her side, and over the sweet curve of her hip, I thought about the future. Not whether I would ever escape the prison of the Palace and evade my father's careful gaze. Not whether I could be free of my brother and his dedi-cated loathing.

But lying awake, I dreamed. Of a life where maybe—just maybe—I could wake up at the start of every turn holding Aia in my arms as I did then. I would kiss her perfect face and watch her glow as I did so. *Perhaps I could find a way to make her something to drink myself without the servants interven-ing—a sweetened tea or a sunrise wine. Oh, and we might read together.* The thought of this made my heart lurch in my chest, for I knew, even if she did not, that she would soon be a gifted reader. There were so many stories we could explore. And she would experience every emotion locked in the pages of a book. Perhaps we would take on some adventures ourselves. Board ships. Taste the salt of open waters. See new forests and sleep in them naked. Perhaps I would tell her what remained buried in my fearful soul. That I loved her. I loved her entirely.

She would keep me in my place. Tell me when I was wrong, and I would get insanely cross with her for it. But she would always be right. And I would give her little pleasures, and great ones as well, after the sun went down. But only the sort she liked. Only the sort she begged for.

Why not say it to her? Why not say it all now while she kisses your neck, while you can feel her breathing against you?

Because. *Because I can not be trusted with someone as perfect as her. Because men like me—Royals like me—only know how to take and nothing of how to give.* I had seen it. Seen how my mother loved my father, but he turned it into malice for his own gain. To have me. To secure her forever as his monument. To ensure no other man could have her. To ensure no other father could raise me.

Loving Aia was selfish. And so instead of telling her what I wanted—to feed her sunrise wine and read her stories in the morning breeze—I told her the truth. Not a fantasy. I told her what my father did, a secret I'd always kept for the sake of his image and for the sake of my own safety.

She would never truly know how I loved her. And it would have to be enough for me.

We fell asleep together, and I prayed heaven would bless my dreams so that they were of the Tree I loved and not of the father who would not let me free of his control.

In my unsettled state of sleep, I thought I heard guardsmen wander by the Wonderful enclave Aia had built with forest trees. They could not find us, and I marveled at how she could harness such powerful Wonder even while we slept.

I did not wake until the sun streaked through the trees. When I stirred, I reached out my hand for my love—the love who would never know how much I adored her.

But there was...no one.

Fear stripped me bare. I sat up and looked around the enclave. She would be present, I knew. Perhaps admiring the bark of one of her trees up close or humming to a little sapling. But I searched and could not find her. I called her name, and she did not respond.

Had she left? Had she gone back to the Palace and left me asleep on the forest floor? I had hoped I would have another chance to hold her, to kiss the place where her heart beat steady. I was not prepared to return to the shambles my life had become, and certainly not without Aia. *But you will have to be without her*, I told myself. *Get used to it, Willen. This is your life.*

I stepped out of the grove of trees and stopped cold, startled by the fleshy corpses of the Wyverns still lying on the ground. Their limbs were mangled, flies already buzzing through their gutted remains. How unusual—no it was beyond unusual, it was orchestrated—for these beasts to come so close to the Palace, past our Wondered seals and shields and through the roof. I had always been told we were impenetrable.

I knew Beralt must have looked for me all night long, and for that, I owed him a hundred apologies of the most sincere manner. I sent a whistle out with a bit of Wonder in case he was still combing the woods searching for me. If he heard it and whistled back, my Wonder would carry it to my ears.

And there it was, on the wind. The return whistle. I sat and waited until the Dwarf barreled through the trees and brush and lunged for me. He shoved me with his short arms.

"You bastard! I thought you were gone. Or *dead*. Why didn't you call out to me sooner?"

"I...."

Beralt pointed a finger at me. "You were with Aia, weren't you?" He growled at me, his beard shaking. "I knew it! That's why I brought limited guard to look for you. Just in case you weren't torn limb from limb but really were off soothing yourself between the legs of—"

"Beralt, enough."

Beralt scowled, but calmed himself. "So we'll need a new whistle tone, then. One that means, 'I'm not dead you Dwarven fool, I'm just seeking pleasures at the most inopportune time in the history of the Palace'."

I inhaled slowly, steadying my own nerves. "I am sorry, Beralt. I know it was not wise and I know I shouldn't have let you wander all night in search of me. I know that now but I did not know that in the moment. I knew nothing in the moment, it seems."

"She has that effect on you. I can't tell if it's good or bad, boy. On the one hand, you have responsibilities. Your life isn't your own to be throwing this way and that whenever you happen to look in her eyes. On the other hand...heaven knows you need to live a little. No one can get everything perfect every time, all the time. She makes you reckless."

"I want what I can't have, is all, Beralt. And speaking of Aia...have you seen her this morning?"

"Have not. Why isn't she with *you*?"

"We were together all night. But this morning...she was simply gone."

"She's got a mind of her own, that one. Did you by chance tell her to stay in one place or do a certain thing a certain way? If so, it would be quickest to assume she's gone and done the opposite. Can't even be cross with her. She just sparkles at me, and I turn to soup."

"That, and she always seems to be right about things."

"Most alluring thing about her, I'd say. Though it's still worrisome that she's up and gone, what with the Palace in shambles and Wyverns flitting about. I can search for her, if you wish?"

I clapped my hand on my friend's shoulder. "You've done enough searching for one lifetime, Beralt. I'll find Aia. Go. Eat and sleep." I wrinkled my nose. "And bathe."

He chortled. "Smell helps keep the Wyverns off."

"Your wife would be ashamed."

"Only because I've never been able to match her pungence!" He slapped his belly, laughing at his own joke. "I'd have an axe to the head for that one. Most certainly."

"Perhaps one turn, I'll actually be able to leave this place. And then you can take me to Dwarf Country to meet her, Beralt."

"Sounds like a good time, Willen, my boy. But first, I'll take that food and that sleep. You find your woman and make sure you can receive forgiveness for whatever your latest offense is.

And then the King'll want answers about these Wyverns, I'm sure."

I nodded, rubbing my chest as we walked back to the Palace. I was more anxious than I expected, my sternum burning beneath my palm.

I sucked my breath in upon seeing what was left of the Palace of the Princes. The spires had been either bent or completely toppled. The roof was gone, nothing left behind but winging rafters and plumes of smoke and ash. Wyverns had no fire in their bellies but they knew how to start them, it seemed.

Servants attempted to sort through the debris, but it would take turns and turns of physical and Wondered labor, if not circles, to rebuild what the Wyverns had taken. For in the Palace, each stone and each stitch had its purpose and place.

My father's attendant quite near sprinted over to me the moment he caught me in his sights. "Noble Prince, oh thank heavens! Your father! He wants an audience with you. With great immediacy. You must hurry."

"Alright, alright, I'm coming," I told him. But all the while I scouted the area for Aia. I thought perhaps Clorente had whisked the Trees away for some sort of horrendous trial, but I saw the girl we'd rescued in the garden that one night. She seemed just as lost as everyone else, turning in tight circles, clutching her dress. I reached out to her, pausing to the dismay of the harried attendant.

"Have you seen Aia?"

"No, I have not, Second Prince." She bowed hastily. "Have you seen—"

But I was rushed on by the attendant. "He wants you now, Second Prince. We cannot slow."

"Where is he? I will use my Wonder and go to him."

"Oh, very good. He is in the—"

But the attendant had no chance to tell me. My father's impatience had reached its pinnacle, and I appeared in the Arena of the Queens. The High King stood alone among the commoners' seats as craftsmen erected the statue of Mida. He so much had the look of Theor in that moment, I was almost afraid to approach him.

"Willen," he said, his voice calloused, no doubt from too many sleepless nights as of late." Are you injured?"

But he did not look at me when he spoke. Only stared straight ahead at the stone statue.

I approached him cautiously. I had not seen my father this upset since I was a young child. I had almost forgotten he could carry so much wrathful disposition. That he could be so...angry.

"My injuries are minor, given the circumstances, and almost all healed."

"You reek of the forest."

I did not know what to say to that. I always thought my father would have had fond memories of the forest since he'd met my mother in one all those circles ago.

"You were quite fond of her," he said. "Of the Fourth Queen. Why is that?"

I swallowed. This was not the line of questioning I'd anticipated. "The Fourth Queen and I had been friends since childhood."

"She always advocated for you. Hoped you could get the chance to see the world. But I argued that I wanted to keep you close. Do you know why, Willen?"

"I believe you have an increased level of fondness for me. Because of your bond with my mother, I assume."

He smiled a bit, but I could detect the hint of a smirk there as well. I shook my head to clear it, for I probably mistook him for Theor rather than the High King.

"Your mother was no ordinary woman. Those are the sort you have to watch out for, Willen. The extraordinary ones." He gestured to the statue of my dear friend. "After Fara, I made certain to choose more carefully. Ordinary ones. It was not so difficult and honestly, quite disappointing. Ordinary women are everywhere, you see. Now I realize, after circles of avoiding them, there seem to be no extraordinary ones left. The only one...she's now dead."

"Yes, I know. I was there."

"You were, weren't you. How unusual. You should not have witnessed it."

"Because then I would know it was all nonsense. And I would not believe in the Ceremony or esteeming Queens or noble sacrifices." I could not believe those words gushed from my mouth.

My father leaned over the railing separating the common area from the seats of the nobles. "I taught you to hold fast to the rules. Did you forget my lessons?"

I shifted my weight, a shiver running up my legs. My father's lessons were not easy to forget. "I remember them."

"They were necessary, child. Your mother raised you with the wildness of her people. Such notions had to be corrected."

"Well, you did an excellent job, King."

"If I had done an excellent job, you would not have openly defied me regarding this unremarkable ordinary woman and her bastard children."

I clenched my fists at my sides. "Defying you was not my direct intention. I only hoped to spare my friend, not to bring you shame."

My father straightened up and turned to me. "I know what you want, Willen, though you don't seem to have wrapped your young mind around the fact that it will never happen. You want me to punish you. Even more, you want me to be done with you. To *banish* you. To send you off, far from me. And you hope you can take your short-legged Dwarf and your seductive Tree with you."

At this, my heart burned, as if something might sear a hole through my spine and leave a gaping wound in my back.

"I will punish you for your defiance. But it will not be what you had hoped, Prince. For I see the truth behind your words and deeds and I will not craft a reward disguised as punishment. I will break your heart and drain your hopes. It will teach you the importance of the rules of the Realm. It will banish the refuse your mother stuffed into your feeble mind."

I waited for his judgment and felt to be a little child once again, motherless and in a strange new place. Unfit for a Palace and unfit to be a Prince. The stories I'd never told. The side of my father even Theor had never met.

"I have sent my men to Dwarf Country. They will wait. If you defy me, they will slaughter the loved ones of your precious Dwarf. As for him, he will remain in my custody. You will be deprived of his friendship from henceforth."

I could not tighten my fists further. I took slower and slower breaths, for letting my Wonder out at my father would only serve to injure me.

"And as for your Tree...."

"She is not—"

"She is. I know she is."

"Father. *Please.*"

"I will give her back to the forest. In high esteem, of course."

"Then I must stop you."

"And lead to the slaughter of your Dwarves?"

My voice broke when I spoke, a sign of incompetent weakness in his eyes. A sign that he still owned me in every way. "You do not have to do this. I will follow your rules."

"Yes. You will." He put a hand on my shoulder, and I wanted to melt away into the shadows but I stood there and I let him. "Willen, you will remain here under my careful eye and my prudent shaping. And when I am gone one turn, Theor will watch over you just as I have."

"If you despise me so greatly, why not simply let me go?"

"You, my son...you are extraordinary. I will never let you go."

"Punish me, then. *Just* me."

"It does not work on you. We have tried that. Your brother is simple. A round of beatings from one of my attendants, and he is tearful and redfaced. But I could beat you to death, and it would not change one thought. This is the only way that works with you, Willen."

"Because this is the way it worked with my mother."

He smiled. "Do not worry, Willen. About anything. Your Dwarf will be safe. Your Tree will be planted. The Wyverns, even, are no surprise to me. The Palace will be rebuilt. In fact, it is the perfect occasion for a Ball Of Desolation. I will issue the announcement. Give the people something to celebrate in these trying times."

"You want to hold a celebration? What could there be to celebrate?"

"That is the point of a Ball Of Desolation, son. You create a reason to celebrate when none exists. It is one of our most valuable traditions. One you will do well to understand. Your attendance will be mandatory, as always. Until our customs are ingrained in your very soul." He nodded. "Go now."

Sometimes I wondered if what my father showed me was the truest form of love. An obsession with another that could not be broken and the unrelenting need to shape that person to hold your expectations for them with immaculate precision. If my father could shape each of my bones to his liking, he would. If he could tie me to a post in the Palace and feed me the rules of his society, he would. He loved me. Everyone knew it. They commented on it. They pitied Theor for his inability to gain my father's affection as I had. "Oh, how Harrod loved Fara. And now look how he loves her son."

Love was a collar around my neck. It was shackles around my ankles. And with Beralt gone and Aia destined for her end, how could I bear the love of my father any longer?

My first instinct, upon leaving the High King, was to find Beralt. *Perhaps we can go for a walk or ride out through the forest? Perhaps we can help in clearing out the fallen Wyverns or clear some rubble in preparation for the ball.*

But Beralt, my friend and my guide, would not be at my side any longer. I tried to save Mida, and instead of being banished as I'd hoped, I lost...everyone.

But at least I can tell Aia in person. I can warn her, and she may flee or seek help from those who might protect her. The True Stone. Maybe even Clorente.

But she was nowhere.

Finally, I thought to visit the place where we had spent the night. It already seemed such a distant memory, my hands on her skin and the cool air flowing over us. Maybe I would find her waiting. We could argue and then find each other's lips once more. Perhaps I could find the courage to read to her as I did in my dreams.

"Where have you gone? Are you truly hiding from me?"

I stopped in the enclave, leaning my shoulder against a tree. But I gasped, pulling myself away. For I swore I felt its bark ripple against my arm.

I stepped back, staring at the rather peculiar tree. For I was certain it had not been there the night before. I would have noticed such a large and brilliant thing in the center of the enclave. Its leaves were unlike any I had ever seen. They glistened in the sunlight, shimmered in the breeze.

"What in all the Realm?"

I circled the tree, examining its strong trunk, its perfectly bending branches. It was magnificent to behold, that was true. Carefully, I extended my hand and touched its gray-green bark once more. And the moment—the very moment—it touched my skin, I knew.

Ep 27

I Would Hate Me

The blood in my veins took on the purity of water. I pulled it from the deep warmth of the earth, lengths beneath the surface. My roots were infinite, it seemed, connecting me through a web of energy to not only every tree alive in the forest, but to every tree that had ever thrived in that soil. Together, we could feel the throbbing of the seeds we would all bear in the coming future. The trees were always mourning the loss of their fallen and always rejoicing over the birth of their seedlings. Beneath the grand boughs of the oldest lived the young saplings. They were proud, those saplings, and often thought themselves to be stronger than they were. But they would learn from watching the old ones. That storms would be carved into their bark and lean circles squeezed out of the rings of their trunks.

I had always been a Tree. That was much clearer when I had my roots deep in the soil and the sun bright on my leaves. Being a human was the anomaly. That was the temporary state. The Treeness had always been me.

The Seed I had given Willen would do the Realm good. I knew this because he was the right person to wield it. He had the courage to protect the Seed above the rules. Perhaps he did not know he had such courage, but I knew. And of all the Monarchs remaining in the Realm, none could be trusted like Willen could. Truly, he was the last.

And if he was the last, so was I.

I had not wished to say goodbye to my Prince. He would not have liked to see me torn apart as I was. It would have scarred him. He would have borne the image of my body's destruction his whole life, and Willen had seen enough of his loves die horrendous deaths he could not prevent.

But I did long to see him once more. How strange that trees and flowers and bushes all long for their familiars to come by from time to time. The mighty red-barked tree across the brook waited every turn for the squirrels to come and play on its knotted branches. The lilacs had their favorite butterflies. And if I was lucky, I would have Willen.

It took until the sun was almost set for him to return to me. I could not see him with my eyes, but I could feel every move he made. I could sense the feelings coursing through his heart, almost as if our roots were laid close together, his and mine.

He wandered through the grove I'd made for us on our last night.

"Aia?" he called. "Where have you gone? Please, answer me!"

He had not yet realized who I was. Had not yet discovered where I had been planted. The Prince looked...tired. Quite exhausted, actually. As if his mind was worn from all its thinking. As if he carried more than the weight of the Realm on his shoulders.

He groaned and leaned his shoulder against me. Still, he could not see that it was me he was so close to. I wanted to reach out and take his beautiful face in my hands and tell him that I was right beside him. That he could lean on me whenever he needed support that would not fail. But I had not hands with which to reach.

So I sent my Wonder out to meet him. It was a difficult thing to do. Trees did not often send Wonder out of ourselves. We were much better at taking it in. But for Willen's sake— and honestly, for mine as well—I made an attempt.

I feared it was not enough, for Willen simply stood up and rubbed his shoulder in confusion. His blue storm eyes still searched the clearing. At least that is what I imagined, for I could not really see his eyes anymore. I could only feel his gaze on my sisters and finally, once more, on me.

He considered. Stepped back to get a good look at the whole of me. Then, he approached with cautious steps and stretched out his arm. When his palm caressed my bark, I tried with all my might to feel like myself for him. Like the Aia he'd known, cloaked in human form and glowing in his arms.

And, I suppose...it worked. For he kept his hand there, his humanity radiating warmth through me. Then he removed that hand, and I felt a quick chill. He replaced it. Removed it. Replaced it once more.

Does he understand now? Does he know it's me?

He shook his head and then backed away. He took to pacing. Toward me and then away from me. Toward me all over again.

Finally, he lifted a tentative hand to my bark another time. He leaned in and whispered, almost as if he wished he wouldn't as he did so, "Aia?"

I sent my Wonder outward as quickly as I could. I felt my leaves tremble and blossoms bloom from the buds hidden on my many branches. I could not see the color or shape of them, but I hoped they were beautiful. I hoped *he* thought they were beautiful.

"No, no. No." He leaned his forehead against me. "No, please."

I knew Willen wept. I could feel the teardrops strike the earth above my roots. Those tears...they would become water in my veins one turn, but I did not think knowledge of that would comfort the Prince.

He went down to his knees and put both hands on me and would not stand up again for some time. He could say nothing besides 'no' and 'please'. If he kept on that way, I feared that the whole forest would weep along with him.

My sisters tried to help. They sent nourishment to me for him, but he was not in a state of mind to receive anything at all. His heart formed a knot, and his mind clouded just like his eyes. He only wanted to hold me. To feel my skin beneath his kiss, but it would not be so. Never again could it be so.

Willen fell asleep beneath me, curled tightly into a ball, his back pressed against my trunk. Gently, I lowered the roots to make sure he was comfortable where he slumbered.

When he awoke, in the darkest part of the night, he whispered to me. "I will come to see you when the sun returns," he said. And I knew it was all he could bear to speak out loud in that moment.

He left, and I thought of nothing else but the sky and how it was not as big as I had believed it was before. And I thought of the places beneath the surface that humans hardly ever saw and how entire worlds resided beneath their feet. And I thought of Willen.

The memories of my human life began to fade more quickly than I expected. I knew I had a brother once, but I could not remember what brothers were for. And I knew I had once walked through a grand Palace but I could not remember why.

I did remember Willen though. He came to me when the sun rose, just as he said he would. In fact, he came most mornings, right as the turn started on its new path.

Often, he brought books. I would have forgotten what those were if he did not always carry them into the forest. He sat with his back against me and flipped through the pages, which, I could hardly believe it, were made out of trees! On the pages were words. The greatest Wonder of humans. The ability to speak and send their Wonder out into the world in magical waves of sound that carried meaning and power with them as they went. The words he read had been carefully chosen and woven together to make things called stories.

He read each story and, if he sensed I enjoyed the tale, brought the book back again for me to hear. Sometimes he slowed down and pointed out the letters to me, making their sounds and tracing the shapes of them onto my roots.

"Little Tree," he would say to me, "I know it's odd, me telling you this, but you often asked me questions requiring such statements. I thought you might want to know. You are a beautiful Tree. Effervescently so. And this turn...you have a bit more rose to your green leaves than a normal tree should. And lavender glows in the grooves of your bark. It's always so easy to find you."

Willen brought the most special water for me as well, spiced with apples and cinnamon. Or sweetened with honey and sugar. "I know you did not have the chance to taste very many of these things," he'd tell me. "I wish I had shown more courage. I should have defied those rules and brought you cakes dipped in lemon glaze. I should have brought you warm milks with ale and watched you discover each flavor."

Other times, Willen came and simply sat and spoke with me. He told me stories of his childhood. Some were dreadful. Old memories of his father's inconsistency. How he loved his mother but traded her freedom for control over him and his life. How he suspected she did not run for fear of risking his own life at the hands of his father. How he had never told a soul that he both treasured and feared his father's visits to him and his mother when he lived in the forest.

"I wish I had told you, though. I wish I could have heard your advice. I wish I had the opportunity to listen to you, to follow what you say."

Sometimes, his eyes filled with tears. He told me how he worried about Beralt but could not gain access to visit his friend. How the Dwarf had been detained because Willen had loved too recklessly. "But I am beginning to think...I did not love recklessly enough. I was duplicitous in my affection, in my devotion. You tried to tell me this, Aia, but I was too afraid to hear you." He paused, and when he looked up to my branches, I felt the tickle of his hair brushing against me.

"Little Tree...is it my fault? What happened to you? Why you became...as you are?" He sighed. "I knew you were too tired that night. Our last night. I knew but...I wanted you. In a way that could not be helped or slowed or diminished. But at night now, when I am alone and without you...I wonder if I hurt you. If I...." He could not complete the expression of that sentiment. He moved on. "And then I think...what if you hate that I visit you like this? What if you loathe my resting against you? Or the sound of my voice when I read to you? What if you resent me? What if I am the focus of your wrath?" He paused. "If I were you...I would hate me."

But alas, I was a Tree and could not speak out against this pattern of thinking. I could not tell him that every turn that went by brought me closer to the earth and the wind and the rain, but I could not tear my attention—my very longing— away from him. I could forget everything about my life except for him.

One turn—I could not say how many had gone by, for trees did not count things like humans—Willen read to me until a rustle caught his attention. I sensed that he closed the book and set it down, standing to his feet as the High King approached.

The King must have waved off his attendants so it was only he and his son present.

"Willen, there you are. Spending all your time in the forests, despite my teachings to find a more worthy occupation. Have I not assigned you enough diplomatic work to keep you busy? Must you sully yourself in nature like the savages of your mother's people?"

Willen bristled at the talk of his mother. I could see love for her pouring from his being. But his father...the love he felt for his fallen Queen was not the same as Willen's. It was twisted, malformed. Tainted.

"It helps me to clear my head. I simply sit and read, My King. I do not mean to offend you."

"Your head need not be clear, it need be filled. Filled with what I teach you."

Willen nodded. "I am doing my best to fill it."

Harrod scoffed. "But you do so for the Dwarf. Not for me. Not because of your love for me. Not because you seek to please me."

"But I *do* seek to please you, father."

"Then come to the Palace of the Kings. Stay within its walls. At my side. Do not leave me as you do every turn to come to this wretched forest."

"I need...air. That is all. I do not go deep into the forest, My King. I remain close." Willen was trying. Trying to say the right words. To please his father. But he wished not to lose the few moments we shared together.

The King lowered his voice. "Your brother. He returns. I received word this morning."

"Theor?" Willen stepped forward, eager. "He will have news of the Tseslarian alliance. Whether it has strengthened or absolved. Whether Morn will be at our door."

"Yes. He will have news. Though I have also received reports of Morn strengthening their numbers and Tseslar reducing their fortifications along the borders we share with them."

I imagined Willen running his hand through his hair, and my core ached to see him as I used to. "But King...that would mean war with Morn is imminent."

"Yes."

"But...why? I do not understand your logic." Quickly, he corrected himself, "I do not *disregard* your logic. I simply don't understand it. Why did you send Theor? I know you wished to stay with...with Mida, but why did you not send me? I would have represented you well."

"You are not to leave my side."

"But why? *Why*?"

"Because you are *mine*!" The King calmed himself in an instant. "You will never leave, Willen. Never."

"Even so"—Willen's voice was tight, controlled—"you could have sent an ambassador to Tseslar and achieved better results. Do you...*wish* for a war?"

The King seemed pleased that Willen had arrived at that conclusion. "Now you are finally using your head, boy."

"A war will destroy the Realm."

"How do you think we became as powerful, as wealthy as we are? Why do you think Tseslar does not prefer to help us? Why Morn wishes to erase us from history? Because we are best at taking. And war gives us a chance to do just that, Willen. We will take what we need to win. And then, when we win, we will take more than we need."

Willen thought for a moment. "You...will take their Trees."

"The Trees Clorente has gathered for us will never supply our needs. Even if one of the two remaining is a True Tree, one Seed will not change our current trajectory. We are depleted of natural resources. We need more."

"So you will take control of lands who have their own Trees. You will then have many at once. And access to the resources their Seeds provide."

"Precisely. But it cannot appear that we have provoked this war, Willen. Our people are soft-hearted. They will defend their righteous King. They will not fight for a tyrant. It must look like we advocated for peace."

"So you sent Theor. The worst advocate of the Realm's history."

"Mighty Theor. Future High King. He will attempt to broker peace and fail. We will have no choice but to fight. And then... naturally...to take." The King sighed. "Do not become indignant and self-righteous now, Willen. You must learn my ways. You must study closely and observe how I implement them."

Willen's heart beat so wildly, I worried for him. I sent Wonder through the ground to his feet and hoped it could fortify his nerves.

"I will do as you say," he responded. "You are the High King. And you are my father. I will learn...I will learn to listen."

"Very well. Very well indeed. For your brother will interrupt our scheduled Ball Of Desolation with the news of impending war. And you will act as surprised as I. The people will rage, as they do at such venting events. And then I will reveal to you our strategy for dominating the lands surrounding the Realm.

"Yes. The ball. I see there is strategy to *everything* you do, father."

"Of course, Willen."

"May I ask you something? I hope it does not offend you."

"Go on."

"When you found my mother in the woods...was it strategy or love that propelled you to lie with her?"

"My son. I will tell you the truth now that it seems you are ready to hear it." The King moved toward his second son and put a heavy hand on his shoulder. "I did not merely find a strange and beautiful woman in the woods and fall madly in love with her. I am the reason, Willen, that she remained in those woods at all. I kept her there, under my careful control, until I had what I needed from her. My most intricate strategy to date come to fruition. I took Fara. And then from her, I took what I needed. Not simply a son, for I knew I could make many of those. I wanted *you*."

Harrod kissed Willen's forehead and left the alcove. Willen stood for quite some time, in silence. And then he knelt and retrieved his book.

"And now I hope you are simply a tree, Aia, and could not hear anything I've said on my visits. Only so that you will not have heard the intentions of my father's heart," he said to me. "But I have heard it, Aia. And I do not know what else I can do now. Besides try. Try to stop him. Perhaps...perhaps the Ancients will have mercy on me for breaking their Law."

I felt his breath on my bark as he kissed me. "At least you are free of this madness, Little Tree. Perhaps soon, I will be too."

I Did Not Mean To

Turns out, there are quite a few things no one wants to be in this world. Of course, there is the role of Queen of the Realm, both beautifully powerless and angled toward unavoidable death. Then of course, there is the poor, noble position of Prince—boys forced to measure up beneath impossible expectations. Then could come the place of a Dwarf in a kingdom of men, wiser than all but somehow coming up short. Designers are not easy parts to play either, for they can only live as long as the ones they style. And, then there are the Trees.

Trees can play human all they want. But they will never be understood.

A Tree sees everything but has no eyes. They feel it all but they have no skin. They hear every scream and every groan of the people though they have no ears. They love without hearts. But they cannot move.

I did not want to dwell in my forest home, drinking in Wonder and sunlight every turn and sharing joy with my sisters. They had grown used to ignoring the sounds of the

humans in need—those praying and begging for trees and
those who had never even seen one.

And I could not ignore the sound of those in the Palace,
readying for some elaborate celebration of disaster. Could
they not see what their High King was doing? Could they not
feel the war facing them, like the greatest Wyvern of them all,
nostrils flared and talons spread? Could they not see their
Second Prince begging for help, for some way to stop it all
from coming to be?

The people of the Realm were not evil. They were trusting.
And they were being manipulated.

I wanted to go to Willen, to tell him to be strong and to
be cunning. Not to play into the hand of his father and not
to forfeit his own life in a vain effort to stop a war that would
come whether the Second Prince was dead or alive. I knew
Willen thought he had nothing left to live for, but I was not
gone. I was not...dead. I lived. I only could not move.

I groaned, my roots shifting in the soil and my branches
shuddering as I stretched.

A Tree cannot concern herself with the affairs of humans,
my grandmothers told me. *You are not them. You never were.*

But he needed me. He was not ready to survive what was to
come on his own, with no help and no love in his life.

If only. *If only he could behold me. See that I would not
leave him as long as he kept his promise and did not leave me.*
But I could not get him to come back to the forest. I had no
voice. I could not speak.

Let me speak to him, I begged. But the Arboreal grandmothers
would not grant my request. They had the power, yes, but
they would not give me a voice that a mere human could

detect. I called out through every tree to reach out to every stone that lay beneath their branches.

I asked them to send Forgotten a message. That he was to look out for the Dwarf named Beralt, locked within his stone dungeon and that, if he could, he should favor my Willen until I could get to him.

But it was not until I witnessed Theor and his crew of fools riding past me, headed for the remnants of the Palace of the Princes, that I knew I could wait no longer.

With all my strength and every bit of Wonder I had left, with the blessings of the trees of the True Tree Forest and the damnation of the Ancient Arboreals upon me, I lifted my roots, one at a time, and *moved*.

The result was agony greater than any I had experienced. More wicked than the torture I endured at the hand of Aman. More exquisite than the trials Clorente put me through. More demoralizing than the brute force of the High King. For Trees were meant to be both still and silent. To watch only, and to glow and grow. Not to move or to change.

When my roots lifted, they were homeless in the air, writhing and confused and lost. Much like I felt when I walked like a human through the Palace. And when they stepped back down, they shot into the earth, wishing to find solace and safety in the dark beneath. But I had to rip them up again. And again. Until each tendril, each length of root screamed in terror.

But forward I went. My roots, they would learn how to endure the pain. They would learn how to move if I just kept on.

My branches struck and crunched against the other trees, causing distress throughout the forest, but I begged for forgiveness and continued, broken boughs falling behind me. My leaves shook loose and floated prematurely to the ground. My buds withered and fell like tiny stones.

But I moved nonetheless, resin leaking from my open wounds.

The closer I got to the Palace, the less I could hear the Arboreals cursing me and the less Wonder I received from my sister trees in the forest. On the stones outside, I fell, unable to continue. It was too much. I had gone too far. There was no soil to stabilize me, to feed me, and the sun had set behind the tops of the leaves. My body shook, wracked with the cold of being utterly alone. I feared I would die there, my bark against smooth stone and my leaves turned to dust.

And what will become of the Seed I have given to Willen? Who will sustain its life?

"You attempt the impossible, Tree."

The graveled voice of a True Stone. I organized my Wonder so it could respond to him. "I must get inside," I told him. "I must."

"You cannot," he said. "You are a True Tree. As I am a True Stone. Your fate is sealed in bark. Anchored to roots. Just as mine is sedimented in ore."

"I must."

"And if you fail?"

"I won't."

"For...what? For what do you defy the Arboreals? For what do you tempt Ancient Law? What will you become, Tree, and *for what*? For the Realm? For some Kings and Princes and Queens? They will forget you. They will leave you."

"Maybe so. But I am not here for some Kings and Princes and Queens. I am here for Willen."

"The boy from the forest? The one who first taught you the ways of Wonder?"

"Yes."

"Very well. A worthy choice. The Ancients will curse me just as they will curse you. Better to be cursed than forgotten."

The smooth stones beneath me began to flutter and then they rolled, pushing me closer and closer to the entrance of the Palace.

At last, the servants took notice and they hurried to help me. But once they came close, their intentions shifted. Some screamed. Some ran. Some said I was a monster from the forest come to avenge the lost Royal twins.

But someone else stopped them from pulling at my twigs and kicking my trunk with their boots. She knelt and threw her arms around me, gruesome as I was to behold. "Aia, my darling!"

"You are not meant to stop here," somebody shouted and pulled at the girl. "It is off to the gallows for you, foolish Designer!"

"Wait!" she cried, trying to throw the guards off her. "Wait! It is not over for us yet!"

Glenne. It was Glenne, heaven bless her. Pulling free of them for just a moment, no doubt by using her Wonder as best she could, she put gentle hands on me and choked back her tears. "My friend, I do not know how to help you. What can I do? How...how can this be?"

I tried to speak to her, but no words came. Only the clashing of my branches.

"You are in pain. Aia, I can take you back to the forest. You need to be planted, sweet Tree. Quickly."

But I shook my leaves in resistance. I would not go back. I had to go forward.

"You are crawling...toward *the Palace*? Aia, people will see you. They are all inside, all the nobles and the Royals. It is the night of the Ball Of Desolation. They will dance and feast among the rubble of the Palace of the Princes. If they see you like this...they will break you into kindling, Aia. I cannot allow it."

It was then I realized Glenne was in chains, leaving the Palace in much the same way as I'd arrived all those turns before.

"Come girl," the guard shouted, yanking her away from me. "Or we will choke the Wonder out of you!"

"Aia, go back to the forest. Go back!"

Glenne struggled to be free of her captors. She would be taken and killed all because they believed I was not the True Tree. All because they believed I could not give the High Prince a Seed.

With everything I could command, I rose to my full height and shone, streaming my Wonder out from every part of me. I could not see what happened to the guards, but they no longer made sounds or took breath.

Glenne gasped, shrieking, the sounds of her chains rattling. "My eyes!" she yelled. "My *eyes!*"

But I did not know how to take back what I'd done. And I had not meant to hurt my dear friend. She heaved on the ground and then she sat very still for so long that I feared she too had perished.

But then she spoke, her words in shambles. "Aia...you saved my life." She reached and searched until her hands found me once again. "I will help to carry you if you can somehow show me the way. I can see nothing."

And so Glenne took my weight upon her, and I shifted our direction until we made it up the grand staircase and through the doorless frame that led to the first great hall. We pushed through the nobles, stumbling over bits of charred wood and glass, the stones moving out of our way like magic.

The more steps I took, the more I felt my roots abandon their shape. The more I felt my branches hang low and smooth. Until finally, after the third demolished hall with its loud music and bright Wondered lights, I felt the sensation of skin beginning to take form over my bark.

Glenne was right. People gasped and screeched and fainted when they saw me. But Glenne did not turn back, and neither did I. Even in her chains, she supported my weight until finally, I could stand on my own.

In the grand hall, my eyes regained their human shape. I could see the blurred images of faces. Of men and women in dark clothing, wearing glittering gems on their necks and hands. The music ground to an abrupt stop, and silence fell over the crowd. A Ball Of Desolation indeed.

But none of this mattered when Willen Vedan noticed me.

He dropped the glass he held and cared not that it shattered to pieces at his feet. He stared and stared. And then he stepped to me, just as he had done in the forest.

I forced words to come from me, though they still held the creaks and groans of bark scraping against bark. "You dropped your glass, Second Prince. Did you do it on purpose?"

His arms encircled me. I was relieved to be able to feel them as I once did. Relieved that I had arms to wrap around him.

The people, they could see us embracing, but Willen did not seem to care at all. He held me for too long. And then I realized it was because he was weeping into my hair.

"You came back," he whispered. "You came back."

I pressed him tighter to me. "I thought...you would break your promise. And leave me."

He groaned at my words but he would not let me go. "I don't know what else to do...."

"We will think of something. Together."

He pulled away, only to kiss me fully and deeply and with every purpose he could find. The crowd gasped, reeling with the realization that I, in fact, was a Tree, and that the Second Prince was violating a long list of rules by enjoying me.

Willen laughed, his eyes still flowing with tears. He smoothed my hair out of my face. "You are very naked, my love." He kissed my forehead. "Would you like clothes?"

"She's *naked*?" Glenne exclaimed. "This is my best design yet! Pity I can't see it."

"Clothes, yes. I forgot about those."

Willen kissed me again, pressing his hands to my back as he did so until I felt the sensation of cloth Wonder over me.

"How?" he asked. "Aia...how? You were a Tree. A True Tree. You were gone. It is impossible...beyond impossible. Never before, not in hundreds of circles—not once has a True Tree ever...come back—"

The sound of nobles being shoved out of the way as the High King and High Prince approached us.

The King began, his shoulders broad and his head lifted high. "Willen, how dare you—"

"Shut up." Theor's voice cut through his father's.

The crowd gasped again. *Anymore gasping and they will inhale us all.*

"Theor...let us speak in private, lest you—"

"No. No speaking in private. I want everyone to hear what I have to say." He filled his broad chest with air and spoke loud enough for everyone to hear him. "I have discovered some truths on my journey to Tseslar. First...not only will they not continue our alliance, they will join Morn in war against us."

Murmurs and gasps abounded.

"Even more troubling...the lies. The lies issued from the mouth of the High King, to all of us. King Harrod did not find the Second Queen Fara in the woods of the Realm. He stole her from Tseslar and forced her to bear him a son. This action is against Royal Law and diplomatic conduct. Meaning...Harrod is hardly a King at all. But rather...a common criminal."

This was met by outcry. Some were enraged at the idea that the King would do such a thing, and others angered by the boldness of the High Prince.

"Theor—" Willen tried, subtly stepping between me and his brother.

"I set my sights on the wrong Royal," he said, cutting Willen off. "I thought my enemy was my weak, pathetic, depressed little brother. But truly...it's the King who keeps me from my full potential. From my power."

"You must be quite finished now," Harrod said. "We are all tired of this."

"We are all tired of you. We have no trees. No resources. And now a war at our door. We are tired of your leadership. And you can do nothing against me, father, for I am your sworn and solemn heir."

"No."

I felt the crowd still at the King's reply. Even my own heart seemed to catch in my throat. In the quiet of chaos, I felt Glenne reach for my hand and hold it tight.

Harrod spoke once more. "Theor Vedan is not and will never be my sworn and solemn heir. For he is not my firstborn son."

I saw Willen's spine stiffen. He took a step back, but there was nowhere he could go. We were packed in by the nobles who lusted to witness what might happen.

"Willen. He was born first. In a forest. And then, second, not a turn later and in a Palace...Theor."

Theor's entire face changed shape, malformed by his rage. His eyes widened, shot with red, and his nostrils flared open. "You are *lying*."

"You know it is true."

"No."

"Tell him, Willen. Tell him what you have always known in your heart."

Willen said nothing. He did not even breathe.

His father lunged forward and grabbed his shirt, ripping it from him in one pull. A clamor ensured, but when the King stepped back, he pointed his finger at *me*.

"Show them!"

"Aia, whatever he is talking about...do not," Willen said, his voice clearer than I'd ever heard it.

"He wants to see the Seed," I said, my voice still carrying the essence of leaves unfurling in the wind.

At this, Willen turned to me, his eyes wide. "What?"

I nodded. "I gave it to *you*, Willen."

"You...*knew*?"

I shook my head.

"Show! Show it now!"

And I did not mean to but I glowed. And when I did, so did the seed buried in Willen's chest.

He reached up and clutched himself, as if trying to hide it. But there was no hiding a Wonderful green glow like that. It filled his torso with soft, beautiful light.

"Only the *High Prince* can receive the Seed of a True Tree!" Harrod cried. "My firstborn and my heir. My most noble possession and one shaped to serve me and to serve this Realm."

But then the King gurgled and froze. His face cemented like stone, and his hands twitched until he fell over onto his stomach, his face bruised and unmoving at our feet. His golden crown slid from his head and clattered onto the ruined marble.

Behind him, a small young thing. Holding a short, light blade. Her round eyes too wide for her slender face. She whimpered, the bloodied knife clattering to the floor beside the fallen King.

There should have been an immediate frenzy, but no one moved for a moment. Not even the guardsmen. Finally, Shrane's squeaky voice broke the silence.

"My love," she said to Theor. "I've done it. Just like we practiced."

With that, and very slowly, as if his mind were turning on for the first time, Theor angled himself toward his brother. For after all his efforts, he still was not rightfully King. The power fell to the one who had never wanted it in the first place.

To Willen.

Everything was expedited after that. Theor lunged for his brother but was propelled backward by the Ancient Law, crashing into the wall.

"Seize him!" Theor cried, pointing to Willen. "And kill his Tree!"

The guards and nobles loyal to Theor rushed toward us, but Willen put his arm out in front of me and prepared his Wonder. I held tight to Glenne's hand, and we stumbled over the feet of those closing us in from behind.

Willen fired his Wonder at the attackers, a few guards coming to his aid. But no one understood who the true High King should be or what had happened to Harrod or who they should rightfully defend.

Until suddenly, a cane cracked the marble floor, sending a long line through the whole of it. A wall of Wonder shot upwards, separating us from our attackers. From the madness of Theor. And Clorente turned her prim head toward us.

"Take them! Take them now and run, child!" she shouted. "We can wait no longer!"

Appearing beside us, Gretaline spread her arms, a spiral of blackened Wonder emanating from her hands. It consumed us, lifting us from where we stood in the midst of the Ball Of Desolation and landing us in a dark forest amid screams and ash and the burning of a strange hillside.

"Morn! Morn soldiers are here!" Mothers grabbed babies and ran uphill. Men charged down with pitchforks and scythes in hand. Meager farmers prepared to give their lives to defend their corner of the Realm from the Mornish siege.

But there we were.

A blind designer. A tainted Wonderer. The High King Of All The Realm, long may he reign.

And the First Dryad.

FROM THE MIND OF TESHELLE COMBS

The First
Collection

The First Dryad 1 & 2

A forbidden love, slow-burn, magically-enchanted romance

The First Stone

An enemies to lovers, arranged marriage, romantic adventure

The First Nymph

A haunting enemies to lovers, star-crossed, fantasy romance

The First Flame

A forbidden love, romantic action, royal drama

The First Breath

A fast burn, forbidden love, mystical, heartbreaking romance

The First Muse

A sweeping, age gap, classical romance

The First Dragon

A chaos-fueled, fated mates romance

The First Spark

A tantalizing tale of romantic obsession

The First Shadow

A twisted story of love and betrayal

More
By Teshelle Combs

Scan to read the
The First Collection
And other books.

Review

This Book

Scan to leave
a review for
The First Dryad

Books

The Twisted Blade Series

"I promise. I am fine—"

"Did he *hurt* you?"

"No."

"Did he *touch* you?" He released me only to take a lap around the room and to smash his fist into the desk, a snarl leaving him that made me jump. Then he returned. "*Did he touch you, Emyri?*"

When I would not answer him, he paced again, his veins raised, his eyes blazing with rage. He came to me again, about to ask me once more what had happened.

Tears down my cheeks. Hot, ridiculous tears. "It is always difficult. And I am always resilient. It is always dangerous. And I am always brave. But for once, can't it be...kind? Or pleasant. Or...." I scrubbed at my tears. "Nkita, just... Be...be *gentle* with me. I—"

What am I even asking? I had seen what a black wing could be. And Rizel cared nothing for my wellbeing, even while thinking I was one of his kind. *Why...why would a black wing, a highborn Teth, a General...a Cryl...be kind to a human spy? My own people. My own people sent me here to die on their behalf. Death at the hands of the Crylia had always been my destiny. Why should it come without suffering? Why should it come gently?*

He will crush me now.

CURRENT TITLES:
RIVERS FOR STORMS
RIPPLES FOR SKIES
REEDS FOR WIND

But he waited. And then he waited. Only staring at me, though I could hardly make him out through my tears.

When finally he spoke, I knew his words should never have been allowed to exist.

"Show me how."

What? What do I...say to this? What do I do with this?

Nkita crossed the room and took my hands in his. His expression did not change. He had not become some different Cryl, overcome with compassion. He was the same. How could he be so different from Rizel? When Nkita told me to take my clothes off for him, I answered him like a Tru. Like a woman. Like myself. I could never have done that with Rizel. I could never have done that with... *anyone* else.

I took his hands, running my fingers along the tip of his, wishing I could know for sure that his talons would not come shooting out to harm me. Then, I wrapped his arms around my waist and leaned into him. My head on his chest. His heart beat quicker than I expected it to.

"Is that all you need?" he asked.

I pressed my nose against his coat. "Mm."

"I don't believe you."

Cryl be damned.

Books
Kindle and Paperback

The Underglow

I confessed to myself that I had paid very little attention to the countless governesses who attempted to explain the general rules of romantic engagement for Femmes of my stature and upbringing. But despite my lack of knowledge of general rules, I had a general sense that I was breaking them, whatever they were. Generally speaking, of course.

Closer should have made me nervous. I was not nervous, however, and so closer I went until there was no separation between his hips and mine. This was a relief to me—one difficult to explain. For I did not think there could ever be such closeness between another living thing and myself. Truly, I did not think, though they claimed to desire it, that any other living thing wanted to be so close to me.

<<You withhold>>, Alexander meant to me, pulling my bottom lip between his before pressing his mouth fully to mine. I felt only the slightest prick of his fangs, for he had not lengthened them. With my head nearly swimming, I wondered if he would sink those fangs into me as he once did. But no. Instead, he intended. <<I will be patient>>.

I detested patience. It was a monster that society told its victims was required, but really, it only convinced us all to work longer hours while they fattened us up for the slaughter. What is the point of patience? Who does it serve but the impatient ones?

I wrapped my arms around his waist and held firmly, but he released my grip rather easily.

<<Patience>>. With a last touch of his thumb to my lip and a final probe of his considerate eyes, he stepped away. <<I will find who hurt you>>.

I truthfully thought he had forgotten about this, as it had left my mind entirely. The idea that he would seek some vengeance on my behalf made my hands go numb, for it led me to envision Alexander strung up in a dark dungeon, awaiting Sleep. Surely he would be captured. Surely he would be enslaved once more. Surely I would not be able to save him. Chivalry was not something I required from this pyre.

But he looked at me—some small distance between us—in such a way that I could not believe it was chivalry compelling him.

<<You do not wish me to find them>>, he meant. The feeling of his meaning came slow and hot, like waves against a stone on too warm of a day. Or like standing too close to a flame. This is what it felt like for Alexander to be cross with me.

I wondered if I should be worried that I enjoyed the feeling.

And then I felt a shift in him, or rather, felt it come from him. <<I will go>>.

Books
Kindle and Paperback

SEVER & SPLIT

His lips grazed my forehead, and everything else was quiet and still. If I lived to be one thousand years old, I would never feel as entirely wanted as I did in that moment.

"Era...when I said you shouldn't touch me.... Before. In the lodge. It wasn't because...I would never...." His words failed him. "I love it when you touch me, Era. I just want to make that perfectly clear."

I nodded my head.

Oteros tucked a loose strand of my hair behind my ear, and I made the mistake of looking up into his eyes. He made the mistake of letting his hand slip down to my neck and allowing his lips to meet mine. For a moment. Just a moment.

Everything...*sang*. It was as though the stars had turned to rain and the wind had turned to music. As if the rhythm of the land danced beneath my feet.

But there was something else. Something...hot and violent and unpredictable. Some part of me that I had always been told should never exist.

More. More now.

And I didn't have time to back away and blush sweetly, to tell Oteros we'd made a mistake. That we were friends and friends are careful with one another. Never reckless. No, I only had time to press myself against him and to thrust my fingers into his hair. To push my hips forward and to part his lips with my tongue.

"Era! Era, where are you?!"

It wasn't until I heard my sister calling from a distance that I pulled myself away from Oteros. I stumbled backward, my eyes locking with his.

"Era, wait—"

But I was gone. Stumbling down the path and away from whatever had overtaken me. I was meant to be solving problems. But it turned out, I was the biggest one of all.

Books
Kindle and Paperback

Slit Throat Saga

"My people," he said, yelling over the toning, "let's celebrate. For today, the one who breaks the laws of nature, the one who moves the unmovable, the one who tests the very hands of God, will be set back on the right path. The Fight is not in vain."

He turned with a flourish to watch with us all as a translucent synthetix blade, held tight in the Moral's fist, sliced across the throat of the girl. A gurgle, then her blonde head flopped forward. Her blood gushed brilliant red. One would think it meant that the Fight was mistaken, that she was just like everyone else—a normal human with no unearthly capabilities, no deadly tendencies. Her blood seemed pure and red, filled with iron just like it should be. But after a few seconds, as her strength faded, the red diluted and her blood ran clear as a mountain river.

She was Meta. Just like they thought and I'm sure as they determined when she was confined in the House of Certainty for questioning. No true metal in her veins. No metal in her whole body. Not even metal in her mind. Instead she could pull it to her. She was a magnet. An abomination. And if left uncaught and unkilled, her kind would destroy the world.

The people—my people—cheered along with the Best Of Us as the Meta's watery blood poured over her small breasts, down her loose linen shirt, over the wooden platform, and through the street. It always amazed me how long Meta could bleed, how much life they held in their bodies. We all waited until the flow pooled beneath our feet, Ender Stream blessing us with one final reminder: *If you are us, you live, and if you are them, you die.*

"Well, Nex," Onur said with a little sigh as the crowd began to disperse, shoes squelching in the remains of the Meta girl, "what must be done is done." He brushed my thick, silver curls behind my ear so he could kiss my temple again, his favorite habit. His pale skin seemed to shine against my dusty red complexion. He looked tired, but he smiled. "We should get something to eat, yes?"

I smiled back at him, turning and tiptoeing so I could reach his lips with my own. His were soft and yielding, warm and inviting. Mine were not quite as full, not quite as tender. I met his eyes, ensuring that my gaze said exactly what I needed it to. *All Fight, no fear.* "Yes, let's eat. We can say cheers to the next one to be found."

I stepped through the Stream, one hand tight in my love's. The other hand I kept stuffed in the pocket of my cotton dress, clenched, but not so firmly that my fingernails might draw blood from my palm. That would not do. For the Stream soaking through my shoes was no less damned than the blood coursing through my veins.

Careful, Nex.

Careful.

Books

Kindle and Paperback

Tuck Me In

I stepped toward him. "Marrow, you walked from There to Here? That must have taken hours. You could have been hurt. You could have been killed."

He nodded. "I did not know that when I set out, but I am aware of the dangers now. There were many."

"So you're not alright. Oh Dios." I rubbed my chest. My heart was definitely not stopped anymore. It raced, banging against its cage. "I might actually be sick."

"Bel...."

I smacked my hands together. "Marrow, what were you thinking?"

He didn't answer. But I found the sadness growing in his dark eyes.

"I'm sorry I'm yelling," I said. And I was so sorry. He didn't know why I was so upset, why the thought of him coming all this way was nightmare-inducing rather than a wonderful surprise.

That's when, without being able to stop myself, I reached out and touched his elbow.

Now, I knew—I knew—I was not supposed to touch my subject. It was on every Grade test I had ever taken. We can't study something if we manipulate it. If we handle it. If we hold it.

But my hand on his elbow led to him leaning into me. He wrapped both arms around me and put his cheek to my hair. And he lingered. In his still, slow way.

I clutched the back of his shirt and pressed my face to his chest and fought the tears that came to my eyes.

"You're okay," he said calmly, with that voice that sounded like magic being born. Like a fantasy opening its eyes.

That was the first time I realized how much everything hurt, all the time, from every direction, and how much I wished it would all stop.

Everything, that is, except for a Glimpse named Marrow.

Books

Kindle and Paperback

CORE SERIES

Ava is the kind of girl who knows what's real and what isn't.
Nothing in life is fair. Nothing is given freely. Nothing is painless.
Every foster kid can attest to those truths, and Ava lives them every
day. But when she meets a family of dragon shifters and is chosen to
join them as a rider, her very notion of reality is shaken. She doesn't
believe she can let her guard down. She doesn't think she can let
them in—especially not the reckless, kind-eyed Cale. To say yes to
him means he would be hers—her dragon and her companion—for
life. But what if Ava has no life left to give?

The System Series

1 + 1 = Dead. That's the only math that adds up when you're in the System. Everywhere Nick turns, he's surrounded by the inevitability of his own demise at the hands of the people who stole his life from him. That is, until those hands deliver the bleeding, feisty, eye-rolling Nessa Parker. Tasked with keeping his new partner alive, Nick must face all the ways he's died and all the things he's forgotten.

Nessa might as well give up. The moment she gets into that car, the moment she lays her hazel eyes on her new partner, her end begins. It doesn't matter that Nick Masters can slip through time by computing mathematical algorithms in his mind. It doesn't matter how dark and handsome and irresistibly cold he is. Nessa has to defeat her own shadows. Together and alone, Nick and Nessa make sense of their senseless fates and fight for the courage to change it all. Even if it means the System wins and they end up...

well...dead.

Poetry
Thoughts Like Words

Let There Be Nine Series

- *Let There Be Nine Vol 1*: **Enneagram Poetry**
- *Let There Be Nine Vol 2*: **Enneagram Poetry**

For Series: Words laced together on behalf of an idea, a place, a world.

- **For Her**
- **For Him**
- **For Them**
- **For Us**

Love Bad Series: Poems About Love. Not Love Poems.

- **Love Bad**
- **Love Bad More**
- **Love Bad Best**

Standalone Poetry Books:

Breath Like Glass

Poems for love that never lasts.

Girl Poet

A collection of poems on the passion, privilege, and pain of being (or not quite being) a girl.

FRAMELESS

A collection of poems for the colors that make life vibrant, from their perspective, so we may share in what they might think and feel.

This One Has Pockets

Narrative poetry about a girl who is near giving up and the boy who tries to save her.

ON THE NATURE OF HINGES

A series of poetic questions from the perspective of someone who has been left behind more than once.

Gray Child

A unique expression of being more than one race, written by a Caribbean American woman, for anyone who cares to read.

Contact Teshelle Combs

Instagram | @TeshelleCombs

Facebook | Tess Combs

Patreon | Patreon.com/TeshelleCombs

Leave A Review

A good review is how you breathe life into my story. Please leave *The First Dryad* an Amazon review and tell a friend how much you love Aia and Willen.

Made in the USA
Monee, IL
06 September 2024

65224317R00208